Snowdrop

'Snow' is what drug deal~~~ cocaine, the deadly white ~~~ millions of lives. And when ~~~ tendent Tommy Fox of the F~~~ Squad finds traces of it at the scene of a brutal double murder, he knows that this is not the ordinary gangland killing that his commander at first believes.

In his search for the killers, Fox discovers that drug smugglers are leaving the 'snow' at a 'drop' on the perimeter of Heathrow Airport to be collected by a contact. It seems all too simple, not least to Her Majesty's Customs who are involved with Fox's inquiries from the outset.

A suave hotelier, his horse-mad wife and their suspiciously charming circle all feature in Fox's investigation . . . Not to mention a blonde air hostess working the London–Rio route and a ruthless killer who blows away his enemies with a shotgun. Fox is convinced that every one of them is somehow implicated. And with HM Customs putting pressure on for a result he must do everything in his power to prove it . . .

SNOWDROP

Graham Ison

MACMILLAN
LONDON

Copyright © Graham Ison 1992

7206R

First published 1992 by
MACMILLAN LONDON LIMITED
Cavaye Place London SW10 9PG
and Basingstoke

Associated companies in Auckland, Budapest, Dublin, Gaborone,
Harare, Hong Kong, Kampala, Kuala Lumpur, Lagos, Madras,
Mancini, Melbourne, Mexico City, Nairobi, New York, Singapore,
Sydney, Tokyo and Windhoek

ISBN 0–333–57719–1

A CIP catalogue record for this book is available from the British
Library

Phototypset by Intype, London
Printed and bound by Billings and Sons Limited, Worcester

Chapter One

The white police Range Rover pulled out of Heston services on to the M4 motorway westbound.

It was one o'clock on Saturday afternoon.

One more hour and then off duty. For two whole days.

But still enough time to do a few more summonses for excess speed.

They had driven about three and a half miles at a cunning 68 m.p.h. when they saw it. A Ford Sierra estate, two-litre Ghia. Red. Parked on the hard shoulder. No hazard lights. Just parked.

'What's this smart-arse up to?' asked Langford.

'Probably decided to bring the kids out for a picnic,' said Phipps. 'Can't beat the M4 on a Saturday afternoon for getting away from it all.' He pulled in behind the Ford and turned on the blue beacon.

The two policemen got out, slipped on their high-visibility tabards, and ambled in a leisurely fashion towards the car.

Langford got there first. 'Oh Jesus,' he said. So did Phipps when he got there. The officers gazed at the car and its two occupants. The windscreen was a gaping hole and the two corpses were unrecognisable, their faces a mass of blood. There was blood and gore on the inside of the roof and on the rear windows. And on the back seats.

Traffic officers of the Metropolitan Police are highly professional. Not only at traffic matters, but at policemanship as well, and they undoubtedly know a traffic accident when they see one. But they also know a crime. And this was no accident.

Phipps was phlegmatic about it. 'Something tells me that we won't be off at two o'clock,' he said and walked to the back of the vehicle. He bent down and touched the exhaust pipe. 'Still hot.' He knew better than to put his fingerprints on the bonnet.

Detective Chief Superintendent Tommy Fox, operational head of the Flying Squad, was at a loose end. He had wandered into the Squad office and made a nuisance of himself, causing certain of his officers to wonder whether he had a home to go to. Then he had returned to his own office and toyed with a few pieces of correspondence, but paperwork was not his forte. He decided that he would go across to the Star and have a drink. Just the one. More if there were any of his cronies in there, and then go home.

'Commander's on the phone, sir. Are you here?'

Fox was standing behind his desk, one finger poised over a file. 'Of course I'm bloody well here. Put him through.'

'Yes, sir.' The DC returned quickly to the Squad office.

'Tommy, what are you doing at work on a Saturday afternoon?' There was an element of amusement in Commander Myers's voice.

Fox didn't like the sound of it. 'Just leaving as a matter of fact, sir.'

'Well I'm glad I caught you. There's been a shooting. Double murder apparently. On the M4. Westbound from Junction Four, just beyond the Harmondsworth Road underpass. Local CID are on scene, but it has all the hallmarks of a gangland killing.' Myers paused. 'Not doing anything particular this afternoon, were you?'

'Well I was,' said Fox, 'but it can keep.' He didn't believe in giving in too easily.

6

'Good. Perhaps you'd take it on. The local lads are a bit tucked up, so the area DAC tells me.'

'Poor buggers,' said Fox. 'It must be hell out there.' He put the phone down and walked into the main office. 'Get hold of Swann . . . and get Mr Gilroy on the blower.' He turned in the doorway. 'Have you heard about this double killing on the M4?'

'Yes, sir.'

'Then why the hell didn't you tell me?'

'Didn't think you'd want to get involved, sir.'

Fox glared menacingly at the DC. 'D'you like it here?' he asked and went out, slamming the door.

Fox's driver, Swann, carved his way through the Saturday-afternoon traffic with the help of a siren and a magnetic blue light on the roof of the Ford Granada. Traffic Division had closed the motorway from Junction Four and imposed on the Thames Valley Police to stop anything entering eastbound from Junction Five. The result was a glorious snarl-up, particularly where the M4 met the M25, as bewildered motorists got lost trying to escape by way of the back doubles around West Drayton, Hounslow and Slough. As the observer of the police helicopter put it, it was like a Scalextric set without grooves. And a quite substantial number of intending passengers found that by the time they got to Heathrow Airport their flights had left without them.

Swann hardly slackened speed as they approached the diversion. He switched on the yelping siren and flashed his headlights, causing a traffic PC to leap for his life. Fox waved cheerfully as they passed.

There were police vehicles all over the place. Two or three patrol cars, a number of white vans belonging to the scientific team, a mobile incident room and a trio of Transit vans that had brought the local territorial support group to this latest centre of police interest. A square of canvas screens hid the murder scene.

Fox didn't like untidiness. Or sightseers. He got out

7

of his car and strode towards a uniformed chief inspector who was clutching a clipboard.

'Name, please,' said the chief inspector.

'Thomas Fox . . . of the Flying Squad.' Fox glared at the assembled vehicles and the odd little groups of policemen, uniformed and plain-clothed. 'What the bloody hell's this pantomime in aid of?'

'Controlling the scene . . . sir.' The chief inspector was uncertain of Fox's rank, but guessed it was probably higher than his own. 'Er, commander, is it, sir?'

'Detective chief superintendent.' Fox gave the chief inspector a disconcerting stare. 'What are all these feet doing here?' It was the disparaging term he always applied to the Uniform Branch.

'Er, controlling the scene, sir,' said the chief inspector again. He seemed fond of the phrase.

'Is that a fact? Well, they don't seem to be doing a very good job. Get rid of them. Now.'

'All of them, sir?'

'Just leave a few traffic men. We certainly don't need that lot.' Fox waved a hand towards the gregarious Transit-van passengers and at two area cars whose crews were gazing out at all the activity. 'And you can go as well. Your DAC tells me that you're all supposed to be desperately busy.'

'Yes, sir. At once, sir.' The chief inspector had never met Tommy Fox before, but he should have known, the moment he had sighted Fox's immaculately suited figure and heard mention of the Flying Squad, that this was a man to be reckoned with. Fox did not suffer fools gladly, whether policemen or villains, proof of which lay in the story of Fox's award of the Queen's Gallantry Medal for disarming a dangerous criminal. It was a story which had become a part of the history and folklore of the Metropolitan Police.

Len Waring, the local detective chief inspector, knew Tommy Fox. Knew him well; he had served under him as a detective inspector and the moment he had heard

8

that Fox was on his way to take charge he had started to tighten things up. But as he didn't outrank the chief inspector with the clipboard, there was not a lot he could do about the Uniform Branch presence.

'Well, Len, what's it all about?'

'Wish I knew, guv'nor,' said the DCI. 'Two bodies in the front of the car. Looks as though they got blown away through the windscreen. Bloody near took their heads off. Probably with a sawn-off shotgun.'

Fox walked through the gap in the screens and studied the Ford Sierra. He put his hands in his pockets, leaned forward and stared through the hole where the windscreen had been. 'There's some messy bastards about,' he said. 'It's completely ruined the upholstery. I just hope there's a hand or two left so that we can get some fingerprints. If those two haven't got form I'll retire.'

'I think your job's safe for a few years yet, guv,' said Waring drily.

'Done a check on the registration, Len?'

Waring flipped open his pocket book. 'For what it's worth, guv, it goes out to a finger called Leach. Norman Leach. Address in Walthamstow.'

'Done anything about it yet?'

Waring shook his head. 'No, sir. Did think of contacting the local CID, but I thought I'd hang on for you. Didn't want to cock anything up.'

'Yeah, good. We'll see what the fingerprints bring us, Len. Have the photographers finished?'

'Just about.' Waring glanced at the senior photographer, who nodded.

'Who found this lot?' asked Fox.

'Couple of lads from Traffic Division.'

'Where are they?'

'In the Range Rover.'

Fox walked back to where the motorway patrol vehicle was parked, its crew lounging in their seats scanning newspapers.

The driver slid back the window. 'Afternoon, guv.'

9

Traffic men called everyone 'guv'. It saved worrying about whether they held rank or not.

'Detective Chief Superintendent Fox . . . of the Flying Squad.'

'Ah,' said Phipps. 'I'll get out, sir.'

'How kind,' said Fox and moved to the side of the road. 'Tell me then.' His glance took in Langford and Phipps.

'Thirteen-oh-seven, sir. Saw this vehicle parked on the hard shoulder and stopped to investigate. The exhaust pipe was still hot, and there's damage to the front off-side. There was no debris on the hard shoulder or the carriageway . . .' Phipps shrugged. 'But with the amount of traffic it wouldn't have been there five seconds anyway. If there was any to start with. The damage looks new, but there again, not that new. Anyway, I sent an All Cars message in case anyone spotted a vehicle with a stove-in nearside that was going like the hammers of hell. Passed it on to Thames Valley, too. But I doubt there's much hope.'

'I hope you told them that the occupants might be armed and dangerous,' said Fox with a grin.

The PC grinned too. 'After that lot, guv' – he jerked a thumb towards the screens – 'you'd better believe it.'

'Any witnesses?' asked Fox hopefully.

Phipps shook his head. 'There was nobody hanging about waiting to assist police when we arrived, sir.'

'That's surprising,' said Fox caustically.

Two more cars arrived. The first contained Jack Gilroy, one of Fox's detective inspectors from the Flying Squad, who had been dragged from a race meeting at Epsom. Gilroy was not particularly keen on racing, but he was very enthusiastic about pickpockets and other sundry villains. And the two always went together.

The man who got out of the other car was short and dapper. He wore a dark suit and carried a case. For a moment he stood still and gazed around as though absorbing the atmosphere through the pores of his skin.

10

Fox shook hands. 'How are you, Dr Harris?'

John Harris appeared to give the question some consideration before replying, but it was a habit that went with the job of being a Home Office pathologist. 'Oh, er, fine thanks.'

'Got a nice one for you today.' Fox led the way through the screens and gestured towards the car containing the two bodies as though proudly displaying a prize exhibit.

Harris adjusted his spectacles and peered closely at what was left of the heads and upper bodies of the victims. Then he stood upright again. 'One thing's certain,' he said.

Fox looked expectant. 'What's that?'

'They're both dead.' There was no trace of a smile on the pathologist's face. Quickly and without fuss, he got to work while the police stood and waited. 'Well,' he said, standing up, 'there's not much I can do here. Certainly looks as though they were blasted with a shotgun . . . straight through the windscreen. You can even see little splinters of glass with the naked eye if you look closely.'

'Take your word for it,' said Fox. 'We'll deliver the remains to your workshop then.' He turned to the senior scenes-of-crime officer. 'Want to do your bit before we move them?'

The senior SOCO shook his head. 'No. I think we'll shove it on a low-loader and give it a good going-over at the lab. It'll be easier. But I'll just get the lads to have a quick look round.'

The quick look round produced one interesting item. When the SOCO opened the tail-gate of the Sierra, he spotted a small deposit of white powder on the floor of the vehicle. Unlike his television counterparts, he did not stick his finger into the substance and taste it. He just looked at it. 'Every picture tells a story,' he said.

'I suppose that means something,' said Fox and turned to DI Gilroy. 'We'd better start then, Jack.'

11

Gilroy nodded gloomily. 'Where, guv?' he asked.

'According to Len Waring, the registered keeper of the vehicle is one Norman Leach of Walthamstow. That seems as good a place as any to start.'

It took Swann ages to get Fox and Gilroy to Waltham-stow, mainly because of the monumental traffic jam which the police themselves had created in the area around Junction Four of the M4, but eventually they drew up outside the police station.

A young lady looked up as Fox and Gilroy entered. 'Can I help you?' she asked.

'Yes, you can open the door.' Fox held up his warrant card. 'Flying Squad,' he added tersely. He did not like the new system of replacing grizzled old sergeants with attractive young ladies. It made it more difficult to bark at them.

They found the CID office and Fox gently pushed the door open with his forefinger. The sole occupant was seated at his desk watching some sort of game show on the portable television set. He wore no jacket, his tie was slackened off and his top shirt button was undone. His shirt-sleeves were rolled to just below the elbows and his feet were propped on a wastepaper basket. He glanced up at his two visitors. 'Evening,' he said. 'Help you?'

'I doubt it,' said Fox. 'I'm looking for a CID officer.'

'Well you've found one. DC Habgood.' The young man grinned. 'And you are?'

Gilroy looked up at the ceiling and winced.

'Detective Chief Superintendent Thomas Fox . . . of the Flying Squad.' Fox spoke slowly, carefully enunciating each word. 'And if it's not too much trouble, you can stand up.'

DC Habgood gulped and sprang to his feet, managing to switch off the television set in the same continuous movement. 'All correct, sir,' he said hopefully.

'Really?' Fox gazed round the office, at the piles of

files on various desks, at the open Duty Book, and at the overflowing trays of correspondence. 'I take it that criminal investigation in this part of London rests entirely with you this evening, does it?'

'Er, not exactly, sir. The DI's on, but he's out with one of the skippers. Meeting an informant.'

'Which boozer?'

'Er, I—' The DC advanced on the Duty Book and pored over its pages. 'Doesn't say,' he said glancing up.

'There's a surprise. Get him, will you. Now.'

The DC looked helpless. 'I'm the reserve, sir. I'm not supposed to leave the—'

Fox pointed at the desk. 'That is a telephone,' he said. 'A wondrous instrument. Use it.'

Seven minutes later the DI appeared. He was clearly distressed at having received a telephone call at his favourite hostelry telling him that the head of the Flying Squad was in his office waiting to talk to him. 'Evening, sir. DI Castle. Ted Castle.'

'Well, Mr Castle,' said Fox gazing round the office once more, 'I can see you run a tight ship here. Tell me about Norman Leach.'

Chapter Two

It transpired that Norman Leach lived in one of the maze of streets bounded by Blackhorse Road and Hoe Street, south of Forest Road.

Apart from that, all that Detective Inspector Castle was able to tell Fox was that Leach had come to the notice of the police on two occasions, mainly for petty villainy. 'Mind you, guv,' he continued, 'we've half a suspicion that he might've been involved in one or two heists. But not on this ground. And nothing's ever come up to connect him with anything.'

'Is he the sort of villain who's careless enough to let someone steal his nice new Ford Sierra estate? A two-litre Ghia, no less.'

'Bloody hell,' said Castle, 'he's gone up in the world. According to my records, he's only got a beat-up old Volvo. A Sierra Ghia, you said?'

'Yes. Mind you, it won't be much good now. The windscreen went on the M4.'

Castle laughed. 'Oh dear. Have an accident, did he, guv'nor?'

'You could say that,' said Fox. 'Someone took it in with a sawn-off shotgun by the look of it. And him with it.'

'Yeah, I heard about that job,' said Castle. 'Didn't know you were dealing with it, though. It was him, was it? Leach, I mean.'

Fox shrugged. 'Your guess is as good as mine. Shan't

14

know until we've taken his dabs. His face was spread all over the upholstery when we found him.'

'What about the other geezer?'

'Same. Both unrecognisable, and nothing on them to identify them. Odd that . . . unless they were on a job. Is there anyone that Leach usually ran with?'

'No one in particular. Could pull a few names, but I doubt that they'd be much help. I always got the impression he was a bit of a loner. If he'd got any oppos they were somewhere else.'

'Is he married?'

'A right little slut, his missus. Works on a check-out in a supermarket. We've nicked *her* a few times, too.'

'Thieving?'

'Yeah. International class. Shop-lifting in Woolies' mainly. I think her best haul was about five quid's worth.'

'Better pay her a visit then,' said Fox. He did not relish the idea.

'Want me to come along, guv?'

'No thanks.' Fox shook his head. 'Wouldn't want to keep you from your informant,' he added cruelly. 'But I'd better take a WPC with me, just in case Mrs Leach has a dose of the vapours. Fix it, will you?'

It was a dilapidated terraced house that shared a porch with the house next door. There were three dirty milk bottles on the step.

The front door was opened a few inches by a woman wearing a tight black skirt and a black leather jacket which had undoubtedly been obtained through a mail-order catalogue. She probably thought it was the very height of trendy fashion. Certainly most of the female inhabitants of Walthamstow seemed to think so.

'Yeah?' The woman looked suspiciously at the two policemen. The WPC was on the other side of the porch, out of sight.

'Mrs Leach?'

15

'Who wants to know?'

Fox held up his warrant card. 'Police.'

'Yeah, I'd sort of worked that out for myself. What d'you want? I was just going out.'

'It's about your husband, Mrs Leach.'

'He ain't here.'

'I think it might be better if we came in.' Fox leaned back slightly and peered at the other, firmly closed, front door. Then he stooped towards Mrs Leach and whispered. 'I think your neighbour's interested,' he said.

Mrs Leach opened her front door wide. 'You'd better come in then. Don't want that nosey cow listening to all my business.'

The front room was furnished with a three-piece suite upholstered in black plastic and a coffee-table with dirty glasses on it. A corner near the window was dominated by a huge colour television set beneath which was a video recorder. Under normal circumstances, Fox would have had the serial number checked against the index of stolen property.

'Sit down if you want.' Mrs Leach perched on the edge of the settee.

Fox examined the surface of the chairs and decided to remain standing. 'When did you last see your husband, Mrs Leach?'

'About half-past eight this morning. He dropped me off at work. Why? What's this all about? You haven't nicked him, have you?'

There was no way out of it. 'We think that he may have been murdered, Mrs Leach.'

'Oh my God!' The woman's hand went to her mouth and she stared at the three police officers. 'What d'you mean, you *think* he might have been murdered? Surely you know.'

'I'll make a cup of tea,' said the WPC they had brought with them from Forest Road.

'Yeah, you do that,' said Fox and turned once more to Mrs Leach. 'What we mean, Mrs Leach, is that a

16

man has been murdered. What we're not sure about is whether it's your husband. It was certainly his car. A red Ford Sierra Ghia estate.'

'It ain't. We've got an old Volvo. On its last legs an' all.'

'And is that what he was driving this morning when he dropped you off at work?'

'Yeah, course. I don't know nothing about no estate. What d'you say it was?'

'A red Ford Sierra Ghia, two-litre. This year's model.'

'You must be joking. Where d'you think Norm'd get the money for something like that? I reckon you've got him mixed up with someone else.'

Fox resisted the temptation to explain about the Police National Computer and the index of registered keepers of motor vehicles. 'Where was he going this morning? After he'd dropped you off?'

'Mini-cabbing.'

'Really? Who does he work for?'

Mrs Leach appeared to give that some thought. 'Can't remember, offhand.' She stood up and crossed the room to a side table. 'I think there's one of his cards here somewhere.' She opened a drawer and started to rummage. 'Yeah. There you are.'

Fox took the card, glanced briefly at it and slipped it into his pocket. 'When were you expecting him home, then?'

Mrs Leach shrugged. 'Usually gone midnight on a Saturday. I know he had a job out to the airport this morning—'

'Which airport?'

'Heathrow. He might have picked up another job out there. There's no telling where he could finish up. I've known him get a run up to Birmingham sometimes. Sometimes he don't come home at all. Leastways not till next day.' Suddenly she remembered why the police were there. 'What d'you mean, you don't know if this bloke's my husband? The one what's been murdered.'

17

'Because we haven't been able to identify him, Mrs Leach,' said Fox.

'So I s'pose you want me to come and have a look . . .' She glanced at her watch. 'I mean, I was going out, but it was only down the Palais.'

'No,' said Fox. 'I don't think that'd be a very good idea. You see we can't identify the man because he's not recognisable. The nature of the injuries, you see . . .'

'Oh my God!' The realisation of what Fox had been trying to tell the woman suddenly dawned. 'But this car. I mean this Ford you was on about. I never knew nothing about that. Could it belong to the mini-cab firm?'

Fox looked doubtful. 'I wouldn't have thought so,' he said. He knew damned well that it didn't. Fox was fairly certain that Leach had been engaged in some criminal enterprise. And probably a continuing one at that. Profitable enough to buy a car that cost nigh on twenty thousand pounds. And not to want his wife to know about it.

Fox watched the WPC as she brought in the tea things and set them down on the coffee-table, carefully pushing the dirty glasses out of the way with the edge of the tray. 'We'll let you know as soon as we hear anything further, Mrs Leach,' he said. 'Meanwhile, I'll leave this officer to pour your tea.'

'Aren't you staying for a cup, sir?' The WPC looked hurt.

'No, but I want a word with you before I go.'

The WPC followed Fox into the tiny hallway, edging past a bicycle to get to the front door. 'Yes, sir?'

'There is nothing I'd like better than to turn this place over,' said Fox, 'but even I'm not that hard.' Behind him, Gilroy looked surprised. 'So keep your eyes open while you're here . . . and your ears. Anything interesting, give Mr Gilroy a ring.'

The owner of the mini-cab firm was called Benjamin

18

Kitchener and he looked suspiciously at Fox's warrant card. 'I guess you gentlemen don't want a cab,' he said, with a nervous grin.

'Norman Leach,' said Fox. 'One of your drivers, is he?'

Kitchener shook his head. 'Not one of mine, man. I ain't never heard of him.'

'His wife says he works for you and that he had a job out at Heathrow Airport this morning.'

Kitchener shook his head. 'Nope. But I'll just make sure.' He walked across his small office and slid back a glass panel. Addressing the back of a man seated at a microphone, he said, 'Winston, you ever hear of some bloke called—' He paused and glanced back at Fox.

'Leach. Norman Leach,' said Fox.

'Norman Leach,' said Kitchener, turning again to the controller.

The controller swivelled round in his chair and shook his head. 'Don't mean nothing,' he said. 'Could try the other firm. It's about two hundred yards up on the other side of the road.'

'The gentleman says he had a job out the airport this morning.'

The controller glanced at a pad. 'Never had nothing out the airport today . . . more's the pity.'

Fox produced the card and laid it on the desk. 'His wife said that this was one of the cards he used.'

Kitchener shrugged. 'We leave those in every Chinese restaurant, every Indian take-away, and every phone box in the area. It don't mean nothing, man.'

'Drove a new Sierra estate, Ghia. Red.'

Kitchener shook his head again. 'All our drivers use their own cars,' he said, 'but there's none of them got one of those.'

'Or an old Volvo?'

'Nope,' said Kitchener.

'Want to check the other one, sir?' asked Gilroy when they were back in Fox's Granada.

19

'I'm not wasting time visiting every mini-cab firm in Walthamstow,' said Fox. 'Get a DC to ring round when we get back. Not that it'll get us much further forward.'

By midday Sunday things had started to come together. The senior fingerprint officer appeared in Fox's office and announced that the two bodies in the car had been identified. One was indeed Norman Leach. The other was called Barnaby Collins. Both had a decent bit of form, Collins more than Leach, and Fox was now more certain than ever that they'd been up to no good. They certainly hadn't been tooled up, as the police say when talking of someone who is armed. But then whoever was responsible for their deaths probably relieved them of any weaponry they had about their persons.

They could have been in the midst of perpetrating any sort of villainy. The criminal record of each showed a catalogue of crime as varied as any calendar at the Old Bailey. Theft, robbery, burglary, demanding money with menaces, assault occasioning bodily harm, both grievous and actual, with and without intent. It was all there. The dismissive view of DI Castle at Forest Road that Leach had 'a bit of form', as he called it, had to be tempered by the fact that compared with many in Castle's parish Leach was a bit of a slow starter.

But the phone call from the Forensic Science Laboratory at Lambeth concentrated Fox's mind in a particular direction. 'The powder in the back of the car, Jack . . .' he said, replacing the receiver.

'Yes, sir?' Gilroy looked up from a statement he was reading.

'Cocaine. About forty per cent purity.'

Gilroy whistled softly. 'Street value about—?'

'About ninety grand a kilo,' said Fox. 'Give or take a few pence.' He swung his chair round and stood up. For a few moments he stared out of the window, gazing down at the street below. 'I've had an idea, Jack.'

'You have, sir?' Gilroy sounded nervous. He'd been

involved in some of Fox's ideas before. They always made him nervous.

'If that car was loaded with cocaine, which seems quite likely, it's an odds-on chance that whoever blew our two friends away stole the said cocaine.'

'Yes . . .' Gilroy spoke hesitantly, not sure what to expect.

Suddenly Fox swung round to face his DI. 'And look where it all happened, Jack.'

'On the hard shoulder of the M4. So what?'

'Practically on top of Heathrow Airport, Jack. And Widow Leach told us that the late, lamented Norm had a job there. I'm beginning to work out just what that job might have been.'

'Well, it wasn't mini-cabbing, guv. At least, not from Walthamstow. The lads have checked them all out. Nothing.'

Detective Chief Superintendent Daniel Jebb was in charge of the Metropolitan Police Special Branch unit at Heathrow Airport. His airy office alongside Terminal Two faced one of the runways and every time he glanced out there seemed to be an aircraft landing or taking off. Not that he had a great deal of time for looking out of windows. His job, with an inadequate number of officers, was to maintain a port watch at the greatest airport in the world. And wherever there were policemen, there was paper. Expenses, duty rosters and reports about every manner of crime . . . and the travelling criminals who committed them. And there was sex. Jebb was convinced that the vast array of attractive young stewardesses working at the airport was a constant temptation to his officers. 'Beware,' he would warn his men, 'they are looking for a husband . . . anybody's husband.' But then Jebb was a pessimist. And as if that wasn't enough, he was frequently troubled by police officers outside his command. Police officers from every force in the country, and sometimes abroad, who wanted help

21

or favours or who just dropped in for a chat and a chance to relieve Jebb of some of his Scotch.

This morning, his visitor was Detective Chief Superintendent Tommy Fox of the Flying Squad.

'Morning, Danny.'

Jebb looked up from his overflowing desk. 'That's all I need,' he said.

'Nice to feel welcome,' said Fox. 'How's the dream factory these days?'

'D'you want something, or have you just called in to waste my time, Tommy?'

'As a matter of fact, Daniel dear boy, I am in need of the sort of expert advice that only you can provide.'

'Bullshit,' said Jebb, and flung down his pen.

'I'm investigating the two murders that took place on the hard shoulder of the M4 on Saturday afternoon,' continued Fox, quite unabashed. 'We found traces of cocaine in the vehicle, like it might have been carrying a load. The chances are, I think, that my two victims were couriers of some sort, and got themselves hi-jacked . . . fatally hi-jacked. Now given that the venue was not a million miles from this prestigious airport of yours, I started thinking.'

The badinage was over. This was professional stuff and Jebb became suddenly interested. 'Yes. Go on.'

'I know that you've got this place buttoned up—'

Jeff scoffed. 'Thanks.'

'But it did cross my mind that some sort of pick-up may have occurred. That our two heroes had a load of coke away and then had it stolen from them.' Fox shook his head sadly. 'It's terrible what some people will do for money,' he added.

'Yes,' said Jebb, 'and if they're really desperate, they join the police and finish up at Heathrow Airport. What have you got in mind?'

'I don't think it was just a kilo. Not worth blowing away a couple of couriers, even for ninety grand. So it must have been worthwhile. A substantial amount. That

22

means it's unlikely to have been brought through Customs. Too risky. How about over the wire?' Fox leaned back in his chair and grinned.

'You must be joking,' said Jebb. He stood up. 'Here, come and look at this.' He walked to the window and pointed at a barrier guarded by one of BAA's security men. 'Every time anyone wants to go through there – and that's only to the cargo tunnel – they have to produce a pass. This place is so tight you can't get away with anything.'

Fox smiled. 'Very good,' he said. 'But supposing he's bent.'

Jebb turned slowly from the window. 'That's always a possibility, I suppose.'

'Yes,' said Fox. 'Now we're making progress. Tell me, were there any dodgy flights in on Saturday? Around lunch-time?'

'Dodgy flights?'

'Yeah. Flights that could have come from a part of the world that has a consuming interest in the production and sale of cocaine. And I do mean consuming.'

Jebb picked up an airport timetable from the window ledge and skimmed through it. 'Bogota,' he said. 'Arrives once a week. On Saturdays. At noon.'

Fox sighed. 'Could anyone get anything off that?'

'Not a chance,' said Jebb. 'Customs have their blokes swarming all over it the moment it arrives. It's a target flight. Too obvious, Tommy, coming from Colombia.'

'What about connecting flights, then?'

Jebb scoffed. 'Now you're asking. See that?' He pointed to a large volume on his bookcase. 'That's *The ABC of World Airlines*. Tells you every flight that connects with every other flight anywhere. The permutations are limitless.'

Fox looked despondent. 'Got any ideas?'

'Well, if you're looking for a South American flight . . .'

'I don't know what I'm looking for.'

23

'There's the Rio de Janeiro. That comes in at about the time you're interested in. The stuff could be brought overland to meet it.' Jebb shrugged. 'It's like looking for a needle in a haystack, Tommy. A hypodermic needle.'

Chapter Three

When Fox and Jebb suggested to Ron Jefferson, the head of security at Heathrow Airport, that one of his staff might just be on the take, he looked grave, but he was not naïve enough to dismiss it out of hand. 'Well, gentlemen,' he said, 'I can certainly tell you who was covering that section of the airport where the aircraft was parked, but I have to say that it seems an enormous risk for anyone to take in broad daylight. The customs people are patrolling all the time, you know, just waiting for something like that.' He reached out for the phone and then paused. 'I take it that this is pure speculation at the moment?'

'Yes,' said Fox. 'What I call a hunch.'

'Right then,' said Jefferson, relinquishing his hold on the phone, 'in that case, I'll be a little more circumspect in my inquiries. I take it you want to catch this fellow in the act . . . at some future time?'

'Ideally,' said Fox. 'But we might be barking up the wrong tree.'

'Understood, but if I start making inquiries about the specific duties of one man, that man will get to hear of it in no time at all. So I'll approach it in a roundabout way and let Mr Jebb know when I've got a result. It won't take long, I promise you.' Jefferson paused. 'I'm not suggesting that all my chaps are lily white, but a maintenance man would be a much better bet, you know.'

'And how many of them are there?'

'Thousands,' said Jebb.

Jefferson smiled. 'Not quite,' he said. 'It just seems like it. If you'd like me to make a few inquiries, Mr Fox, I'd be more than willing. I probably know my way round this airport better than most.'

Fox nodded gloomily. 'That would be a help,' he said. 'Provided it was done discreetly.'

Jefferson just smiled. 'I was a policeman once, albeit in Africa . . . and a long time ago,' he said.

The Collector of Customs and Excise was less than happy about Fox's speculations and promptly called in another officer. 'This is Mr Ramsay, the SIO from ID,' he said.

'I'm very happy for him,' said Fox, 'but what does that mean?'

'Senior Investigating Officer, Investigation Division,' replied the Collector a little tersely. 'And if there's any indication that drug smuggling is taking place on the scale you visualise, Chief Superintendent, something will have to be done about it immediately. And by Her Majesty's Customs.'

'Wouldn't you like to know where it's going?' asked Fox mildly.

'Well of course, but—'

'Then I've a suggestion to make that ought to get us both out of a spot.'

The Collector looked dubious. 'We can't just let this stuff run and then hope for the best, you know.'

'I'm aware of that,' said Fox, 'but two people have been murdered already. In this sort of game, others may be killed. But then I don't have to tell you that.'

The Collector nodded.

'If we play our cards right, though, you'll get your drug smugglers and I'll get my killers.' He leaned back in his chair and grinned. 'There, can't say fairer than that, can I?'

'What d'you have in mind, then?' asked the SIO. The Collector still looked unhappy.

'See how this grabs you, old son,' said Fox, and leaning forward began to outline his plan.

The head of security at Heathrow Airport had been very thorough. Certain members of his staff had certainly been patrolling near the M4 and at a time when the Rio de Janeiro flight had arrived, but there was nothing to indicate whether any of them had been involved in cocaine smuggling. Not that Fox had any evidence to link the murders with the airport other than that they had occurred within spitting distance of it, and that traces of cocaine had been found in the victims' vehicle. Even he had to admit that it was a long shot.

But Jefferson did provide the names of the maintenance crew which had serviced the aircraft. The men worked for a firm of specialists who held several contracts, usually from airlines who found such an arrangement cheaper than employing a full technical staff of their own at every airport they used.

Fox stared at the list of names and decided that he would do some digging. Or more to the point, that some of his men would dig. He sent for Detective Inspector Henry Findlater, sometime head of the Criminal Intelligence Branch surveillance team, but now a member of the Flying Squad and a natural choice for what Fox had in mind.

'Henry, I am passionately interested in learning more about a merry team of artisans at Heathrow Airport.'

Findlater gazed mildly through his owl-like glasses at Fox. 'Do we have any more details than that, sir?'

'Indeed we do, Henry. They are all maintenance engineers, cleaners and in-flight caterers and they all live near the airport . . . I should think.' Fox smiled benignly and pushed a piece of paper across his desk. 'Those are their personal particulars.'

'Right, sir.' Findlater picked up the piece of paper and turned.

'And, Henry . . . discreetly, eh? I don't want these fingers to know of our interest in them.'

Findlater frowned. Slightly. 'Of course, sir.'

Findlater assembled his usual team for the job. It included Detective Sergeant Percy Fletcher and Detective Constable Ernest Crabtree, both of whom were accustomed to being lumbered with Findlater's surveillance jobs. They weren't enthusiastic about these observations, but that was the way it was in the Flying Squad. Show that you were proficient at something just once, and you were lumbered for ever after.

One of the fascinating things about discreet inquiry work is that most of the information the police need is already recorded. Somewhere. The trick is to discover where. But Percy Fletcher knew. In common with many policemen, he was essentially lazy. That meant that he would only move from his desk as a last resort, and one of the perverse laws of criminal investigation is that idle policemen are often the most efficient.

But there comes a time when there is no alternative to leg-work, and after two days of letting their fingers do the walking, both on the telephone and the computer, that point was reached.

There followed ten days of boring observation before the Flying Squad struck lucky. The name, when it came, meant nothing. Not officially. Nor for that matter any other way. But their man was called Stanley Reynolds.

Fortunately, Stanley Reynolds was either over-confident or careless, although it amounted to the same thing in the long run. But whichever it was, he never once spotted any of the scruffy vans or run-down motor cars from which the police were keeping watch on his house in Harlington, whether it was early in the morning, in the middle of the day, or late at night. Every time he came out of his house he got into his seven-year-old Austin Maestro without a glance up or down the street and drove to the airport. Once there, he would wave cheerfully at various friends and colleagues, and there were a lot of them, sometimes even sounding his horn to attract their attention. Having left his car in the staff car park, he would amble slowly across to the duty room and then on to wherever he happened to be assigned for that particular shift.

During breaks, Reynolds would play cards or darts or a frame of snooker, but always boisterously, shouting, laughing and generally chi-iking everyone around him. He seemed to be without a care in the world. And without a guilty conscience.

But Reynolds eventually gave himself up. In a manner of speaking.

Fletcher, huddled in a nondescript observation van, was somewhat surprised to see Reynolds emerge from his house apparently intent upon going to work. Surprised because the shift rosters which the police had discreetly obtained showed that Reynolds should have been off duty. But he was wearing his 'uniform' of blue jeans and a blue denim shirt. As usual, he carried the small holdall which they now knew would contain his sandwiches, a set of darts and a pack of cards.

Fletcher promptly radioed Findlater, who, with Crabtree, was parked up near the house of another suspect some three miles away, and told him that Reynolds was going to work after all.

Findlater was not unduly surprised by this turn of events and was pleased that enough of his team were not too far away. Today was a day when a Rio de Janeiro flight was due to arrive and it was beginning to look as though Reynolds had swapped duties so that he could be there to meet it.

'Just had a call from Henry Findlater, guv,' said Gilroy. 'Reynolds left the house at seven o'clock this morning, dressed to go to work. Looks as though he's done a swap.'

Fox stood up and rubbed his hands together. 'Aha!' he said. 'Cunning little bastard. Better give our customs friend a ring, I suppose.'

But Stanley Reynolds did not go to work. He drove on to the M25 motorway, switched to the M3, and carried on south-west for a further thirty miles leaving at Junction Seven. Ten miles more and he pulled into the driveway of a secluded house near Preston Candover. Waiting only to see Reynolds put his car into a double garage next to a Porsche, Findlater and his team made for the nearest phone box.

'What now, sir?' asked Gilroy.

'Now,' said Fox, 'we get a Home Office warrant to put an intercept on his phone. Should make interesting listening. Anything else?'

'Yes, sir. Ramsay and the customs boys at Heathrow kept discreet observation on the Rio flight . . . from afar.'

'I should bloody well hope so. And?'

'Nothing, sir. Clean as a whistle.'

'Good.'

'Good, sir?'

'Yes, Jack. Reynolds wasn't there and nothing happened. I think we're looking in the right direction.'

'Oh!' Gilroy was non-committal. For him there were too many negatives to make the information of any use.

Fox had authorised the withdrawal of the surveillance team. Findlater had told him that they would be too exposed to maintain a discreet observation, and Fox agreed that it would endanger the operation if they were spotted. It was not that they thought Reynolds was alert enough to notice them, but at this stage the police didn't know who else was in the house. But Fox meant to find out and Fletcher's fingers started walking again.

It was apparent that friend Reynolds was not taking any chances with petty officialdom. He was registered for poll tax and the records showed two adults living in the house. A check on the registration number of the Porsche, which Findlater had been able to get before the garage door had been closed, indicated that Stanley Reynolds was the registered keeper and gave the Preston Candover address.

Fox decided that he would have to take the local police into his confidence and telephoned the head of the Hampshire Constabulary CID. Before ringing Fox back, the Hampshire detective had made a call to the uniformed constable who was responsible for the area where Reynolds seemed to have a second home. The officer, a man of twenty-eight years' service, was a mine of information. Yes, he knew of Reynolds . . . and his wife. But it was a different wife from the one living in Harlington. The one in Hampshire was about twenty-five and good-looking. The local policeman didn't know what Reynolds did for a living, but he was often away from home. He seemed to have plenty of money and tended not to mix with the locals.

'Looks like he's living two lives, guv,' said Gilroy.

'He's going to need nine by the time I've finished with him,' growled Fox.

Reynolds's next tour of duty at the airport was on the following Tuesday, but he had returned to Harlington the previous evening. Three days later he was off to Hampshire once more.

'I wonder how he explains his absences to his missus,' said Gilroy. 'His Harlington missus, I mean.'

'Probably spins her some fanny about times being hard and having to work overtime,' said Fox gloomily. 'You know, like you do.'

*

Fox's inquiries into the background of Barnaby Collins, the other victim of the M4 shooting, were disappointing. Which was no more than he expected. Collins's criminal record showed his last address to be in the backwaters of New Malden. There was no reply. As Fox and Gilroy retraced their steps, a helpful neighbour appeared from next door.

'She's out.'

'Thank you, madam,' said Fox. 'I'd come to that conclusion myself. Do you know when she's likely to be back?'

'No idea. I think she works.'

'I see. Thank you for your kind assistance.' Fox's sarcasm was lost on her.

They had just got into the car when a woman came round the corner of the street. She was attempting to control a push-chair with one hand while carrying a bulging shopping bag with the other.

'Could be,' said Gilroy.

It was. When she reached the door of the house that Fox and Gilroy had just left, the woman stopped and started searching her bag for keys.

'Mrs Collins, is it?'

The woman looked up. 'Yes.'

'I'm a police officer, madam,' said Fox, and glancing at Gilroy, said, 'Help the lady, Jack, there's a good fellow.'

In the cramped front room of the house, Mrs Collins unstrapped her child from his enforced confinement. Fox eyed the child benevolently as he promptly went berserk, running about and screaming at the top of his voice.

'Darren, shut that bleeding row,' said Mrs Collins mechanically. 'Go and play with your cars.' It had no effect. She turned to Fox. 'What d'you want?'

'It's about your husband, Mrs Collins. I take it your husband is Barnaby Collins?'

Mrs Collins smiled. It was only the police who called

him Barnaby. 'Barney? He don't live here any more. What's he been up to, anyway?'

'You say he doesn't live here.'

'No. We split up. Went off with some bird. We got divorced. Good riddance, too.'

'I see. You don't happen to know where he went to live, I suppose?'

Mrs Collins shook her head. 'No idea. Didn't care neither. Anyway, what's this all about?'

'I'm sorry to have to tell you that he's dead, Mrs Collins.'

'Oh!' Mrs Collins spoke the word flatly, an automatic response devoid of any emotion. 'What happened to him then?'

'I'm afraid he was murdered, Mrs Collins.'

The woman nodded, as though accepting an inevitability that she had expected for some time. 'Can't say I'm surprised. He mixed with a rough lot, you know.'

'When did you last see Barney?'

Mrs Collins lit a cigarette and dropped the match into an overflowing ashtray. 'About five years back, I s'pose. Last time he went in nick.'

'I see.' Fox was aware that Collins had been sentenced to five years' imprisonment for his part in a robbery. Knew also that he had been released just over eighteen months ago after receiving full remission for what passed these days as good conduct in Her Majesty's prisons. 'And you've not seen him since then?'

'No.'

'You mentioned a divorce. Didn't you see him then?'

'No,' she said again. 'It was all done by post.'

'You mentioned that he'd gone off with some other woman,' said Fox. Mrs Collins nodded. 'Do you know anything about her?'

'The solicitor said something about her being a hostess in one of them clubs, up Fulham somewhere I think, but I can't remember her name. Matter of fact, I don't think I ever knew it.'

'You don't happen to remember the name of the solicitor, do you?'

Mrs Collins walked across to an old and scratched sideboard. After taking out a variety of papers, a napkin ring, two old pens and a mail-order catalogue, she produced a letter and handed it to Fox. 'There it is.' It was a note from the solicitor telling her that the decree had been made absolute and giving details of the maintenance she could expect to receive.

'Did you receive any money from Barney?' asked Fox.

Mrs Collins scoffed. 'You must be bloody joking,' she said. 'I go office cleaning in the mornings, and work in a pub at nights.'

'What about him?' Fox nodded at the rampaging Darren.

'Take him with me, don't I.'

It had taken a great deal of persuasion to secure a warrant to tap Reynolds's Hampshire telephone, and it was only after a lot of teeth-sucking on the part of Home Office officials that it had eventually been granted. But it was some days before anything remotely interesting turned up.

'I've got the latest transcripts, sir,' said Gilroy. 'Starting to get interesting by the look of it.'

'About bloody time,' said Fox.

Until then, all that the intercept had proved was that the woman who lived with Reynolds in Hampshire was called Sherry Martin and she spent an inordinate amount of time on the phone, chatting with friends or making appointments with either her hairdresser or with her beauty salon for facials and manicures.

Fortunately for the police. Sherry Martin was in the house alone when the first telephone call to excite Fox's interest was made.

'A woman rang and asked for Mr Reynolds,' said Gilroy. 'Sherry told her that Reynolds wasn't there, and asked who it was. The woman said that she was the

34

receptionist at the hotel, but didn't say which hotel. So Sherry asked. The woman said that Stan would know.' Gilroy looked up and grinned. 'You'll notice, guv, that suddenly Mr Reynolds has become Stan. Then she asked the caller what the telephone number was. The receptionist said Stan would know that too, and said, "Just ask him to ring the hotel." Anyway, Sherry eventually got the message, as you might say.'

'Is that all?' asked Fox.

Gilroy flipped over a page of the intercept report. 'No, sir. When our Stanley got in, which seems to be about an hour later, he's straight on the trumpet and asked for Miss Clark. She's presumably the receptionist – the lads on the taps reckon it was the same voice – and indulged in a strange conversation, and I quote. Clark: "Thank you for ringing back, sir. I just wanted to confirm your reservation." Reynolds: "Thank you. It is still as telephoned by my secretary." Clark: "Right then, sir. I'll make sure there's a porter available." ' '

Fox took a cigarette and tapped it thoughtfully on the case. 'And Miss Clark had reverted to calling him sir. Interesting. That's it, is it?'

'Not quite, sir. Earlier today Sherry Martin also made one or two calls to the operations room of an airline at Heathrow Airport.'

'Oh? What about?'

'Confirming duty times.' Gilroy looked smug. 'It would appear, sir, that she's a stewardess . . . on a South American run.'

'Well, well.' Fox's fingers played a little tattoo on his blotter. 'Things are beginning to come together, Jack. It looks as though our Mr Reynolds, who seems to be living beyond his means, is going to take a short holiday. I'm beginning to think he's the courier, Jack. And that Sherry Martin is helping him.' Fox held out a hand for the intercept report. 'This hotel . . . do we have an address for it?'

'Yes, sir. The number that Miss Clark rang from, and

the number that Reynolds called back, were one and the same.'

'What a surprise.'

'That's it there.' Gilroy pointed. 'Goes out to a hotel in Gloucestershire, the owner of which appears to be one Charles Norton.'

'Know anything about it, do we? Or him?'

'Not yet, guv'nor. We've only had the information for about ten minutes.'

Fox shook his head wearily. 'Long enough, Jack,' he said. 'Long enough.'

Chapter Four

Charles Norton's hotel was about ten miles from Cheltenham. In fact, it was about ten miles from anywhere. As far as the local police were concerned it was a properly regulated establishment and neither Norton nor his hotel had ever been a problem. 'He did say it was a very expensive place, sir,' added Gilroy.

'Who's "he", Jack?'

'The detective chief superintendent, head of CID, guv.'

Fox scoffed. 'Yeah, I know him,' he said. 'As far as he's concerned, anything he can't get for nothing is expensive. Tell me about the place.'

'Converted country house with a separate block of modern bedrooms built on. There are conference facilities and a health club complete with indoor swimming pool. Sounds all very kosher, guv. I suppose that friend Reynolds is going to have a dirty weekend there with his bird.'

Fox appeared to give that some thought before speaking again. 'Why should he bother, Jack?' he asked at last. 'He's already shacked up with her in an expensive drum in Preston Candover. No, there's more to it than that. Some woman called Clark speaks to Sherry Martin and says tell Stan to ring the hotel. Right?' Gilroy nodded. 'When Stanley does so, Miss Clark calls him sir, and sounds all official.'

'I think we can thank Sherry Martin for that, sir. Miss Clark obviously expected Reynolds to answer the phone the first time she rang. But Reynolds was out and his daft bird answered instead, started asking stupid questions and Miss Clark got flustered.' Gilroy ran a hand round his chin. 'Trouble is there's no way we can put an obo on Reynolds at his place in Hampshire. As Henry says, we'd stick out like a sore thumb.'

'Don't think we need to, Jack. Have a word with Henry – he's got a copy of the maintenance crew's duty roster – and find out when Reynolds has next got a day or two off duty. And get Henry to have a word with Special Branch at Heathrow as well. See if they can help with a duty roster for Sherry Martin. If she's off duty as well that will be when the pair of them go to this hotel in Gloucestershire. And if we're very lucky, it'll be shortly after the next flight from Rio.'

'So what do we do, sir?'

'What we don't do is to put an obo on him, Jack. At least, not all the way. We'll let Henry Findlater see him off and we'll wait at the other end for him to arrive.'

'Right, sir,' said Gilroy. 'And who do we get to do that?'

'Fancy a weekend in an expensive hotel, Jack, courtesy of the Commissioner?'

There is a failing among senior policemen. It is a misplaced concept that they, and only they, can do the job properly. On the arduous climb from constable to commissioner they are convinced of their own competence to carry out their duties faultlessly. But when they are promoted, they find that those who have replaced them in the ranks below are somehow not nearly as competent as they were themselves when they were down there. Consequently they assume an overwhelming desire to do the job themselves. This aberration is excused by such self-deluding thoughts as not having joined the job to shuffle paper, drive a desk, attend meetings about reorganisation, discuss budgets, or enter into serious debates about whether policemen should salute each other. Detectives don't salute anyone anyway.

But Fox really did hate paperwork. His idea of a day's sport was to sally forth and joust with London's villainry.

Although it had been his original intention that Detective Inspector Jack Gilroy should go by himself to Charles Norton's hotel for a bit of a poke about, Fox eventually convinced himself that he should go as well.

'If they happen to sus me out as Old Bill, Jack,' said Fox, 'they'll start running around like a disturbed ants' nest. And what I want you to do is keep your ear to the ground and watch what comes up.'

Gilroy refrained from suggesting that Fox was doing a bit of metaphor-mixing or that the answer could well be ants. 'But if they sus you out, guv,' he said, 'they'll know who I am.'

'We will not talk to each other, Jack.'

'But if we arrive together—'

'Nor will we arrive together, Jack. I shall go by car and you will go by train.'

'But what about the expense, sir?' That wasn't the reason at all. Gilroy hated trains.

Fox appeared to give that some thought. 'Exactly, Jack. You know what the Commander's like about expenses.'

'Yes, sir, I do know what the Commander's like. But it'll be cheaper by car, even if I travel separately. Anyway, it'd look a bit strange for a businessman to turn up at a hotel without a car. Everyone's got a company car these days.'

Fox considered that. 'What we'll do, Jack, is travel down by car – my car – and I'll drop you at the station. Then you can get a taxi and turn up as though you don't know me.'

'God Almighty!' said Gilroy. When he was back in his office.

The solicitor was very cagey about discussing a client's

affairs. Even a loathsome, one-off client like Barnaby Collins.

'Client!' said Fox. 'He's a bloody toe-rag—'

'Be that as it may, Chief Superintendent—'

'And he's been blown away by some hood whose collar I'm going to feel before he's much older.'

The solicitor blinked behind his rimless spectacles. 'Blown away?' He visualised his client having been swept off some cliff-top by a mischievous gale and immediately foresaw a claim for heavy damages against an authority too negligent to fence such a dangerous promontory. He was very good at conveyancing too, and a positive wizard at finding his way through some labyrinthine trust, but the earthier language of the underworld was something of a mystery to him.

'He was blasted into eternity by some low-life with a shotgun,' said Fox patiently.

'Oh!'

'Exactly,' said Fox. 'So his last known whereabouts would be of inestimable value to me. As would the name of the woman he went off with.'

'Ah!' The solicitor flicked a switch on his office inter-com and asked for the file concerning Collins against Collins. After some seconds, a young lady appeared with a slim folder. 'Yes,' said the solicitor, 'I think I can let you have his last address.'

But the building wasn't there. It had been pulled down and a half-completed office block now stood in its place.

Percy Fletcher went back to the records again but found that the address provided by the solicitor was the only one contained in any official documentation concerning the late Barnaby Collins apart, that is, from the one at New Malden which had already proved a blow-out.

'Sod it,' said Fox.

'Well, is that it, guv?' asked Gilroy.

'Too bloody right. I'm not wasting any more time on him,' said Fox. 'As far as I'm concerned they can bung him in a pauper's grave. And the sooner the better. But,' he added, 'this Tracy Barlow . . .'

'The bird his wife divorced him over, you mean?'

'Get Percy Fletcher to find her. And tell him to have a little chat with her.'

It was only five days before Stanley Reynolds's next scheduled two days off duty coincided with Sherry Martin's two days leave. Fox promptly set off for Gloucestershire accompanied by a muttering Gilroy, still irritated that Fox was intent upon dumping him at Cheltenham railway station.

The hotel was set in a few acres of countryside, and proved to be exactly as the local police had described it. Fox registered, had a quick shower, and made his way downstairs. It was seven o'clock in the evening.

Gilroy turned up some forty minutes later. But of Stanley Reynolds there was no sign.

Not particularly wanting to chance having anyone listening in if he rang New Scotland Yard through the hotel switchboard from his room, Fox made for a pay phone in the lobby.

'I was just going to ring you, guv'nor,' said Henry Findlater. 'He's down in Preston Candover. Doesn't look like he's coming in your direction, either. According to the intercept we've got on his line, he's just booked a table for two in Basingstoke.'

'Didn't know there were any restaurants in Basingstoke,' said Fox acidly, and slamming the receiver back on its rest made his way to the bar.

It was richly furnished and dimly lit, but the oak beams were undoubtedly genuine. There were comfortable leather chairs, and small tables fashioned from half-barrels with brass trimmings. It had an air of quality that met with Fox's whole-hearted approval.

As Fox entered, a man detached himself from a little group at the far end of the bar and strolled towards him

41

with his hand outstretched. 'Good evening. I'm Charles Norton. I own the place.'

Fox shook hands. 'How d'you do?'

'Let me get you a drink . . .' Norton raised an eyebrow.

'Scotch, please.'

'Your first time with us, isn't it?' Norton was an impressive man. Some six feet two in height, he was elegantly attired in a hacking jacket which must have cost the earth. Cavalry twills, highly polished brogues and a check shirt with a yellow cravat completed the ensemble. He fingered his moustache and smiled.

'Just a bit of business in Cheltenham,' said Fox.

'Ah yes. Get a lot of businessmen here, y'know. What line are you in, as a matter of interest?'

'Pest control,' said Fox and picked up his glass. 'Cheers.'

'Yes, good health, old boy.' Norton took a longish draught of real ale. 'Pest control, eh? Must say you don't look like a rat-catcher.'

'Appearances can be very deceptive,' said Fox. 'Nice place you've got here.'

'Try to do our best, old boy, but times are hard.'

Fox nodded in an understanding way. 'Been in the business long?'

'Since I came out of the army as a matter of fact. Came to the conclusion that I wasn't going to get any further than captain, and . . .' Norton paused to sip his beer again. 'Well, to be frank, there's not a lot a public school chap can do after the army. No qualifications. That sort of thing. So here I am, so to speak.'

'Must have been difficult.'

'Difficult?'

'Yes. Coming out of the army and not knowing what to do.'

'Oh, I see. Yes, but still, we manage to scratch a living. Come far, have you?'

'Not really. Hampshire.'

'Oh, whereabouts?'

'Just outside Basingstoke.'

Norton nodded. 'Nice part,' he said. 'Well, if you'll excuse me, I must pop out to the kitchens. Make sure the cook-sergeant's got everything under control, if you know what I mean.' Norton laughed and drained his glass. 'Feel free to make use of the facilities,' he said. 'Swimming-pool, sauna, all that sort of thing.'

'Well that was a blow-out, Jack.' Fox and Gilroy were on their way back to Scotland Yard. And on speaking terms again. Fox had aborted their visit to Norton's hotel the morning after their arrival, when he received Henry Findlater's message that Stanley Reynolds had returned to Harlington. 'Norton's a public school man and ex-army . . . a captain apparently,' he continued. 'He's a bit over the top, but he seems the genuine article . . . bit too genuine for my liking. What did you learn, Jack, anything?'

'Not a lot, sir, no,' said Gilroy, 'but I did bump into his wife. Literally. We collided in a doorway.'

Fox nodded sagely. 'Yes, you would, Jack.'

'A horsy type. Tight-fitting riding breeches, silk blouse. Long brown hair . . .' Gilroy grinned. 'In a pony-tail.'

'Naturally,' murmured Fox. 'Name?'

'Letitia.'

'How d'you find that out?'

'She told me.'

'I don't know about you, Jack.'

'I am a qualified detective, guv.'

'Apart from the description, anything useful?'

'Got the impression she was very county,' said Gilroy. 'Wouldn't mind betting she's got a wardrobe full of ball-gowns . . . and green wellies.'

'Not to be worn at the same time, I trust,' said Fox mildly. He paused in thought for a moment or two, then said, 'Get hold of Percy Fletcher, Jack. I've got a job for him.'

But Percy Fletcher was still working hard at the first of Fox's quick-fire string of tasks.

'Help you, squire?' The blue-chinned bouncer at the sleazy drinking club in Fulham looked as though the last thing he wanted to do was to help anyone. Except out of the club . . . with optional violence.

'Doubt it,' said Fletcher, holding his warrant card so close to the bouncer's face that he had to move his head backwards to see it properly. 'Unless you can tell me where to find Tracy Barlow.'

'In the bar some place, I s'pose,' said the bouncer, not wanting to appear too co-operative, but at the same time not wishing to upset this hard-nosed detective. Hard-nosed detectives could make life very difficult for the bouncing profession. He cocked a thumb at a set of double swing doors covered with faded red baize.

Fletcher pushed his way through, stopped and came out again in time to see the bouncer on the house phone. 'I'll remember you,' he said.

The bouncer looked at the handset as if it had appeared by magic in his hand. 'Wrong number, guv,' he said nervously.

Tracy Barlow was perched on the stool at the far end of the bar surveying the unrefined clientele that lounged about the tables of the club. A cloud of cigarette smoke hung permanently just below the ceiling and that, coupled with the dim lighting, helped her to appear almost attractive. But Fletcher knew that in the harsh light of day, she would look the haggard tom she so obviously was. Her breasts almost spilled out of her low-cut red dress, and the carefully arranged split in the skirt went all the way to her thigh.

'Are you Tracy Barlow?'

'Sure am,' said the girl in a pseudo-American accent. 'And who are you, big boy?' She fluttered her false

44

eyelashes so violently that Fletcher thought they might fall off.

'Detective Sergeant Fletcher of the Flying Squad.'

'Oh!' The smile vanished. 'And what d'you want?' The transatlantic twang had been replaced by a coarse voice with an unmistakable trace of Liverpool.

'When did you last see Barney Collins?'

Tracy Barlow scoffed. 'That loser,' she said. 'I haven't seen him in months.'

'How long?'

Tracy thought about that. 'Must be at least four or five,' she said. 'Why?'

'Know anything about a red Ford Sierra estate he had?'

'Well, he had one, yeah. What about it?'

'Did he own it?'

'What d'you mean, did he own it?'

Fletcher sighed. 'Was it his?'

The girl shrugged. 'I s'pose so.'

'Did he ever mention a man called Norman Leach?'

'No.' Tracy looked expectantly over Fletcher's shoulder at a group of men who had just entered. 'What's this all about, anyway?'

'What it's about is that Barney Collins managed to get himself murdered.'

'Murdered?' The girl's gaze was suddenly riveted on Fletcher's face. For some seconds she continued to stare. 'Well, like I said, I haven't seen him for ages.' She quite definitely did not want to get mixed up with any murder inquiry. 'He shacked up with some slag he met up west.'

An old saying about pots calling kettles black passed through Fletcher's mind. 'Know her name?'

'No. Don't want to either.'

'Is there some trouble, officer?' An unctuously smooth individual in a silver-coloured suit appeared at Fletcher's shoulder, obviously alerted by the bouncer to the presence of police in his establishment.

Fletcher's sweeping glance took in the entire club

45

before he turned and studied the man. 'If I were you,' he said, 'I'd do something about your fire exits before the fire brigade pay you a visit. After all, you might be the one trying to escape.'

It was another two weeks before there occurred what Fox described as a confluence of events. That is to say, Reynolds was on duty and a Rio flight – with Sherry Martin as one of the stewardesses – was due. As a result, Fox, Gilroy and the rest of the team assembled at Heathrow Airport. Ramsay, the customs investigator, was there too with a squad of his men.

'Right,' said Fox. 'The situation is this. Reynolds is on duty this morning. He is also assigned to the maintenance crew that will service the Rio flight. And the Rio flight has his bird on it.' He grinned at the assembled company. 'Things are beginning to look promising.'

'What evidence is there to suggest that Reynolds is the bloke having this stuff away, Mr Fox?' asked one of the customs team.

'Nothing whatever,' said Fox cheerfully. 'Except this.' He tapped the side of his nose. 'But I have come to an agreement with Mr Ramsay. All I want is the finger – or fingers – who rubbed out Messrs Leach and Collins. The drugs, gents, are all yours.' He beamed benevolently at the customs men.

'Our interest,' said Ramsay, 'is to find out where this cocaine is going. If, in fact, any cocaine is going anywhere. It'd be easy enough to nick this bloke, but it looks as though he's only a cat's paw.' Fox nodded approvingly. 'But,' continued Ramsay, 'we want the dealer. However, in order to assist Mr Fox to arrest his murderers we will proceed with caution. In other words, this morning's exercise is purely a surveillance.'

'They'll be kissing each other in a minute,' said DS Buckley quietly to DC Crabtree. To most of the officers present, police and customs, this sort of inter-departmental liaison was almost unprecedented.

'Well, if anybody cocks it up, it'll be our guv'nor,' said Crabtree moodily.

Buckley shot him a sideways glance. 'There are times, Ernie,' he said, 'when I think that you don't really like the job.'

The giant Boeing 747 touched down on time, but most of its four-hundred-plus seats were empty. As Fox drily observed, the citizens of Brazil did not exactly seem to be fighting their way on to an aircraft that would take them to England.

Unaware of the interest that their arrival had attracted, the passengers alighted and were led along the finger into the arrivals lounge. But that was not what the watchers were waiting for.

The boarding customs officers secured the bar box and cast a perfunctory eye around the vast cabin before going on to the next arrival. They had been warned not to search the Rio flight too thoroughly.

Ten minutes later, a swarm of maintenance technicians and cleaners started work, an in-flight caterer's lorry appeared . . . and a battery of surveillance equipment was brought to bear on the huge aeroplane and the activity that now surrounded it. So far nothing untoward appeared to be happening.

'Ah!' said Ramsay, who was next to Fox in a vantage point which gave excellent coverage of the area where the 747 was parked. 'That looks interesting.'

Reynolds, carrying a small canvas toolbag, had emerged from inside the aircraft. He swung casually down the maintenance ladder which had been put in place once the passengers had disembarked and dropped the bag on to the tarmac before walking round the other side of the aircraft apparently intent on examining one of the ailerons. A few moments later, he returned to the bag, picked it up and slung it casually on to the front seat of a Land Rover. Then he walked round the vehicle and got into the driving seat. Watched by at least twenty pairs of eyes in different parts of the airport, he drove some distance to a point close to the perimeter fence and slung the bag over so that it fell into some long grass close to Northern Perimeter Road.

'Well, the double-dyed bastard,' said Ramsay. 'That's not fair. It's too bloody simple. We always expect something a damned sight more complicated than that.'

'That's the way it goes,' said Fox, enigmatically, and pointing to Gilroy's personal radio, went on: 'Better make sure our chaps clocked that little caper, Jack.'

Within seconds, a blue Montego pulled up on Northern Perimeter Road and a man leaped out and picked up the bag. Obviously not wishing to get involved with the police for speeding – one thing usually leading to another – the Montego then drove off eastwards at a sedate pace, turned across Bath Road and joined the M4 at Junction Four. From then on, it was fairly straightforward as teams of unidentifiable police and customs surveillance vehicles tracked the suspect car.

Two hours later, the Montego drew into the car park of Charles Norton's hotel ten miles from Cheltenham. Two men, each dressed in a dark suit and carrying a briefcase, alighted from the car and registered at reception.

'Well that's all very satisfying.' Fox glanced up as DI Findlater entered the room. 'You've missed all the fun, Henry,' he said.

'Not completely, guv'nor,' said Findlater. 'I've been making a few inquiries. Discreetly, of course.'

'Of course,' said Fox. 'And?'

'And, sir, I've discovered that one of the stewardesses on the flight from Rio was Sherry Martin, common-law wife of Stanley Reynolds and well-known resident of Preston Candover.'

'Oh dear, Henry,' said Fox. 'You'll have to move faster than that if you're going to keep up.'

Chapter Five

Detective Inspector Denzil Evans was convinced that he had only been put at Heathrow Airport to make up the numbers. But his was the team that had finished up following the suspect Montego into the car park at Norton's hotel and he now found himself at the sharp end of Fox's murder inquiry. Faced with the inevitable dilemma of any subordinate, he pondered the options open to him. He could leave it right there and telephone Fox, by which time any handover could already have taken place, or book into the hotel and keep casual observation in the hope that he would learn something of value. But on the basis of previous experience, he knew that whatever he did would probably be wrong in Fox's eyes. Mentally tossing a coin, he opted to go in, and he and Detective Sergeant Ron Crozier presented themselves at the reception desk. Right behind the two suspects.

'May I help you, sir?' asked the young lady receptionist, smiling the standard welcoming smile as taught in the best hotels.

'I'm not sure,' said Evans, which was perfectly true, 'but we're half expecting to meet a colleague here. If he turns up, we shall need to book in for the night.'

The girl smiled again. 'That's quite all right, sir. We have plenty of rooms available tonight. May I suggest that you have a drink – the bar's still open – and wait.' She half turned towards the message rack. 'Perhaps your friend's here already, sir. He may have left a message. If you can give me your name . . .'

'Evans.'

'And your friend's name, sir?'

'Er, Runciman,' said Evans, conjuring up an unlikely name from his distant past.

The girl examined the rack and shook her head. 'No, there's nothing, sir, but if Mr Runciman arrives, I'll tell him you're here.'

'Thank you.' Evans turned away from the counter. 'Anything, Ron?' he asked when they were out of the receptionist's hearing.

'Yeah. I clocked the registration slip for one of them. Calls himself Leo Bridge, address in Wandsworth. Probably duff,' he added despondently.

'And the other one?'

'Dunno,' said Crozier. 'Couldn't see it.'

Evans looked around. 'Where did they go?'

'Bridge booked into room two-twelve. The other finger's probably next door.'

'Well that's a bloody write-off.'

'Best I could do, guv,' said Crozier.

Evans shook his head. 'Can't be helped, Ron, but if those two bastards have got a briefcase full of coke, and this Norton bloke that the guv'nor's got it in for wanders into their room, there's no way we're going to see a handover, is there?'

After a few brief moments of introspection, Evans telephoned Fox, told him what had happened and asked for directions.

'Stay there,' said Fox.

'And do what, guv'nor?' asked Evans plaintively.

'Use your initiative.'

Gilroy's information that Norton's wife was called Letitia had been Detective Sergeant Percy Fletcher's starting point. After a few hours at St Catherine's House, he had found the entry for the Nortons' marriage at Chelsea

Register Office five years before. Norton was described as an hotelier and Letitia as a model. From there, Fletcher had used the ages given at the time of the wedding to find the entries for their births. Charles Norton had been born on the 25th of July 1954, and Letitia, née Pearson, on the 16th of October 1960.

So far, so good.

Fletcher sighed and dialled another number. It was all getting rather tedious.

'What have you got, Perce?' asked Fox, nodding towards a chair in his office.

Fletcher sat down and started to shuffle his assortment of papers. 'Got dates of birth, sir. For both of them.'

'Good.'

'I've also got his national insurance number, his national health number, his driving licence number—'

'Terrific, Perce. I'm sure you've been flogging yourself to death, but have you got anything that is in the remotest bit bloody useful?'

Fletcher grinned. He always pushed out the trivia first. In that way, it made what little he had got seem valuable. 'I tried the Ministry of Defence, sir. Officers' records . . .'

'And?'

'Nothing, sir. They have no record of a Captain Charles Norton. They did have a Major Geoffrey Norton, though.' Fletcher sniffed mournfully. 'But he was killed in the Normandy Landings,' he added.

'Doesn't surprise me,' said Fox. 'I'd begun to think that Norton was a bit of a parvenu.'

'No he wasn't, sir,' said Fletcher. 'He was a corporal.'

Evans and Crozier returned to London. All that they had got from their sortie into Gloucestershire was a good description of the two men who had picked up the canvas tool-bag at Heathrow, the name that one of them was using, and the registration number of the Montego.

51

'Well I'm buggered,' said Crozier, peering more closely at the screen of the Police National Computer, 'his name really is Leo Bridge.'

'Well that's something, I suppose.' Evans was still smarting from Fox's reaction when he was told that they had been unable to witness the handover of the tool-bag – if handover there had been – much less to discover its contents. Fox seemed unwilling to accept that it had been an impossible task. 'See if he's got any form, Ron,' said Evans, looking over his sergeant's shoulder.

Crozier tapped in the name of Leo Bridge and an approximate date of birth, based on their assessment that the suspect was about thirty-six years of age. 'Bingo!' Crozier pressed a variety of keys and watched as the printout of Bridge's criminal biography emerged. 'There you are, guv'nor,' he said, tearing off the printout and handing it to Evans. 'A typical South London villain by the look of him.'

Fox was slightly mollified by this information and gazed at the printout with a wry smile on his face. 'Oh dear,' he said. 'Just look at that. Robbery, GBH with intent and half a dozen assorted thefts and handlings.' He stared thoughtfully at Evans. 'I reckon there's an employment agency somewhere that specialises in these bloody toe-rags, Denzil.'

'Looks like it, sir,' said Evans, relieved that the governor seemed to be in a lighter mood.

But he wasn't. 'Pity you didn't follow them back home when they left, Denzil.' Fox had the ability to make a passing comment sound like a criticism.

'Thought we might show out, sir,' said Evans.

'I see.' Fox sounded unconvinced. 'Tell you what, Denzil,' he said, 'put an obo on this Leo Bridge. With any luck, he'll lead us to his little friend.'

'Little friend, sir?'

'Yes, dear boy, the nasty piece of work who accompanied Mr Bridge to Cheltenham.'

*

The house where Bridge was living – or at least where the computer had said he was living – was in the crowded territory east of Garratt Lane in Wandsworth. Evans had decided to drive down the street just to see what the house looked like and whether there was any chance of mounting a discreet observation. But when they got to Bridge's turning it was taped off and a policeman flicked his fingers in that imperious way that policemen have, indicating that they should carry on along the main road.

It was eight o'clock in the morning, and Evans was not in the mood for prima donna constables. 'Pull up, Ron,' he said to Crozier, who was driving, 'while I find out what that prat's supposed to be doing.'

As Evans got out of the car, the PC strode towards him. 'You can't stop there . . .' he began.

With all the dexterity of an accomplished conjurer, Evans produced his warrant card and practically stuffed it up the PC's nose. 'DI Evans, Flying Squad,' he said.

'Oh, sorry, sir, I—'

'What's happening?'

'Fire, sir, in a dwelling house down on the—'

'Number twenty-seven, is it?'

The PC was clearly impressed by this. 'Yes, sir, but how did you know that?'

'I guessed, son,' said Evans. 'I'm very good at guessing. That's why I'm a DI on the Squad. What's it all about?'

'I don't know, sir. I'm only on traffic, but our DCI's down there.'

'Thought he might be,' said Evans darkly.

Detective Chief Inspector David Blunt had been stationed at Wandsworth for eighteen months. During that time he had dealt with practically every crime in the calendar. And it showed. He stood now in the centre of a tangle of hoses, his shoulders hunched inside a Barbour and his hands in his pockets. Although he had reached that stage in his service when he was rarely shocked by anything, he was, none the less, mildly surprised by the arrival of two Flying Squad officers.

'Morning, guv,' said Evans.

'What the hell are the Squad doing here at this time in the morning, Denzil?'

'Oh, we never sleep,' said Evans. He jerked a thumb towards Crozier by way of introduction. 'Ron Crozier, my DS.'

Blunt nodded an acknowledgement. 'Have you got an interest in this, Denzil?'

'Does the name Leo Bridge feature anywhere in this unfortunate conflagration, guv?'

Blunt grinned. 'Yeah, you could say that. His body's in a plastic bag in the back of that.' He inclined his head towards an ambulance.

'In that case, I'm interested. Or at least, Tommy Fox is.'

'Oh, Jesus,' said Blunt. 'That's all I need.'

'What's the score, then?'

'PC in a panda passed the house at about half six this morning, saw flames and called the brigade. Well alight when they got here. Two bodies in the front bedroom upstairs. One male, one female. Fire chief's first reaction was that it was arson, which is why I'm here. Both bodies were quite badly charred, but the cause of death'll probably be smoke inhalation. That's what the pathologist said, anyway. He's doing the PM this afternoon.'

'Who ID'd the bodies, guv?'

'No one yet. We're just assuming that it's Bridge and his wife . . . or some slag he's kipping with. There was a jacket on the floor of the bedroom with some papers in it that suggested that it was Bridge, but . . .' Blunt shrugged. 'We'll have to wait for a formal identification. What's Tommy Fox's interest then, Denzil?'

'He's doing the M4 job. But there's a suggestion of drugs. Frankly, guv, it's getting too complicated for me.'

'You and me both,' said the DCI. 'Let's have a word with the fire chief. See if he's got anything for us.'

They strode across to where a station officer from the London Fire Brigade was conferring with some firemen and making notes.

'What d'you reckon, Chief?' asked Blunt.

The station officer pushed his helmet back slightly to reveal a white forehead that contrasted with his smoke-grimed face. 'Arson, without a doubt,' he said. 'As far as we can see, a substantial amount of petrol was poured in through the letter-box and ignited.'

'But that wouldn't be enough, surely?'

The fire chief shrugged. 'Depends how long it was burning before your bloke spotted the flames,' he said. 'But it looks as though the kitchen window was forced and petrol spread around the downstairs rooms as well. Difficult to tell, mind you. There was a minor explosion that took the windows out, but there's no doubt about there being several seats of fire. It wasn't helped by having a lounge suite made of combustible foam, either.'

'Bloody marvellous.' Blunt turned to Evans. 'I suppose there's no chance of Tommy Fox taking this one over, is there, Denzil?'

Evans just grinned.

Fox and Evans met at the entrance to New Scotland Yard.

'You're back early, Denzil. I thought you were setting up an obo on friend Bridge.'

'Got there too late, sir.'

Fox looked cynical. 'I don't believe he goes to work, Denzil. At least, not that early.'

'No, sir. We arrived in time to see his body being carried out of his drum. Someone set light to it during the night. Him and some bird got burnt to death.'

Fox raised his eyebrows. 'What, in Wandsworth?'

'Yes, sir, in Wandsworth.'

'Funny place for a barbecue,' said Fox.

*
55

'I've been trying to get some more information about Norton, sir,' said DS Fletcher, 'but the MOD seem a bit reluctant to tell me anything. I think there's probably more to him than meets the eye.'

'That,' said Fox, 'is a racing certainty. Who did you speak to?'

'Some civil servant, guv. Said that it was confidential information and he couldn't divulge it.'

'Did he now?' Fox gazed across his office and smiled. 'In that case, Perce, we'll by-pass him.'

Lieutenant-Colonel George Lloyd was head of the Special Investigation Branch of the Royal Military Police for London District. Despite having such an impressive-sounding title, he had only a poky little office on the second floor above the Central London Recruiting Office in Great Scotland Yard. He knew Tommy Fox and Tommy Fox's arrival had the same effect on him as it had on most other people.

'Oh, God! Tommy Fox. And to what do I owe this doubtful pleasure?' Lloyd stood up, shook hands and made his way straight to his drinks cabinet.

Fox waited until Lloyd had placed two glasses on his desk and poured a liberal quantity of Scotch into each. 'Corporal Charles Norton, retired,' he said.

Lloyd pushed a jug of water towards Fox and sat down. 'Norton? What about him?'

'That's what I want to know,' said Fox. 'Ever heard of him?'

'As a matter of fact, I arrested him. About six or seven years ago it must have been. I was a captain in Germany, at Munchen-Gladbach.'

'Interesting.' Fox took a sip of his Scotch. 'What d'you nick him for, George?'

'Smuggling,' said Lloyd.

Fox leaned back and crossed his legs. 'Did you now? That's very interesting. What was he smuggling?'

'Booze. And pornography.'

56

'Oh! That's a shame. I was hoping you might have said drugs.'

'Probably would have done, given the chance. Hang on a minute.' Lloyd walked across to a filing cabinet and pulled out a docket. 'Always keep the papers on my jobs,' he said. 'Going to write my memoirs one day,' he added with a grin. 'Yes. Here we are. Remember it now. He was orderly to a major-general at Bielefeld.'

'Big cheese, eh?'

Lloyd gave a wry smile. 'From where I'm standing he is.' He flipped over a few sheets of paper in the file. 'Among his other duties, he used to pack all the general's gear whenever he went on leave. Then he'd accompany the general and unpack it all again at the other end.' Lloyd looked up. 'Got the drift, Tommy?'

Fox laughed. 'Nice one. Presumably the general didn't get turned over by customs.'

'Got questioned once or twice, but purely a routine stop, I suspect. The general was a stickler for observing the regulations. Nothing was ever found. But Norton came unstuck when the general finished his tour in Germany and got posted back to the UK. Down the road to the MOD, as a matter of fact.'

'And he got caught by customs, I suppose?'

Lloyd laughed. 'Yes, I'm afraid he did.'

'How dreadfully unfortunate,' said Fox. 'How did that happen?'

'The usual routine is that you take all your boxes or crates or whatever to the local German customs office together with lists of what they contain. They will check the lists and seal the boxes. Once they've been sealed in that way, and given that it's a general's kit, the British customs don't usually bother too much.'

'What went wrong?'

'The old story, I'm afraid. A new customs officer, seeking to impress his superiors, decided to give the general's boxes a bit of a going over.'

57

'And he found the booze and pornography heretofore mentioned, I suppose.'

'Exactly.' Lloyd smoothed his hand across his blotter and picked up his glass. 'The general went potty,' he said mildly.

'I can imagine that. And that's when you got involved, was it?'

'Yes. As we say in the army, Corporal Norton's feet didn't touch. He'd been at it for some time apparently. Used to drive up to Denmark, to the crossing at Flensburg – in an army vehicle would you believe, saucy bastard. It's a good two hundred and fifty miles. He'd buy up a load of porn movies and then calmly pack them in the general's gear on his next leave, unpack them at the other end, and flog them round Soho.'

'And the booze? Duty free, I suppose?'

'Yes. There was a knock-on from that which we put the way of British customs. Apparently Norton had an ex-army mate who kept a pub in Aldershot. He used to flog him a case or two of Scotch, and that would pay for his leave.'

'What happened to him?'

'Court-martialled. Got busted, six months in chokey and discharged with ignominy.'

'Well why isn't there a CRO file for him?'

Lloyd shrugged. 'I don't know, Tommy. He got done in Germany. Does that make a difference?'

'God knows,' said Fox. 'Admin was never my strong point.'

'I think we'll have an intercept put on Charlie-boy Norton's phone, Jack,' said Fox.

'You'll never get a warrant for a hotel, guv'nor.'

Fox pondered that. 'No,' he said, 'you're probably right, but he's bound to have a private line somewhere. In his office, perhaps. That'll do for a start. Get the paperwork organised, Jack.'

Chapter Six

'I have been speaking to the Commander Operations on Five Area, Tommy,' said Commander Alec Myers.

'I thought you might have been, sir,' said Fox gloomily.

'And he thinks it would be a very good idea if you were to take over the murder of Leo Bridge.'

'I'm sure he does, sir. Wants a bit of expert assistance to pull his chestnuts out of the fire for him.'

Myers pursed his lips and studied Fox over the top of his glasses for a moment or two. 'Yes . . .' he said when eventually he had decided that Fox was being no more insolent than usual. 'It seems that the local chaps haven't got very far with it.'

'Far enough to bugger it up, I expect,' said Fox. 'Who's dealing with it, sir?'

Myers glanced down at the notes on his desk. 'A DCI Blunt at Wandsworth. Know him?'

'Probably,' said Fox, 'but in any event I'm sure he'll get to understand my ways very quickly.'

'Well it wasn't Five Area Commander's intention that you should tie up his officers, but rather—'

'Couldn't possibly do without them, sir,' said Fox. 'Local villain, and all that. Absolutely essential to have someone who can beat on the ground and see what comes up.'

'Your commander seems to think you're not up to solving this tuppeny-ha'penny murder,' said Fox. He walked across to the DCI's notice board and examined it. Fox was an inveterate reader of other people's notices.

'Can't match the expertise of the Flying Squad, sir.' Blunt moved a large docket into the centre of his desk. 'Cup of coffee, sir?'

'Is that the best you can do?'

Blunt smiled and produced a bottle of Scotch and two glasses. 'It's all there,' he said, prodding the docket with a forefinger. 'Fire report, lab report, post-mortem—'

'What about the inquest?'

'The usual, sir. Evidence of death and adjourned.'

'Just one other thing. Who killed Leo Bridge?'

'Haven't got a clue, guv'nor.' Blunt poured out the Scotch and pushed one glass across the desk. He knew Fox of old, and knew his bluster. It might have intimidated a lesser man. But not David Blunt.

'No suspects?'

'No, sir.'

'Not one?'

'Not one, sir.'

'Oh!' Fox drained his Scotch at a gulp. 'Who was the woman?' he asked.

'Mary Gibbons. She'd been living with him for a couple of years. Got about three previous for tomming, but I don't think she'd been on the game for a while. Working as a barmaid recently. Bridge's wife,' continued Blunt, forestalling Fox's next question, 'cleared off and left him some years ago.'

'Why?'

Blunt shrugged. 'No idea. Got fed up with him, I expect. She was quite a decent soul apparently. Had a couple of kids by him, but trying to cope when he was in stir was probably too much for her. Last time he came out, she was gone. Nobody knows where.'

'You've done house-to-house, I suppose?' It was a tongue-in-cheek inquiry on Fox's part. He had known the answer before he asked the question. Any attempt on the part of the police to obtain assistance in the sort of area where Bridge and his like lived was doomed to failure from the outset. But it had to be done, otherwise someone would ask why it hadn't.

'We tried, sir.' Blunt grinned. 'But no one knows anything in that part of the world. Don't want to know either. There's just one other thing, sir.' He sounded hesitant. 'Might not be connected—'

'Give it a try,' said Fox.

'The area car was in Garratt Lane at about twenty past six—'

'Night duty?'

'Yes, sir, they work an eleven to seven. To overlap the foot duty that comes on at six.'

'So we're talking about six twenty a.m.?'

'Yes, sir. They saw a blue Datsun doing about fifty. In the opposite direction. Damage to the rear offside wing—'

'Get to the point.'

'As soon as chummy spotted the area car, he took off at high speed. They gave chase but lost it.'

'Brilliant. They didn't happen to get the number, I suppose?'

'Yes, sir.'

'And?'

'Goes out to a pantechnicon in Dundee.'

Fox sighed. 'What you're trying to tell me is that it was nicked and on false plates.'

'Yes, sir. They circulated it, but so far nothing.'

'You'd better put it on the computer as possibly connected then.'

'Done that already, sir. And circulated it in *Police Gazette*, asking for a special search of streets. At two in the morning.'

'Good,' said Fox. 'If you're not careful you could well finish up on the Flying Squad.'

'I don't think my wife'd like that too much, sir,' said Blunt with a grin.

61

'It's not her I want. Incidentally, have you found Bridge's Montego yet?'

'Not round here, sir. Didn't realise he had one.'

'Well, he did,' said Fox. 'And a dark suit. And a friend who had a dark suit. And both were seen in another part of the country. And they were at it. Any idea who his little friend might have been?'

'No, sir. My information was that he was a bit of a soloist.'

'Interesting,' said Fox. It seemed to him that so far most of the participants in this business had been villains who had no regular accomplices, and yet Leach and Collins had been together, and Bridge and one other. Fox sighed. Again. 'Oh well,' he said, 'I'd better have a look at that docket.'

'Station Officer Lovell?'

'Yes.'

'Detective Chief Superintendent Thomas Fox . . . of the Flying Squad.' Fox stuck out a hand. 'I believe you dealt with the fire that toasted the unfortunate Mr Leo Bridge and his lady friend.'

Lovell grinned. 'That's right. Take a pew.' He waved at a vacant chair.

Fox looked gloomily round the fire chief's office and dismissed any hope of getting a glass of Scotch. 'I've read your report—'

'Well there's nothing to add.' Lovell bridled slightly.

'Not suggesting you've missed anything out,' said Fox. 'Just wanted to get a first-hand account.'

'I reckon we arrived about half an hour after the fire started. God knows why it wasn't spotted before, but in that neighbourhood . . .' Lovell shrugged. 'There was a time when people worried about their neighbours, but not any more. Anyway, by the time we turned up it had got a good hold. Most of the ground floor was gone. The three-piece suite was foam . . . the old type. They'd have gone under from inhaling that long before the fire reached them. But there's no doubt in my mind that petrol had been spread about the ground floor by an intruder. There were several seats of fire. Too widespread for it to be accidental.'

'Yes,' said Fox. 'Our lab people found marks on what was left of the kitchen window-frame that indicated a possible forced entry. Maybe.'

'There you have it, Mr Fox. I'm sorry not to be able to add anything.'

'Well, it'll do for a start, I suppose,' said Fox.

'A start?' Lovell did not look happy.

'Yes. Once we get going on the report for the Crown Prosecution Service, we'll need detailed statements, you see.'

'That was detailed.'

'Really?' said Fox. 'Oh well, we'll have to do what we can with that, I suppose.'

'Have you arrested someone then?'

'Not yet . . . but it's only a matter of time.' He stood up. 'Well, haven't got time to waste. It's all go in our job, I can tell you.' He beamed at Lovell.

'It's not exactly beer and skittles in the fire brigade either . . . and we don't get your money,' said Lovell. 'Bloody coppers,' he added as the door closed behind Fox.

'The Datsun's been found, sir,' said Gilroy.

'Where?'

'In a car park on Beachy Head.'

'Right, Jack,' said Fox. 'Get it on a low-loader and brought down to Lambeth. I want the lab to go over it with a fine-tooth comb.'

'Thought you might, sir. All in hand. Should be there by about two o'clock.' Gilroy paused at the door. 'Incidentally, guv, it was burned out.'

The next flight to arrive in London from Rio was on a Saturday when Stanley Reynolds was on duty, but his maintenance crew had not been assigned to service the aircraft. At the last minute, however, Reynolds engineered a swap with a mate, and so was once more in a position where he could pick up the consignment, if consignment there was.

But the customs investigators were beginning to get impatient. 'If drugs are coming in, we ought to be doing something positive about it,' said Ramsay.

'We don't know that it is drugs,' said Fox blandly. 'Might be porn videos for all we know, and although that's unlawful, it's not exactly a threat to either the stability of the country or to the revenue.' He raised an eyebrow and smiled. 'Is it? After all, the only evidence we've got is traces of the stuff in the murder vehicle. The rest is bloody guesswork.'

Ramsay was not to be outdone. 'If it's porn, then we're wasting our time,' he said.

Fox sensed the need for a little placation. 'Let's give this flight a run and see what happens, eh? Tell you what, just to keep the overtime down, we'll watch the pick-up at the airport, and I'll have a couple of my chaps down at the hotel to watch it come in. Then I think we'll have to start nicking a few. How's that grab you, Mr Ramsay?'

Ramsay grinned. 'You're on,' he said. 'Name's Peter, by the way.'

'They've come up with a set of prints on the Datsun, sir,' said Gilroy. 'And we've got a match.'

'Whose are they?' asked Fox.

'A villain called Farmer, Edward Farmer. Aged twenty-nine. One previous for wounding, and two for GBH.'

'Has he now. Sounds just like the sort of nasty little bastard we ought to go and talk to.'

'Is that wise at this stage, sir? We don't want to warn anyone off, do we?'

'No, but if he's connected – and it's a big if – he's

sufficiently far removed for it not to matter.' Fox put his cigarette case and lighter in his pocket. 'To the casual onlooker,' he continued airily, 'we are investigating a burned-out car. Apart from anything else, Jack, we can't allow people to go marauding about the place committing crime without *some* intervention on our part. A waiting game's all very well, but there is a limit . . .'

'When then?'

'Once we've dealt with the little matter of Heathrow Airport's forthcoming attraction, Jack.'

It was the mixture as before. Almost. The combined customs and police team at the airport lay in wait. Reynolds emerged from the aircraft with a toolbag and slung it over the fence at exactly the same point as before. The same Montego arrived – a surprise that, considering that its owner now lay in the mortuary at Battersea – and stopped just long enough to allow a man to leap out and grab the bag.

DI Evans and DS Crozier waited at Norton's hotel, having parried the receptionist's awkward questions about whether they had eventually found their friend, the fictitious Mr Runciman, the other day. They waited and waited. But nothing happened. The only snippet of interest that Evans was able to report to Fox in a later telephone call was that Charlie Norton appeared to be slightly agitated. But only slightly.

'Something's gone amiss, Pete,' said Fox. 'The bloody stuff hasn't turned up.'

Ramsay frowned; he didn't like having his name shortened. 'Then there must be more than one handover point,' he said. 'Perhaps we should have sat on their tails after all.'

'Yes,' said Fox thoughtfully. 'On the other hand, some malcontent might just have nicked it. In which case there could well be a couple of bodies in a lay-by somewhere, waiting to be investigated.'

*

Evans and Crozier had been instructed to book into the hotel until further notice, just to see what happened next.

'But I haven't even got a toothbrush, guv'nor,' Evans had complained.

'Then buy one,' Fox had said. 'A cheap one.'

But Fox fretted about two of his officers being in the only place where there was likely to be any action. After a few minutes of careful consideration, he rang the hotel. 'Denzil,' he said, once the receptionist had located Evans, 'I'm coming down. Now when I get there, don't talk to me. Act as though you didn't know me and I didn't exist.'

Evans put the phone down. 'There is a God after all, Ron,' he said.

'Do what, guv?' asked Crozier.

It was seven o'clock in the evening when Fox strode into the hotel. As an acknowledgement to its being Saturday, he was wearing his favourite hacking jacket and a pair of lovat-green trousers, both from Simpsons of Piccadilly. A Harrods check shirt, an Angelo tie and a pair of brown McAfee brogues completed the picture of an English gentleman enjoying a bit of leisure.

Norton saw him the moment he entered the bar. 'Mr Fox, nice to see you again. I suppose pest-control's a bit of a twenty-four-hour job.'

'No,' said Fox, 'but I thought I was entitled to a weekend off. This being a good hotel, I decided to spend it here.'

'Splendid, splendid,' said Norton with a little more enthusiasm than Fox's decision seemed to warrant. 'You must meet my wife.' He reached out and took the arm of a woman who was standing at the bar with her back to him. 'Darling . . .'

The woman turned. She was wearing a bottle-green silk dress, low-cut, and her brown hair was now loose round her shoulders. 'Charles?'

'I'd like you to meet one of our guests, darling. This is Mr Fox. D'you remember my telling you about him. The gentleman who's in pest control.'

'How d'you do. Letitia Norton.' She held out a pale hand. Fox noticed that the fingernails – plain varnished – were cut short, and he presumed that long nails didn't go with the horses that Gilroy had said she was keen on. 'How fascinating. Tell me, what sort of pests d'you specialise in?'

Fox shrugged. 'Oh, the usual. Rats, bats, mice and cockroaches. That sort of thing.'

'Oh, that's splendid.' Letitia Norton spoke with a cultured voice. A convincingly cultured voice. Fox had met a few pretenders in his time, but was certain that this was the genuine article. He thought it likely that Mrs Norton knew nothing of the nefarious activities in which Fox was convinced that her husband was indulging, particularly since hearing Colonel Lloyd's revelations about the former batman. 'You see, Mr Fox, I've got this trouble with rats in the stables. I wondered if you could possibly take a look and—'

'I don't think that's really on, darling,' said Norton. 'Mr Fox is down for a bit of a break. That's right, isn't it, Mr Fox?' He swung his gaze back to his guest.

'I'm afraid that we're more into the big commercial stuff,' said Fox without hesitation. 'I dare say I could put you in touch with a small man locally.' He paused, intent on changing the subject before it got out of hand. 'D'you know, Mrs Norton, I could swear that I've seen you somewhere before. You're not an actress, by any chance, are you?'

It worked. The one sure way of flattering a pretty woman was to suggest that she was famous because of her looks. Mrs Norton lifted her chin slightly. 'As a matter of fact, I used to be a model,' she said. 'Before I married Charles.'

'That must have been it,' said Fox. 'Probably seen

your picture in *Vogue* or *Harper's Bazaar* . . . something like that, eh?'

'Quite possibly.' Letitia turned to her husband. 'I think you should buy our guest a drink,' she said.

Fox accepted with alacrity. He knew that Letitia Norton's modelling career hadn't even got off the ground. Percy Fletcher's inquiries had discovered that most of the agencies to which she had applied had concluded that she was neither quite tall enough nor of the right proportions to succeed. But she looked all right to Fox. 'Have you got many horses?' he asked.

'Six, as a matter of fact. I'd like to open a racing stables, but Charles is not all that keen. It's terribly expensive, you know.'

'It's not that so much,' said Norton, 'but once you get into that sort of thing, you're open to inspection. People from the Jockey Club, or whatever it's called, wandering about the place checking up to see if your damned nags have been doped.' He laughed. But it sounded rather hollow.

'Is that so?' Fox contrived to look interested. 'It's surprising what happens these days, isn't it?' He could quite understand why Charles Norton wasn't particularly keen on people wandering around his property looking for drugs. At least, he thought he could understand.

Chapter Seven

After dinner, Fox returned to the bar for a brandy. Norton and his wife were still holding court and it seemed almost as though they were running the hotel as a private club for their cronies rather than for any commercial profit. If the number of guests in the hotel that evening was the norm, the business was not sufficient to support the rich lifestyle of Mr and Mrs Norton. Fox decided that at the conclusion of the case he would let the Inland Revenue and the VAT inspectors have a bite of the cherry as well.

'Ah, come and meet some of my friends, old boy.' Norton hailed Fox from the far end of the bar where a little coterie was gathered around Letitia Norton who was clearly the centre of attraction.

'As a matter of fact, I was just going to have a brandy and go to bed,' said Fox, who had no intention of retiring if there was a chance of getting to know some of Norton's acquaintances.

'No rush, old boy, surely? You did say you were having a weekend off.' He turned to the barman. 'A large Cognac for Mr Fox . . . on my bill.' The barman moved towards an optic. 'Not that one, for God's sake, Trevor. Give Mr Fox some of the decent stuff.' He turned towards Fox. 'Managed to get a case of Courvoisier XO last week,' he said.

'Your good health,' said Fox, taking an appreciative sip of his brandy.

'Let me introduce you, old boy.' Waving a hand round

his circle of friends, Norton reeled off names. But it was the last one in the group that interested Fox. 'And this is Jock Cameron.'

Cameron shook hands. 'You're the rat-catcher, Charlie tells me.'

'One way of putting it,' said Fox mildly. 'I can be relied on to spot a rat at fifty paces.' He didn't smile.

'What? Oh, yes, very good.' Cameron bellowed with laughter and the rest of the group – Fox included – joined in. 'Bit of a strange profession though, isn't it?'

'Someone has to do it.'

'S'pose so. Get abroad much, do you?' Cameron's question was incisive, and posed in a confidential voice.

'Fortnight in Portugal about once a year. Why?'

'Just curious, old man,' said Cameron.

Fox wondered why a man like Cameron should be interested in whether a rat-catcher, whom he had only just met, went abroad. In the circumstances of Fox's investigation it was an interesting question, and one which decided Fox to look more closely at the man. Although casually – but impeccably – dressed, he had sharp features and a thin moustache. And that, for no good reason, other than gut reaction, aroused Fox's suspicions. He had met many Jock Camerons in his professional life. And locked up a fair few of them.

'Jock more or less lives here,' said Norton. 'One of our permanent guests, as you might say.'

'Really?' said Fox. 'How fascinating. Retired, are you, Mr Cameron?'

'Call me Jock, old man. Retired? Good heavens, no. Still keep my hand in, you know. Doing a bit of this and that. Import and export mostly. But this is a very comfortable place to use as a second headquarters. Especially when mine host keeps dispensing this very good brandy of his.' He pushed his glass towards the barman. 'Same again all round, Trevor, there's a good fellow. And one for yourself.'

Fox stayed for two more rounds. One was paid for

70

by a foppish individual who obviously fancied Letitia Norton like mad, and the other by Fox, although he was determined that it would be the Commissioner who finally footed the bill. Then he went to bed. But not directly to bed. On the way he called into Denzil Evans's room.

'Denzil, I want you and Ron Crozier to do a bit of spade-work on a nasty-looking piece of work called Cameron. He's one of Norton's cronies, but if ever I saw a villain, he's one. No visible means of support. See what you can find out. While you're about it, you may as well have a go at the others too. There's a pansy-looking tosser called Jeremy Studd. Aptly named, the way he was fawning over the beautiful Letitia, and some clown called Rodney Bingham. Look into them, there's a good chap. But discreetly, mind.'

'Of course, sir.' Evans wondered if Fox would ever trust him to get on with a job without adding some cautionary caveat. 'What are you going to do, sir?'

'Go back to the Yard,' said Fox. 'First thing in the morning. The bloody crowd they've got here will drive me up the wall . . . and quite possibly bankrupt the Commissioner into the bargain.'

Fox had directed that details of the Montego registered in the late Leo Bridge's name should be circulated to all police forces, but so far there had been no result. It obviously hadn't been kept at Bridge's Wandsworth address – at least, it wasn't there at the time of the fire – and he was keen to learn who was using it now. But he was also tired of seeing crimes being committed without taking any action. It went against his innermost feelings.

'Jack,' said Fox.

'Yes, sir.'

'This Edward Farmer whose dabs were found on the burnt-out Datsun.'

'Yes, sir?'

71

'Where does he live?'

'Wanstead Flats, sir.'

'That reckons,' said Fox. 'Get a warrant and assemble a team. We shall go and have a conversation with Master Farmer. Probably in Wanstead nick. By the way, have we had anything useful from the intercept on Norton's phone?'

'Depends what you mean by useful, sir,' said Gilroy. 'Apart from the usual business calls to suppliers, he's been having one or two chats with a woman called Daphne Lovegrove. Her number goes out to an address in Stokenchurch . . . on Thames Valley's ground.'

'What's that all about, then?' asked Fox. 'Bit on the side?'

Gilroy smiled. 'Could well be right, guv,' he said.

Edward Farmer actually lived slightly north of Wanstead Flats, in that area of Greater London known as Snaresbrook, a hotbed of villainy if ever there was one.

The first thing that caught Fox's eye as the Flying Squad team entered the street – from both ends – at six o'clock in the morning, was a well-known Montego.

'Aha!' said Fox, rubbing his hands together. 'The gods are with us, Swann.'

'Could have fooled me, guv.' Swann, Fox's driver, was not greatly enamoured of driving to Snaresbrook at six on a Sunday morning. Or for that matter, at any other time.

'Oh yes. And Mr Farmer is about to discover that Uranus is in the fourth quarter,' said Fox mysteriously.

'Nothing wrong with my anus, guv,' said Swann, and pulled into the kerb outside a mean-looking terraced house.

The man who answered the door was unshaven, and wore a dirty singlet and filthy jeans.

'Edward Farmer?' asked Fox.

'Yeah. What d'you—?' was all that he managed to say before the Squad was through the door and Gilroy had Farmer with his face against the wall and his arm up his back.

'Good morning, Ted,' said Fox affably. 'Thomas Fox . . . of the Flying Squad.'

'I don't give a monkey's who you are, you're breaking my bleeding arm.' Farmer's complaint came out in a strangled cry.

Fox nodded sympathetically, but forbore from pointing out that it was actually DI Gilroy who was breaking his arm. 'And that's only a start,' he said. 'We have a warrant to search these premises.'

'Clean, guv,' said Gilroy, standing back after conducting a lightning search of Farmer's person.

'That's a matter of opinion,' said Fox, casting a distasteful glance at the piece of human detritus who now stood with his arms folded truculently across his chest, glowering at the assembled detectives. 'Right, lads. Get to it. You know what I want first. In the meantime, Mr Gilroy and I will have a little chat with our friend here.'

'What the bleeding hell's this all about?' asked Farmer.

'Wondering that myself,' said Fox, leading the way into the front room. 'Sit down.'

'You're not coming barging in my house telling me what—'

Fox pushed Farmer gently in the chest so that he fell into a chair that had undoubtedly seen better days.

'Here, that's assault, that is—'

'Oh, shut up,' said Fox, staring round the room. There were worn patches on the carpet, and the Formica-topped coffee-table, which had cigarette burns along its edges, overflowed with recent editions of the tabloid press. The chair in which Farmer was now hunched did not match the other one, or the settee. In one corner stood the inevitable television set and video-recorder. 'Get one of the lads to check the serial number on that,' said Fox. He turned to Farmer and lit a cigarette. 'Well now, Ted,' he began.

73

'I want my brief.'

Fox affected surprise. 'Whatever for? Have you committed some crime?'

Farmer's mouth opened in astonishment. 'Well, if I haven't, what the bloody hell are you lot doing here?'

'It just so happened that we were passing through Snaresbrook this morning, Ted, and it suddenly occurred to me what a nice idea it'd be to drop in on you for a chat . . . about a burnt-out Datsun that an eagle-eyed constable happened to notice at Beachy Head.'

'Don't know what you're on about.'

Fox let that pass and watched, with apparent interest, as DC Crabtree pulled the video-recorder from under the television set and examined the serial number with a small magnifying glass.

'Who's he? Sherlock Holmes?' asked Farmer insolently.

'Well, he's not the man from Granada, that's for sure,' said Fox. 'Now, about this Datsun . . .'

'I said I don't know anything about a Datsun.'

'Got your fingerprints on it.' Fox gazed at Farmer through a haze of cigarette smoke.

'Couldn't have—'

'Why? Because you set fire to it?' Fox shook his head. 'Oh dear, Ted, you've a lot to learn about the miracles of modern forensic science.'

'Is this what you're looking for, guv?' DS Fletcher put his head round the door of the sitting-room and held up a set of car keys.

'Ah! Quite possibly, Perce. Give it a try.'

'Right, guv.'

''Ere, what's he doing?' Farmer strained to look out of the window.

'Just testing,' said Fox non-committally, and leaning over the coffee-table started to read an article in one of the open newspapers.

DC Crabtree was the first to return. 'Nicked, guv.'

'What the television . . . or the video?'

74

'Both,' said Crabtree with a broad grin. 'Proceeds of a warehouse robbery in Greenford six months ago.'

'Well now, there's a thing. What have you go to say about that, Ted?'

'Bought 'em down the market,' said Farmer.

Fox gave an understanding nod. 'From a bloke whose name you don't know, who you'd never seen before and who you haven't seen again.'

'Yeah, that's right. How did you know?'

'Not the first time it's happened,' said Fox. 'But it's usually in a pub. However, I'm not here to worry about little things like nicked videos.'

'Oh!' That statement disconcerted Farmer. He knew from his long experience of the law that the Flying Squad usually took a passionate interest in such things. The fact that they weren't apparently bothered bode ill . . . for Farmer. It meant that they were after bigger fish. And right now, Farmer had that nasty feeling that he was just such a fish.

'They fit, guv.' Now it was Percy Fletcher's turn.

'Oh, splendid.' Fox turned to Farmer with a beaming smile. 'It's turning out not to be your day, old son.'

'What—?'

'Perhaps you'd care to explain how you came by that expensive Montego that is currently languishing in the kerb near here, Ted.'

'Don't know anything about it.'

'Then how come that my officers found the keys to the said Montego beside your bed?'

'They weren't by my bed, they were in the—' Farmer suddenly stopped, realising that he had just talked his way into a verbal cul-de-sac.

Fox smiled benevolently. He always smiled benevolently when confronted by a push-over. 'The motor vehicle in question,' he said, 'is registered in the name of one Leo Bridge of Wandsworth.'

'I was looking after it.'

75

'Why should Mr Bridge want you to look after his car, Ted?' Fox looked genuinely puzzled.

'I never knew that was his name.'

'Oh!' Fox looked round for an ashtray. 'And I suppose you met him down the market, too.'

'No, in a pub.'

Fox yawned and dropped the butt of his cigarette into a teacup that appeared to have been on the mantelshelf for several days. There was a slight hissing noise as the dregs extinguished it. 'Right,' he said, 'I've had enough of your poncing about. You're nicked.'

'What for?'

'The unlawful possession of a video recorder and television set. That'll do for a start. If you own a shirt, you may care to put it on.' Fox turned to Gilroy. 'Get that Montego on to a low-loader, Jack, and get it up to the lab. The usual.'

Gilroy laughed. 'There's so many parked cars up there, guv, it's beginning to look like—'

'The M25,' said Fox.

Detective Sergeant Ron Crozier was a much smoother operator than Detective Inspector Denzil Evans, but at least Evans had the good grace to admit it. 'Ron,' he said, 'get alongside Mrs Norton. See what you can find out. I shall devote myself to the odious Cameron.'

It wasn't difficult. At lunch-time on the Sunday, the inevitable gaggle of hangers-on were assembled in the bar. At its centre, as usual, was Letitia Norton, dressed exactly as she had been when Gilroy first saw her: skin-tight riding-breeches and an equally tight-fitting blouse that left little to the imagination. Her hair was drawn back into the pony-tail she affected when riding and her highly polished boots added a faint air of sexuality that was absent when she was more formally dressed.

'Morning.' Charles Norton nodded to Crozier, waited until he had bought himself a pint of bitter and then invited him to join the group. 'Always like everybody

76

to know everybody else,' he said. 'After all, a hotel should be like a second home, what?'

'I'm Letitia Norton.' Charles Norton's wife held out her hand and appraised Crozier carefully. 'Staying long, Mr Crozier?'

'Haven't decided yet. Depends on business.'

'What business is that?' Letitia eventually relinquished his hand. To the obvious relief of Jeremy Studd. Norton himself appeared not to notice.

'Travel business.'

'What, air travel, holidays? That sort of thing?' Norton took a sudden interest.

'Yes.' Crozier was on safe ground there. His wife had recently gone back to her former job as an airline booking clerk, now that the girls were at university.

'Bit of a tricky market at the moment, isn't it?'

'Could be better.' Crozier said it with feeling. His wife had recently been warned that redundancies were in the offing.

'Mmm! Perhaps we could have a talk later on. Been thinking about encouraging foreign tourists, y'know. Got a lot to offer here. Apart from the hotel, I mean. It's glorious countryside. And there's golf, fishing, all that sort of thing.'

'Darling, I'm sure that business is the last thing that Mr, er—' Mrs Norton hesitated as she struggled to remember Crozier's name.

'Crozier.'

'Yes, of course. I'm sorry, I've got a dreadful memory for names. I'm sure that business is the last thing that Mr Crozier wants to talk about at the weekend.'

Norton smiled indulgently at his wife. 'There's always time to talk business, my dear,' he said. 'Another drink, Mr Crozier. Bitter was it?'

'Anyway, you left out riding, darling.' Letitia pouted at her husband and sipped at her Martini. 'Are you interested in horses, Mr Crozier?'

77

'Only the sort of rank outsider that wins with good odds,' said Crozier.

Norton laughed. 'That's more my fancy, too,' he said.

Letitia was not to be rebuffed. 'Perhaps you'd care to have a look at the stables after lunch, Mr Crozier.' She swept an elegant hand round the assembled company. 'This lot will probably be sleeping off their excesses.'

'Thank you, Mrs Norton. I'd like that.' Crozier noticed that Studd looked decidedly unhappy.

'Call me Letty, why don't you?' said Letitia. 'Shall we say half-past two?'

Norton's wife came alive the moment she got among her horses, her feigned languor disappearing completely as she conducted Crozier round the stables, excitedly telling him the name of each horse, how old it was, and listing its competition record with obvious pride.

'I must say it all looks very clean and tidy,' said Crozier, desperately trying to find something sensible to say about a subject of which he knew absolutely nothing.

'Thank you.' Letitia Norton preened herself at the compliment and led him into the tack-room, where she stood with her hands on her hips and boasted a little about the battery of red and blue rosettes – mostly red – which were pinned to the wall.

From time to time, she would stress some important point by laying her hand on his forearm: Letitia Norton was a very tactile person. She complained, too, that her husband had no interest in riding, but seemed obsessed with business matters. The inference that Crozier drew, and was meant to draw, was that Mrs Norton was a neglected wife. 'And just to crown it all,' she added, 'he's going away tonight, on some business junket. I ask you, on a Sunday.'

Fox was interested to learn that Norton was going away, but decided against assigning Evans and Crozier to keep the hotelier under surveillance. That would undoubtedly

78

compromise their cover, and he didn't want that. In any case, he knew where Norton was going. The intercepts on his phone had revealed that two days previously Norton had telephoned Daphne Lovegrove in Stokenchurch and arranged to spend Sunday night with her, adding the gratuitous information that he had told his wife that he was going away on business.

But just to make absolutely certain that Norton wasn't much more devious than he seemed, DI Henry Findlater, who thought that he was having a Sunday evening off, came in for a surprise. The surprise was that he had to assemble a surveillance team in one hell of a hurry . . . and get to Norton's hotel before he left.

But what came as no surprise was an incident which occurred that night at the hotel.

Crozier had been for a stroll through the extensive grounds of the hotel to clear his head, and had returned to his room just after midnight. As he turned the corner of the corridor, he was just in time to see Letitia Norton entering a room at the far end. Jeremy Studd's room.

Chapter Eight

Fox examined the pathetic figure huddled in a chair in the interview room at Spratt Hall Road police station and slowly shook his head. 'Well, Ted, you're in a bit of bother, my old love.'

'So, what's a nicked telly and video?'

'A mere bagatelle, Ted.'

'There wasn't no bagatelle. You must've planted that. Anyway, I ain't seen one of them in years.' Farmer was still hoping that Fox's visit this morning was a mere accident, a ghastly coincidence. But he was not having much success at convincing himself that the police had happened on him by chance.

'It's about this Datsun, Ted. It worries me.'

It worried Farmer too, but he confined himself to the standard answer of the villain caught on the hop. 'Don't know nothing about it.'

'Oh dear,' said Fox with a sigh, 'we're not going through all that again, are we?' He grimaced at the smell of cooking wafting through from the canteen, and sat down. 'Like I said, Ted, this Datsun was found in deepest Sussex by an astute officer whose suspicions were aroused by the fact that it was burnt out, and that the police had been looking for it. Now your problem, Ted . . .' He paused to light a cigarette. 'Your problem is that your fingerprints were found in the said vehicle.'

'Yeah, well I had it nicked off of me, didn't I?'

'Oh, that's all right then.' Fox glanced across at Gilroy. 'He had it nicked, Jack.'

80

'Happens all the time, sir,' said Gilroy.

Fox looked back at Farmer. 'Well, if you just tell me at which police station you reported this diabolical theft, Ted, we can probably clear it all up very quickly.'

'Don't be daft. I never reported it. What's the good of that? Your lot wouldn't have found it. Waste of bleeding time.'

'But they did find it, Ted. Now then, that Datsun was seen a few days ago driving along Garratt Lane in Wandsworth. With false plates on it. Plates that indicated that it was a Dundee pantechnicon.' Fox paused. 'Don't happen to know any Scottish removal men, I suppose?' Farmer looked blank. 'No? Never mind. Anyway, Ted, it was going quite fast and when the driver saw a police car, it went even faster. Now that's a bit odd, wouldn't you say? Furthermore, Ted – and I hope you don't mind me going into detail over all this, but I do want to be fair – furthermore, it was at about the time that someone set light to a certain Mr Leo Bridge's house, incidentally setting fire to Mr Bridge at the same time, to say nothing of his bit of crackling . . . to coin a phrase. Both done to a turn, Ted. And talking of coincidences, whose motor car should we find outside your drum in Wanstead Flats? The same Mr Bridge's. And the keys to the said motor were in the chest of drawers in your bedroom. How's that for starters, Ted?' Fox sat back and waited.

'I don't know what you're talking about.'

'In that case, I've got a better idea, Ted. As we don't seem to be making much progress this way round, it'd probably be simpler if I just charge you with murder, and then work backwards from there. Can't say fairer than that, can I, old sport?'

'Murder!' Farmer's stomach gave a nasty lurch. No wonder Fox hadn't been interested in a bent video recorder. 'God's honest truth, I don't know nothing about no murder.'

81

Fox tutted. 'Well then, let's try again. Where were you at the time of Mr Bridge's sad demise?'

'In bed at home, wasn't I?' Farmer stared at Fox with a baleful expression on his face, willing the detective to believe him. He should have known it was a waste of time.

'Were you really, Ted? Interesting. In fact, very interesting, particularly in view of the fact that I haven't yet told you the date of the murder.'

'Well I'm home in bed every morning, ain't I? Specially since the accident.'

'What accident's that?'

'Fell off some bleeding scaffolding we was putting up.'

'Careless,' said Fox with no trace of sympathy. 'But why should your being in bed in the morning absolve you from this dastardly crime? I didn't mention the morning either.'

Farmer ran a hand round his rough chin. He'd done it again. 'Look—' he said, and then dried up.

'I am looking. In fact, I've been looking at your potted history, Ted. Wounding and GBH.' Fox shook his head. 'Seems to me you've got to be a front-runner for this little lot.' He stood up, suddenly. 'Well, if that's it, Ted, we'll get the paperwork done.' Addressing the far wall, he intoned, 'In that you did murder Leo Bridge, against the peace.' Then he smiled down at the hapless Farmer. 'That sounds about right, Ted. Should be able to get you up before the beak first thing tomorrow, followed by a nice little eight-day lay-down.'

'I want my brief,' said Farmer.

'Want him!' Fox scoffed. 'You couldn't possibly do without him, dear boy,' he said.

'You can do the business at Bow Street in the morning, Jack,' said Fox on the way back to the Yard.

Gilroy shook his head slowly. 'The Crown Prosecution Service aren't going to like this one, guv'nor,' he said.

'There's not a shred of evidence to connect Farmer with Bridge's topping.'

'I know,' said Fox. 'Exciting, isn't it?'

Detective Inspector Henry Findlater and his team of surveillance officers only just arrived in time. Ten minutes after they were in position, Charles Norton's Bentley left the hotel and made south for the A40. Skirting Oxford, he drove on to the M40 unaware that his every move was being monitored by the police.

Leaving at Junction Five, Norton eventually pulled into a car park in Stokenchurch and then walked about a quarter of a mile to a block of flats. He pressed the bell-push for number five, and after a crackling conversation through the intercom was admitted.

'I make application for bail, sir,' said Edward Farmer's solicitor.

The magistrate nodded and switched his gaze to the Crown Prosecution Service solicitor. 'Well?'

'There are objections, sir,' said the CPS lawyer.

'Go on.'

'In view of the seriousness of the offence, and that the defendant has previously failed to surrender to bail, sir. In addition, other persons not in custody are believed to be involved and the defendant may be at some personal risk.'

The magistrate nodded again and glanced at Farmer's solicitor. 'Mr, er—'

'It would seem that the evidence is very sketchy, sir, and—'

'Sketchy? What do you mean by sketchy? I don't think I'm familiar with that word in relation to evidence, Mr, er—'

'Er, that is to say, not very strong, sir.'

'Oh! Get on then.'

'My client vigorously denies the charge, sir, and as he was not involved, he cannot be at risk from any other person and I ask for bail. My client is willing to surrender his passport . . . sir.'

The magistrate glanced briefly at the sorry figure of Farmer standing in the dock. 'Does he have a passport, then?'

Farmer's solicitor had a hurried and whispered conference with his client before turning back to the magistrate. 'Er, no, sir. It would seem not.'

'Doesn't make any difference then, does it,' said the magistrate, writing in his ledger. 'Remanded in custody for eight days.' He looked up. 'Next.'

At eleven o'clock on the Monday morning, just as the Bow Street magistrate was telling Farmer's solicitor the inevitable result of his application for bail, Charles Norton emerged from the block of flats where he had spent the night, and drove back to his hotel outside Cheltenham.

'Sod it,' said Findlater. Which was unusual for a strict Calvinist like him.

'Well? How did it go, Jack?'

'Eight-day lay-down, guv,' said Gilroy.

'Told you.' Fox grinned at his DI. 'Anything else?'

'The CPS solicitor wasn't too happy, sir. Wondered if there was going to be any evidence before the next remand hearing.'

'Saucy bastard.'

'Farmer's solicitor reckons his client has a complete answer to the charge.' Gilroy grinned.

So did Fox. 'What is this complete answer, Jack? Guilty?'

'Don't know, guv. The beak didn't take a plea this morning. Just evidence of arrest.'

Detective Sergeant Percy Fletcher sidled into Fox's office with his customary furtiveness. 'The Volvo's been found, sir.'

84

'What Volvo?'

'The one owned by the faceless one . . . Leach, sir.'

'Ah! Where?'

'Richmond Park, apparently.'

'What the hell was it doing there, Perce?'

Fletcher shrugged. 'Could be that's where the meet was, guv.'

'What meet? What the hell are you talking about?'

'Well, it was locked up. No sign of it having been nicked from anywhere. Just parked there. I reckon that someone else, Barney Collins perhaps, met Leach in the park with the Sierra – the one found on the M4 – and he took it over.'

'What makes you think that, for Christ's sake?'

Fletcher looked hurt. 'Well, Leach's missus reckoned she'd never seen the Sierra. Didn't know he owned it. But it must have been kept somewhere. If Leach was on an earner from this cocaine business and didn't want anyone to know, like his missus – or us – it would make sense.'

Fox thought about that. 'You could be right, Perce. What about prints? Been done yet?'

'In the process, guv. I'll let you know as soon as we get a result.'

'Right. Keep me posted, Perce.'

'I'm getting a lot of pressure from above, Tommy,' said Peter Ramsay. 'My people think that we ought to start nicking a few people.'

'Her Majesty's Customs and Excise getting a bit twitchy, are they?' said Fox.

'It was that last load that did it. The one that didn't get to Norton . . . if Norton's the dealer, that is.'

'That's just the point, Pete. We don't know. Supposing that there was another handover at the hotel, and that Norton's got nothing to do with it. Don't forget that Denzil Evans didn't see where the gear went after the Montego arrived there. It might just be that it's a convenient place to do the business. You know, way out in the country.' Fox spread his hands. 'Makes sense when you think about it. A bloke books into a hotel and waits for it to snow, so to speak. Then he moves on to lay it off on some other punter, miles away.'

Ramsay looked thoughtful. 'But you've been there, Tommy. What about these dodgy characters you saw?'

Fox stared at the customs investigator with a sorrowful expression on his face. 'Oh, Pete,' he said. 'If we nicked everybody who looked a bit dodgy, the prisons would be overflowing. And for that matter, half the offices at New Scotland Yard would be empty.'

'Wouldn't argue with you there, Tommy,' said Ramsay.

'It was you who rang earlier, I presume,' said the bank manager when Gilroy entered his office. 'Something about Leo Bridge's account.'

'Yes, I've a warrant under the Police and Criminal Evidence Act to examine it.'

'Oh!' The manager looked disappointed. 'I was hoping you'd come to pay off his overdraft.'

'You're joking,' said Gilroy.

The bank manager smiled. 'Yes I was, I'm afraid. I've long given up hope of that.'

'No, I meant that you were joking when you said he'd got an overdraft.'

'Not at all. He's about three hundred in the red. What's your interest anyway, or shouldn't I ask?'

'He's been murdered,' said Gilroy. 'So I would say that you've got no chance of getting his overdraft paid off. Unless he owned his house.'

'He didn't,' said the manager gloomily. 'He was a tenant. And we paid the rent . . . in a manner of speaking. Anyway, you're welcome to do what you can with this lot.' He pushed a pile of paper in Gilroy's direction. 'There's just one thing though.'

'What's that?'

'We received a letter recently. Addressed to Bridge care of the bank, with a request for it to be forwarded.'

'Who was it from?'

'We didn't open it,' said the manager defensively. 'That would be contrary to bank policy.' He smiled. 'But it was from the Abbey National Building Society . . . at least, that's what was on the envelope.'

'What did you do with it?'

'Sent it on to him, of course.'

'We followed Charles Norton on his so-called business trip on Sunday evening, sir,' said Findlater.

'Naturally,' said Fox. 'And?'

'Spent the night at a flat in Stokenchurch, sir.'

'Thought he might have done. What was that all about then?'

'It would appear,' said Findlater, a sour expression on his face, 'that he went there for the purpose of committing adultery.'

'Oh good!' said Fox. 'For a moment I thought you were going to surprise me, Henry. With whom did he perform this outrageous act?'

'According to discreet inquiries in the vicinity,' said Findlater pompously, 'the flat is owned and occupied by Mrs Daphne Lovegrove, a divorced woman, aged about thirty. I gather that she entertains Mr Norton quite regularly.'

'You mean she's on the game?'

'No, sir. It seems to be a steady liaison that's been going on for about a year.'

'Dear me, Henry,' said Fox. 'What an immoral world it is.'

'Forgive me for saying so, sir, but none of this seems to be a surprise to you.'

'It's not, Henry,' said Fox, 'but that's why I'm a detective chief superintendent and you're a detective inspector.'

*

'I've got the lab report on the Montego, sir,' said DI Evans. 'The one that Fletcher lifted from outside Farmer's place.'

'Splendid. What news?'

'Well for a start, there's absolutely no trace of cocaine. But the lab people said that if it was in sealed packets inside the sort of canvas bag that was used at Heathrow, it's quite likely that there wouldn't be.'

'I suppose that makes sense,' said Fox.

'The vehicle contained quite a few fingerprints. One set's been identified as Bridge's and there are at least two other sets, but neither of them are on record.'

'That's bloody inconsiderate. What about Farmer's dabs? They must have been there somewhere, surely?'

Evans shook his head. 'No trace of his, sir. Either he wore gloves, or he was just minding it. But the interesting bit,' he continued, 'is that the vehicle was nicked.'

Fox sat up sharply. 'What was it, Denzil, a bloody ringer?'

'A classic, sir. We didn't find out until the lab blokes examined the engine and chassis numbers. They'd been erased and overstamped, but they were able to bring up the originals.'

'Damn clever, these scientific chappies,' said Fox. 'Let's have chapter and verse then.'

'It was nicked from the railway station car park in Farnham about four months ago. The thieves had obviously kept obo on the owner, saw him leave it there every morning at eight and pick it up again at about seven in the evening, so they had plenty of time. They gave it new engine and chassis numbers and sent the details off to Swansea along with a duff receipt and registered it as new. Got a fresh registration number for it and a genuine log-book.'

Fox sighed. 'Some things never change, Denzil,' he said.

'And of course it's still on the books at Farnham nick as not recovered, sir.'

'Any joy with the duff receipt?'

Evans grinned. 'There is such a garage, sir,' he said. 'In Wanstead.'

'Well I never,' said Fox. 'Get a warrant, Denzil, and we'll give it a spin.'

'Right, sir.' Evans turned to go.

'By the way, Denzil . . .'

'Sir?'

'I've just got your expenses claim for your enforced night's stay at Norton's hotel.'

'Yes, sir.'

'I must say that two quid's a bit strong for a bloody toothbrush.'

'Only one they had, sir,' said Evans displaying his teeth. 'It was a very good one.'

Chapter Nine

Fox had been looking at the display of shiny new cars for some time before an unctuous salesman appeared. He had a little plastic badge on his lapel that gave his name and proclaimed him to be the sales manager.

'Very popular model that, sir,' said the salesman, nodding towards the car Fox was looking at.

'Yes,' said Fox non-committally.

'Anything in particular take your fancy, sir?' The salesman absently primped his breast-pocket handkerchief.

'Yes, a blue Montego sixteen hundred, as a matter of fact.'

The salesman pursed his lips and looked appraisingly around the showroom. 'Don't have one of those in stock at the moment,' he said. 'But we can easily get you one . . . very quickly.'

'So I gather,' said Fox and produced his warrant card.

'Ah!' said the salesman. 'Very popular with the police, Montegos,' he added nervously.

'Not right now, they're not,' said Fox. 'Shall we adjourn to your office?'

'Of course. Follow me.' The salesman led Fox into a glass-walled cubicle in the corner of the showroom. 'What can I do to assist?' he asked, even more unctuous than before.

'Tell me about this vehicle,' said Fox, sliding a piece of paper across the desk. 'I'm told you sold it about four months ago.'

The salesman picked up the slip of paper. Slowly. As if it were contaminated. 'I shall have to check our records,' he said. He stood up and walked towards a filing cabinet. 'Is there some problem?' he inquired as he opened a drawer.

'Only for you,' said Fox cheerfully.

After searching for several minutes, the salesman slammed the drawer shut. 'I'm sorry,' he said, 'but I can't find any trace of having sold such a vehicle. Are you sure that you've got the right garage?'

'Positive. I have a photostat copy of the original receipt, if that's any help.'

The salesman studied the form that Fox produced, and sucked through his teeth. 'Ah!' he said. 'That explains it.'

'What explains what?' Fox looked at the salesman with an amused expression on his face.

'About six months ago, we took on a new chap in sales. Then about three months ago, we found that one or two receipts had gone missing, together with some of these forms . . .' He tapped the photostat. 'They're the standard forms that most car dealers use. They set out the cost of the vehicle, car tax, VAT, allowance for trade-in. All that sort of thing.' The salesman shrugged. 'We couldn't prove anything, but we had our suspicions.'

'Did you report it to the police?'

'We mentioned it to the local beat bobby, but he said that there was nothing to go on. That the forms had probably got lost.'

'Idle sod,' said Fox under his breath. 'So what did you do?'

'The managing director got to hear of it, and sacked the bloke straight away. He's a bit like that, our MD.' He lowered his voice. 'Tends to go off at half-cock, you know.' Fox nodded. 'But after he'd gone, we didn't lose any more receipts.'

'So you can't shed any light on this particular transaction?'

''Fraid not, no. Is there something wrong with that car, then?' But the salesman knew. He had been in the trade too long not to know.

'Yes,' said Fox. 'It's a ringer.'

'Oh, Christ! The old man'll do his nut when he hears about that.'

'Very likely,' said Fox and stood up. 'All I need to know now,' he continued, 'is the name of this light-fingered fellow you sacked.'

'Rodney Bingham,' said the salesman.

Fox was sitting sideways on to his desk, one leg crossed nonchalantly over the other, gazing at his picture of the Queen and gently tapping one elegantly trousered knee with a paper-knife. 'I think,' he said, 'that it's time to summarise the situation.' He looked thoughtfully at his three detective inspectors and at Peter Ramsay, the customs investigator.

'Good idea, sir,' said Evans. 'I'm totally confused.'

Fox stared at Evans for some seconds. 'Yes . . .' he said eventually, to Evans's great discomfort. He dropped the paper-knife on to his blotter and swung round so that he was sitting with his elbows on the desk. 'What we have here is a dog's dinner. Two villains get blown away on the hard shoulder of the M4. Their vehicle contains traces of cocaine. We then take a quantum leap, thanks to copper's nose . . .' He tapped the side of his nose and grinned at Ramsay. 'That's what we call policeman's intuition,' he said.

Ramsay nodded. 'Yeah,' he said. 'We call it revenue nose, but it amounts to the same thing.'

'Revenue nose.' Fox savoured the phrase. 'Yes, I like that. However, that led us to Stanley Reynolds, who's shacked up – from time to time – with a stewardess who just happens to have been the stewardess on the next flight to arrive from Rio. That flight was serviced by the maintenance crew of which our Stanley was, by some quirk of fate, a member. Reynolds then goes gently

92

berserk and throws his toolbag over a fence, whereupon, miracle of miracles, it is found by two hoods driving along in a Montego. The Montego goes to a hotel owned by Charles Norton and from where a Miss Clark has had enigmatic telephone conversations with the afore-mentioned Stanley Reynolds—'

'Who doesn't exist,' said Evans.

Fox peered at his DI. 'What?'

'We made a few discreet inquiries while we were there, Ronny and me . . .' Evans grinned at DS Crozier who scowled back. 'And we learned from the reception-ist that there is no Miss Clark working in the hotel, nor has there ever been.'

'Thanks for telling me,' said Fox sarcastically.

'That's all right, sir,' said Evans.

'As I was saying,' continued Fox, 'among the habitués of this hotel is one Rodney Bingham. By yet another quirk of fate, a man of the same name was a one-time car salesman in Wanstead, but got the chop after a few receipts went adrift, one of which turned up at Swansea with an application to register the said Montego – which had been stolen in Farnham, four months previously – in the name of Leo Bridge. Mr Bridge got fried in Wandsworth and his Montego then turned up outside the residence of one Edward Farmer – who happened to live in Wanstead – and who has now been charged with the murder of Leo Bridge.' Fox glanced at Gilroy. 'How am I doing, Jack?'

'With you so far, guv'nor.'

'Good. Farmer's Datsun – bearing false plates – was seen near the fire that did for Leo Bridge, and was later found by an enthusiastic constabulary, burnt out at Beachy Head. Mr Leach's Volvo – Mr Leach being one of our two M4 victims – was found abandoned in Rich-mond Park.' Fox paused. 'Incidentally, have we got any result yet on the prints found in that Volvo, Denzil?'

'Yes, sir. His and hers.'

'What's that supposed to mean?'

'Norman Leach's and his wife's.'

'That was quick.'

'Yes, sir,' said Evans. 'But Mrs Leach's prints were on record already. If you remember, she'd got previous for shoplifting.'

Fox shook his head slowly. 'What a tangled web,' he said. 'Well, we won't get much mileage out of the Volvo.'

'Probably not, sir,' said Evans. 'It already had about a hundred thousand on the clock.'

Fox shot a sour glance at Evans. 'While you're feeling so clever, Denzil, perhaps you'd pop down and cast your eyes on the aforementioned Edward Farmer. Just in case he was the bloke you followed down to Norton's place . . . with the late, lamented Leo Bridge. However . . .' His glance took in the others once more. 'There is nothing positive to connect Norton, formerly one of Her Majesty's corporals, with the whole sordid business, nor indeed to suggest that the toolbags that occasionally get lobbed over the perimeter fence at Heathrow ever really contained cocaine either.' He swung round and stared out of the window. 'All we've really got,' he continued, with his back to his audience, 'is that Charlie-boy Norton is having it off with a lady called Daphne Lovegrove in Stokenchurch, while Letitia Norton is almost certainly doing ditto with Jeremy Studd, another habitué of the hotel.' He turned back from the window. 'Which begs the question, where the hell do we go from here?'

'There's a couple of things which might help, guv,' said Gilroy.

'Thank God for that,' said Fox. 'Like what?'

'You remember the WPC we took with us when we interviewed Mrs Leach, the late Norman's wife?'

'Yes.'

'The WPC kept in touch apparently. Thinks she's a social worker.'

'Don't they all,' murmured Fox.

94

'Got a call from her this morning. Mrs Leach bumped into her in the street and told her that when she was clearing out Norman's things, she found a pass-book from the Halifax Building Society in one of his jacket pockets. It had fifteen grand in it. She wanted to know if it was hers now.'

'Well, well,' said Fox.

'But that's not all, guv. I did a Part Two warrant on the Abbey National – result of my chat with Bridge's bank manager – and they turned up an account for Bridge with twenty-five grand in it . . . and fourpence.'

Fox banged the top of his desk with the flat of his hand. 'The bastards are at it,' he said. 'Well, Pete,' he continued, looking at Ramsay, 'I think the time's come to start nicking a few. What d'you reckon?'

Ramsay grinned. 'Long overdue, Tommy.'

'But before we do, I'd just like to know a bit more about this Cameron character, well-known bar-fly at Norton's hotel. My copper's nose tells me he isn't quite right.'

'From what you say, my revenue nose tells me the same,' said Ramsay.

The DC stuck his head round the door. 'Phone call from Mr Evans, sir. He says that Farmer's not the bloke he followed to Cheltenham. Make sense to you, sir?'

'Nothing in this bloody inquiry makes sense,' growled Fox.

The Driver and Vehicle Licences Authority's records at Swansea – always a useful source of information – revealed that Rodney Bingham now lived not far from Cheltenham. Quite close in fact to the hotel owned by Charles Norton. Swansea further revealed that some three months before he had advised the DVLA that he had moved there from Woodford which, as any London detective will tell you, is not a million miles from Wanstead. Just to make absolutely certain, DS Fletcher rang up his contact at the Department of Social Security who imparted the glad news that Bingham's last recorded employment was when he had worked for three months as a car salesman at a dealership in Wanstead. That it was the same dealership that had furnished the false receipt for the Montego found outside Edward Farmer's abode came as a surprise to no one. No one concerned with the Flying Squad's current inquiry, that is.

'We shall visit Master Bingham, Jack,' said Fox. 'With a search warrant.'

'Right, sir. That'll be Cheltenham Magistrates' Court, presumably.'

'You presume incorrectly, Jack. Get it from Bow Street. It wouldn't surprise me to discover that one of Bingham's smart-arse drinking companions is on the local bench, and I don't want him alerting Bingham to our consuming interest. But . . .' Fox hesitated. 'We will wait and see what Denzil Evans has to say about the odious Jock Cameron. Only fools rush in where angels fear to tread, Jack.'

'That is true, guv'nor. Very true.'

For a moment or two, Fox stared icily at Gilroy.

Evans and Crozier were greeted like old friends when they arrived at Norton's hotel. Crozier was made to feel particularly welcome by Letitia Norton, but he hoped that her effusiveness was prompted only by the interest he had displayed in her horses. But he had the feeling that there was more to it than that.

The usual gang were assembled in the bar, even though it was a Wednesday, and a casual onlooker might have been forgiven for wondering what they did for a living. Evans and Crozier, however, were becoming more and more convinced that they knew.

'And what did you think of my horses when you saw them the other day, Ronny?' Letitia Norton had somehow manoeuvred herself so that she now stood beside Crozier. Evans smirked but remained silent.

'Superb animals, Letty,' said Crozier. 'And good jumpers, if all the rosettes are anything to go by.'

'They are rather, aren't they. As a matter of fact, I'm going to have a jump tomorrow.'

Crozier caught sight of Evans's face just before the DI turned away. Evans knew of Letitia's nocturnal visit to Jeremy Studd's room, and his policeman's sense of humour had got the better of him.

'Are you really?' said Crozier, trying desperately to keep the amusement out of his voice.

'I was wondering if you'd care to come and watch.' Letitia smiled. 'Unless you'd like to have a go yourself . . .'

Crozier took a longish draught of beer before attempting to answer. 'I'm afraid I've got a business meeting tomorrow, in Cheltenham,' he said eventually. 'Anyway, I think I prefer a horse that has got my money on it, rather than me on it. I'm very much a townie, you know.'

'Never mind,' drawled Letitia in her county accent. 'There'll be another time, I expect.' She turned to the ever-present Studd. 'Jeremy, be a dear and get me another drink.'

'Yes, of course, Letty.' Studd was obviously delighted to have been brought back into the conversation. He reminded Crozier of a spoilt lapdog.

'I see Jock's not here today,' said Evans to no one in particular.

Norton glanced sharply at him. 'Jock? No, old boy. Away on business, as a matter of fact. Went last Sunday. No idea when he'll be back. Comes and goes, you know. Comes and goes.'

'Still, import and export is a bit like that,' said Evans. 'I think that's what he said he was in.'

'Yes, so I believe,' said Norton.

'Well, you can't afford to miss a profitable line when one crops up in that game, eh?'

'Are you in that business then?' asked Norton, suddenly interested. Until then, he had regarded Evans as a tiresome little Welshman. Probably an accountant.

'No, not any more. Used to be some years ago, but it's hard work.'

'Yes, I suppose so.' Norton pushed his empty glass towards the barman and nodded. 'Get abroad, do you, in your present job?'

'I'm afraid not. My boss is one of those chaps who wants to do it all himself. To be perfectly honest, I'm not much more than an office-boy.' Evans spoke with feeling. 'Sends me to Cheltenham, but he goes to Cannes.'

Norton laughed. 'Cannes isn't all it's cracked up to be,' he said sympathetically. 'What exactly is your line of business, then?'

'Well—'

'Mr Evans?' The hall porter appeared at the edge of the little group of drinkers and peered round.

'Yes, that's me.'

'Telephone call for you, sir, in reception. A Mr Reynard.'

'Your boss, is it?' asked Norton.

'Sounds like it,' said Evans.

'Bad luck,' said Norton and laughed.

Evans walked through to reception and picked up the phone. 'Evans.'

'Denzil, it's Fox.'

'Thought it might be,' said Evans.

'Go to the nearest nick and ring me, Denzil. It's urgent.'

'Right, guv.' Evans paused. 'Any idea where the nearest nick is, guv?'

'Not a clue, Denzil. But you're down there, not me.'

Evans didn't know whether it was the nearest police

98

station, but eventually he came across a blue lamp out-side a house in a village about four miles from the hotel.

Even though the constable examined Evans's warrant card with some care and a measure of suspicion, he still seemed reluctant to accept that a Flying Squad detective inspector should suddenly materialise on his doorstep. Just as reluctantly, he showed Evans into the office and pointed at the telephone. 'That's the phone, sir,' he said.

'Good gracious, so it is,' said Evans, and dialled Fox's number. 'It's Denzil Evans, sir,' he said when Fox answered.

'Denzil, what's happening down there?'

'Nothing much, sir. The usual crowd are hanging round the bar, with the gorgeous Letitia holding court . . . and chatting up Ronny Crozier.'

'Who?'

'Ronny, sir. That's what she calls him.'

'Oh, so that's what your sly comment was about the other day. I'll remember that. Who's there exactly?'

'Norton, of course, and Studd and Bingham. All the usual hangers-on. Cameron's away on business, so I'm told. Norton said that he went on Sunday night. But that was after Norton left for Stokenchurch, because Cameron was still here in the bar . . . and so were we. No idea where he went, but he obviously didn't go with Norton otherwise Henry Findlater would have spotted him. What's the problem, guv?'

'The problem, as you put it, Denzil, is that Cameron's body was found on Monday morning, stabbed to death.'

'Oh, bloody terrific,' said Evans. 'How come we've only just heard?'

'Because the local police didn't know we had an interest, Denzil, that's why.'

'Where was it found then?'

'On a golf-course at Princes Risborough.'

'Where the hell's that, guv?'

'As the crow flies,' said Fox, 'about five miles from Stokenchurch.'

Chapter Ten

Senior Investigating Officer Peter Ramsay of Her Majesty's Customs and Excise was not a happy man. He had listened to Tommy Fox's report and was singularly unimpressed that he seemed no nearer arresting any of the cocaine smugglers. He was aware that Fox had a greater interest in the four murders which had taken place, but Ramsay's priorities were different from those of the police, and so he went to see his boss, the Chief Investigating Officer.

As Chief Investigating Officer, Duncan Mayfield rated as an assistant secretary in the Civil Service, and the only way he had of equating with people outside that service was to look at the pay scales. On that basis he had a rough parity with a commander in the Metropolitan Police and although he had not had any dealings with Fox before, he knew Commander Alec Myers quite well. He decided that it was time to pay him a visit.

'It would appear, Alec,' Mayfield began, 'that cocaine is being illegally imported into this country at intervals by way of the Rio flight into Heathrow. Now, we have afforded every co-operation to the police in this matter, but we can't just let it roll.'

'Are you sure?' asked Myers mildly, peering at Mayfield over his glasses.

'What? Am I sure of what?'

'That cocaine is being smuggled in? My detective chief superintendent assures me that all that has been seen so far is a canvas toolbag being thrown over a fence on the perimeter of the airport. Twice.'

'Yes, I see your point, but it's obviously something that the people concerned don't want customs to know about.'

Myers raised his hands. 'Oh, I agree,' he said, 'but there is no evidence that it's cocaine . . . apart from the traces found in the murder victims' car on the M4 a few Saturdays ago.' He smiled disarmingly. 'I have got that right, haven't I?'

'Well yes, but if we go on at this rate, we're not likely to have any evidence, are we, Alec?'

'What are you proposing then, Duncan?'

'Peter Ramsay, the SIO dealing with our side of it, has suggested that he puts one of his men on the Rio flight that has Sherry Martin on board and which will be serviced by Reynolds's crew, just to see if anything happens.'

'Won't that look a bit obvious? Going out and coming back, I mean.'

Mayfield smiled the sort of smile he reserved for people who clearly did not grasp the finer points of a customs investigation. 'We wouldn't send him out and back on the same flight, Alec, only back on it. He would get to Brazil by a circuitous route, as you might say,'

'Yes, I suppose you might say that,' said Myers enigmatically. 'There's just one point, though.'

'Yes?'

'We had a case only last year of an aircraft cleaner who was stealing those tiny jars of marmalade that they serve on breakfast flights. When we nicked her she had over sixty little jamjars about her person.'

Mayfield frowned. 'I don't see what that has to do with—'

'I just hope that when you eventually open one of those toolbags, it isn't full of little jamjars, that's all,' said Myers.

*

101

Contrary to popular opinion – which these days is usually formed by television fiction – there is no great animosity between police forces, and the detective chief superintendent who headed Thames Valley's CID was not at all averse to Fox taking an interest in the murder of Jock Cameron. He knew Tommy Fox and invited him to go to Princes Risborough to have a look. In fact, he even hoped that the Metropolitan officer might be persuaded to add the case to his own growing list of victims on the grounds that all four seemed inextricably linked. But he didn't know Fox that well.

Nor did Detective Chief Inspector Kevin Donaldson, the officer investigating the killing. Which probably accounted for his general feeling of well-being. But that was about to change.

'Nicked anybody for it?' was Fox's opening question when he arrived at the incident room with Gilroy.

Donaldson grinned. Nervously. 'Not yet, sir, no.'

'Oh!' Fox contrived to look both disappointed and censorious.

Donaldson's air of confidence gave way to one of inferiority. 'We've only been at it for twenty-four hours, sir,' he said apologetically.

'As long as that?' said Fox airily. 'Oh well. Tell me about it.'

'The body was discovered early yesterday morning by a man out walking across the golf-course, or rather by his dog. It was hidden in some bushes in the rough near the fairway leading to the seventh.'

'Is that near a road by any chance?'

'Yes, it is, sir,' said Donaldson. 'And the pathologist is adamant that Cameron was killed elsewhere and taken there . . . probably by car,' he added, and immediately wished that he hadn't.

'I didn't suppose it was in a wheelbarrow,' said Fox drily. 'Any sign of a murder weapon?'

'I've got teams out searching the golf-course for it,

102

but in view of what the pathologist said, I doubt we'll find it. At least, not there.'

Fox nodded. 'What else did he say?'

'Death was caused by a single stab wound to the stomach by a right-handed assailant. He reckons that it more than likely started with the arm full length, sweeping upwards, and was probably a man because of the extent of the penetration.'

'Which was what?'

'About six inches, sir, and he's putting money on it being a weapon with a blade between one and two inches wide.'

'Terrific. Any defensive wounds?'

Donaldson shook his head. 'None, sir. Looks as though Cameron was taken completely by surprise.'

'Time of death been established?'

Donaldson made a rocking movement with his right hand. 'The pathologist gave us the usual mumbo-jumbo about night temperatures and all that, but the up-and-down of it is that he reckons somewhere between ten o'clock the night before and one in the morning. He can't get closer than that.'

Fox grinned. 'Looks as though you'll have to make do with that then. Anything from your scientific people yet?'

'No, sir. We've done all the usual. Soil samples, shoes, fingernails, tyre-marks.' Donaldson yawned. 'But I've got this nasty feeling that it's all going to come to nothing.'

'Could be right,' said Fox cheerfully. 'On the other hand, you might just get a helping hand from the Met. Never know your luck.'

John Williams had to change flights twice in order to get to Brasilia, the capital of Brazil, which is where protocol demanded that he went first. But as a member of the Customs and Excise Investigation Division, he was quite accustomed to being mucked about.

103

When eventually he arrived at the British Embassy, he found that they had not received the telegram informing them of his arrival. Either that or they had mislaid it. Whichever it was, Williams's appearance seemed to come as a complete surprise to Her Majesty's Ambassador Extraordinary and Plenipotentiary to the Republic of Brazil. On more than one count. Williams had long hair, longer than normally associated with a law-enforcement officer, and a straggling moustache reminiscent of the Che Guevara style of the sixties. His suit, which had not been a very good one to start with, was creased and in urgent need of cleaning. He looked like a travel-weary and unsuccessful businessman. Which was exactly the impression that he intended to convey.

Fox decided that the time had come to arrest Rodney Bingham. He would have been quite happy to do it alone, but the house had to be searched, and that would risk getting his suit dirty. It also meant writing things down. It was even possible that statements might have to be taken. And that meant writing, too. So Fox took Gilroy, Evans and Fletcher with him.

Bingham lived in the sort of rural cottage that had sold in great numbers and at vastly inflated prices in the eighties when the owners or the owners' executors realised that large profits were to be made from yuppies who fancied a place in the country.

A red Jaguar filled the driveway so that Fox and Gilroy had to walk on the grass to avoid it. Bingham opened the door and paused briefly as he struggled to place Fox. 'Ah,' he said, 'it's the rat-catcher,' and laughed. 'What on earth are you doing here?'

'Working,' said Fox, and produced his warrant card.

To say that Bingham was surprised to learn that Fox was a police officer would have been a monumental understatement. He was shattered. But Fox knew that it was not that revelation alone. It was the implication. In other words, guilty knowledge.

104

'I want to talk to you about a false receipt and other papers used to register a stolen Montego as if it were new . . .' began Fox.

'I've no idea what you're talking about,' said Bingham nervously.

Fox glanced at Gilroy, standing to one side with pocket book out and pen poised. 'Got that, Jack?'

'They ought to print it at the top of every page of a police pocket book,' said Gilroy. 'Save us having to write it down.'

It took three hours to search Bingham's cottage, but nothing of an evidential nature was found. Fox was not surprised. It merely hardened his belief that Bingham was a bit more clever than he had appeared at first. And the possibility that he was not involved in anything more than one bent motor car did not even cross Fox's mind.

'Which nick, guv?' asked Gilroy as the handcuffed Bingham was escorted down the path.

'Bow Street, of course,' said Fox. 'Are there others?'

Williams formed the opinion that Britain's diplomatic mission to the Republic of Brazil was like a boat that had been adrift for a long time in a foreign sea, its occupants out of touch with reality. The only member of the staff who seemed to have any understanding of what Williams was trying to do was a young second secretary who suggested that he make himself known at the United States Embassy where there was some sort of drugs liaison officer . . . he thought. He was about to make a telephone call to arrange it when Williams reminded him that telephone conversations in that part of the world might just be tapped.

Consequently the second secretary fixed up an apparently innocuous meeting with his opposite number at the American Embassy and passed Williams over . . . with obvious relief. Visitors from outside the closed little world of diplomacy were always an encumbrance: one just didn't know what to do with them.

But things improved radically when Williams met Sam Martino, a special agent of the Drug Enforcement Administration who had been attached to his country's embassy for two years. About forty, with a crew-cut that consisted entirely of grey stubble, Martino had a craggy face with a scar that ran down the left side of his chin. And he knew his stuff.

Over a bottle of bourbon, Williams told Martino the story of the toolbag that had been thrown over a fence at Heathrow Airport, half expecting the American to dismiss it as too trivial for his professional attention. But Martino was obsessive about drugs. To him it didn't matter whether it was a gram or several thousand kilos . . . or 'keys' as he called them. It was his job and he loved every minute of it.

'The first thing we'll do,' said Martino, 'is introduce you to Sanchez.'

'Who's Sanchez?'

'Sanchez is my contact. He's a *delegado*. At least I think that's his rank – it's something like a captain – and he's the only guy who gives a goddam cent about drugs. To everyone else, it's a shrug of the shoulders, and surrender. It's one hell of a problem and most of the guys in the Feds—'

'What's that?'

'It's a sort of federal set-up.' Martino grinned, the scar on his chin making it a lop-sided sort of grin. 'I nearly said like the FBI, but even I can't be that hard. They're responsible for investigations here in the capital and at airports, seaports and land frontiers.' He sloshed more whiskey into Williams's glass. 'Not that I blame them for being laid back. Poke your nose in too far in this god-forsaken place and you'll get your damn head blown off. A few of the local fuzz have gone that way. Houses getting burned down in the middle of the night, and cars with an ignition that blows you into little pieces when you switch it on. The truth of the matter is that law-enforcement has broken down here. If the locals

106

come across a thief, they lynch him. Sure as hell they don't waste their time talking to the fuzz.' He shrugged again. Martino did a lot of shrugging.

'How have you survived then?' It was of especial interest to Williams now that he was in the battle zone.

'Keep your eyes and ears open. Drop money into the right pockets . . . and never go anywhere without this.' Martino pulled his jacket back to reveal a holstered .45 that seemed to occupy most of the left-hand side of his body. 'Got a piece?' he inquired casually.

'We don't carry them,' said Williams.

For a few seconds, Martino stared at the British customs officer as though he were raving mad. Then, without comment, he walked across to his safe, took out a pistol and laid it on his desk. 'I got a holster some place,' he said. 'You can give it back to me when you leave.'

Williams hesitated for only a moment. 'Right, thanks,' he said.

'OK, like I said,' continued Martino, 'we'll take Sanchez out to dinner and fill him up with so much cheap wine it'll blow his mind.' He laughed. 'He's the only guy who can help you . . . and he knows his way round Rio de Janeiro Airport, too. Even though it's six hundred miles away.'

The Crown Prosecution Service solicitor who was handling the case of The Queen against Farmer, was sitting in his office staring dejectedly at the Form 151 which he had received from Detective Inspector Gilroy on the morning of Farmer's first appearance at court and which outlined the salient facts of the police case. At least, it was supposed to outline the police case, but even with his lack of experience he could see that the so-called evidence was likely to be laughed out of court on the very first occasion that it was given an airing.

His confidence was not boosted by the reaction of the colleague with whom he shared an office and whose

107

advice and assistance he had sought. All the while his friend was skimming through the Initial Report Form, he was shaking his head and tutting. Not that he had time for too many shakes or tuts. But when he reached the name of the officer in the case, he laughed outright. 'Tommy Fox,' he said. 'Christ, Mike, you've got a load of grief there. Your best bet is to resign and offer to handle Farmer's defence. It's the only way you'll win.'

'Thanks. You're a great help.'

But then the solicitor had a telephone call from Farmer's solicitor, Isaacs, who said that his client wished to see the police. Mr Farmer, it seemed, wanted to make a full statement about his part in the demise of the unfortunate Mr Leo Bridge. This, Isaacs emphasised, was contrary to the advice which his client had been given, but there it was.

Suddenly the CPS solicitor felt a whole lot better. He rang the Flying Squad and left a message for Detective Chief Superintendent Fox to contact him. Urgently.

Chapter Eleven

Rodney Bingham had not been in a police station before, except for such mundane matters as the production of his driving licence or to ask the way to somewhere, and he was obviously shaken by the starkness of the interview room and the indifferent attitude of the unsmiling and silent constable who had positioned himself just inside the door. But Bingham did his best to give the impression that he was unconcerned by this terrifying turn of events. He crossed his legs, nonchalantly took a cigarette from a silver case, and endeavoured to create a positive picture of a victim of mistaken identity who would be released with profuse apologies the moment that the police realised their error. But this attitude did not fool Fox. Neither, for that matter, did Bingham fool himself.

But Fox was somewhat put out. During the journey back to London, the Flying Squad office had relayed the message from the CPS that Farmer wanted to make a statement. If Fox had been able to visualise such an unlikely occurrence, he would probably have delayed Bingham's arrest. As it was, Bingham was now in custody at Bow Street, and the Police and Criminal Evidence Act demanded that something be done one way or another. Quickly. Farmer would have to wait. After all, he wasn't going anywhere.

But neither was Bingham. Fox was adamant about that. The last thing he wanted was Norton getting to hear of Bingham's arrest.

'Right.' Fox placed his cigarette case and lighter on the table, carefully inspected the chair and sat down. 'I haven't got time to bugger about. You were responsible for abstracting a number of receipts from the car showroom where you worked in Wanstead . . . before you got the sack, that is—'

'That was never proved.' Bingham spoke with the sort of strangulated accent that marks out a man who had been to a minor public school, usually because he had no brains but his father had got money. 'I was wrongly dismissed,' he added and stubbed out his half-smoked cigarette.

'Is that a fact? I'll put you in touch with the industrial tribunal people, if you like. You've probably got a case there, you know.'

For a moment, Bingham took him seriously, but then, dismissively, 'I really don't know what all this nonsense is about,' he said. 'I'll say it again. It wasn't proved.'

'Don't you worry about that, my son,' said Fox. 'You leave the proving to me. But I will tell you this. You then conspired with others to re-register a blue Montego motor car well knowing it to be stolen. That car was subsequently used to convey smuggled cocaine.' That was pushing it a bit. There was very strong suspicion but no proof. 'And I need hardly tell an educated fellow like you, who obviously reads the quality press, that Her Majesty's judges tend to come down like a ton of bricks on that sort of thing.' Fox paused and studied the interview room door. Then he looked back at Bingham. 'I'd say the going rate for that, these days, is about eight years, rising twelve.'

Bingham's dandified appearance and affected demeanour started to evaporate. He had never had dealings with the Criminal Investigation Department before and Fox's hard-nosed attitude had frightened the wits out of him. But there was still a tiny element of resilience left. 'That's a very good try,' he said, 'but it won't wash. You can provide me with two things. My solicitor . . .

110

and some proof of what you're alleging. In that order.'
He turned away disdainfully and lit another cigarette.
'Until then, I have nothing to say.'

Fox stood up. 'Your choice, old son,' he said. 'We'll
talk again later.'

'What now then, guv'nor?' asked Gilroy once he and
Fox were outside the interview room. 'Does he get a
solicitor?'

'As far as I am concerned, Jack, he can have the
whole of the Queen's Bench Division. You and I are
going to Brixton . . . to see a man about a statement.'

'I am reliably informed,' began Fox airly, 'that you wish
to make a statement.'

'Yeah, well—'

'I must caution you that you need not do so, but that
anything you say will be taken down in writing and may
be given in evidence,' said Fox for the benefit of Isaacs,
Farmer's solicitor, who was sitting next to his client.

'Yeah, well—'

'Then you may begin,' said Fox. He was convinced
that his journey to Brixton was going to be a waste of
time. On frequent occasions in the past, he had interviewed prisoners who had suddenly decided that they
wished to confess all, only to find out that they were
doing their inadequate best to row themselves out,
rather than row someone else in.

'It's about the burning.'

'What is?'

'What I want to talk about.'

Fox sighed. This was going to be a tedious business.
'Well just do it, instead of telling me that you're going
to, Ted.'

'That morning, what you was talking about, when you
saw my motor down Wandsworth . . .'

'Yes?' Fox decided not to explain that the car had
been seen by other officers.

'Well, I knew about it, see. Some geezer come down

111

my drum the night before and said as how he wanted to borrow it—'

'Who was this clown?' asked Fox.

'Dunno. He just like—'

'This isn't another of your man-in-pub stories, is it?'

'Nah! I ain't never seen him before. But he turned up and said he wanted to borrow the motor. And when he come back next morning, he said I was to get rid of it. And he said I was to take it down Beachy Head and set fire to it.'

'Ted, dear boy . . .' Fox yawned and lit a cigarette. 'As I understand it, some finger that you've never set eyes on before turns up at your drum, borrows your jamjar, brings it back the next morning and tells you to take it to Sussex and set fire to it. Is that about the strength of it?'

'Yeah, that's it.' Farmer's face cracked into a crooked grin.

Fox leaned forward, confidentially, as if about to explain some adult problem to a particularly dim child. 'D'you think I came up the Clyde on a bicycle, Ted?'

This concept clearly baffled Farmer. 'I dunno,' he said.

'I do think that my client's doing his best to assist you, Mr Fox,' said Isaacs.

Fox stared at the solicitor. 'For the moment, Mr Isaacs,' he said, 'I think that you and I will have to agree to differ on that point.' He turned to Farmer again. 'Personally,' he continued, 'I've never heard such a cock-and-bull yarn in all my life. I think you'd better start fleshing out your little attempt at a joke, Ted, or there's a danger I shall miss the punch line.'

'Oh!'

'Oh, indeed, Ted. Now tell me, how much did this dark stranger bung you?'

Farmer glanced at Isaacs who, clearly as irritated as Fox at having his time wasted, nodded.

'Four grand,' said Farmer.

112

'Bit of a high price to pay for an old Datsun, Ted. How old was it? Ten years?'

'Eleven.'

'Yes, well, not exactly a *Glass's Guide* price, was it. So obviously there was a payment for something else. What was that?'

'Well there was the petrol. It's a long way to Beachy Head.'

Fox laughed. 'If you spent about three grand on petrol – and I reckon that to say the car was worth a thousand is pushing it – then you must have gone a damned long way round to get to the seaside.' Even Isaacs had the grace to smile at that. 'So what was the extra for?'

'I dunno, Mr Fox. Honest.'

'Oh dear. Let me put it another way, then. To be offered four thousand pounds for the use of your car and its eventual destruction, being well over the odds for its value, must mean that the borrower was up to no good. What d'you reckon?'

'I really don't think that my client's in a position to speculate about that, Mr Fox,' said Isaacs.

Fox swung round on the solicitor. 'What's your view then, Mr Isaacs?'

Isaacs coughed. 'It's not for me to say,' he said. 'I'm here merely to advise Mr Farmer.'

'Yes,' said Fox, 'well, I would suggest you advise Mr Farmer that his acceptance of that proposition amounts to guilty knowledge. Or is he so naïve that he imagined his caller to be a good fairy who just happened by?' He faced Farmer again. 'You say you don't know who this person was, Ted.'

'No, he never give his name.'

'And did you ask him if he was insured to drive your vehicle? Or was it insured to cover any driver?' Fox grinned at the prisoner.

'You needn't answer that,' said Isaacs.

'What did he look like, this man with no name?'

113

Farmer gave that some thought. 'About the same as him.' He nodded towards Gilroy.

'What? Same height and build?'

'Yeah.'

'Colour of hair, eyes?'

'Never noticed, Mr Fox. Sort of dark, I s'pose. But he did have a la-di-da accent.'

'Is that a fact? Well, well. And would you know him again, Ted?'

'Yeah, I reckon so.'

'Well, Jack. What d'you think?'

'Could have been Bingham, I suppose. But I don't think Farmer was telling us all that he knew.'

Fox stared acidly at his DI. 'That, Jack,' he said, 'is a statement of the bloody obvious.'

Delegado Vicente Sanchez was not a very tall man, but he was big. A good twenty stones in weight, he had black hair and a black moustache that straggled its way down both sides of his mouth. All in all, he looked like a story-book Spaniard. Except that he was a Portugese-speaking Brazilian. And he drank red wine like he'd just heard that an acute shortage was imminent.

'This is John Williams, from British Customs,' said Sam Martino.

Sanchez collapsed into a chair that looked as though it would not last the evening under his immense weight, and sighed deeply at the effort. Then he took a crisp linen napkin and tucked it into the collar of his shirt. Without being asked, he filled a glass with wine from the carafe on the table and took a deep draught. Then he put his glass down, nodded, and stuck out a podgy hand in Williams's direction. 'Sanchez,' he said. He didn't seem at all surprised that a British customs officer should suddenly appear unannounced in Brasilia.

'Before we get down to business, Vicente,' said Martino, 'I've lent John here a piece. Can you fix up for the permit?'

'Is no problem.' Sanchez devoured a bread roll.

'Not that anyone bothers much around here,' continued Martino, 'but if you wing someone, they start getting all official. Isn't that right, Vicente?'

'Is right!' Sanchez refilled his glass with red wine, and then turned and flicked his fingers at a passing waiter. As far as he was concerned, the fact that Martino was paying was a mere formality. He knew that eventually the bill – along with the claim for the monthly stipend that Sanchez received from US Government funds – would find its way to the Drug Enforcement Administration's headquarters in Washington, DC.

It was obvious that Sanchez had to settle the matter of food before any serious conversation could begin, and it was not until he had a huge dish of chilli in front of him that he was prepared to enter into any meaningful discussion. 'So,' he said, between mouthfuls. 'You have a problem, *O Senhor* Williams?'

'John, please,' said Williams, and went on to give the Brazilian policeman details of the Heathrow Airport operation.

From time to time, Sanchez nodded, all the while alternating great mouthfuls of chilli with draughts of wine. By the end of the meal, Williams estimated that the Brazilian policeman must have consumed nearly a litre.

When he had finished eating, Sanchez leaned back in his chair and placed his hands across his huge belly, presumably to give some aid to his shirt buttons which looked as though they were about to abandon the unequal fight. 'So, you think someone is putting the cocaine on this plane at Rio de Janeiro, eh?'

Williams nodded. 'Looks that way,' he said. 'And it's probable that the stewardess is transferring it to this canvas toolbag. We don't know that for certain, but she lives with the man who collects the bag. It would be a pretty big coincidence if she had nothing to do with it.'

Sanchez laughed, a deep rumbling laugh. 'I should think so,' he said. He took another mouthful of wine and looked longingly across the room at a table spread with sweetmeats. 'OK,' he said. 'I look into it for you. If this is happening, I tell Sam and he tells you. OK?'

'Yes, fine. Thanks very much.'

'Is no problem,' said Sanchez, and suddenly giving up on the idea of eating more, levered himself into an upright position. 'OK,' he said. 'Now we go to my favourite bar and have a drink.'

'You're absolutely certain that Charles Norton spent the whole of that Sunday night in Daphne Lovegrove's flat, are you, Henry?' asked Fox.

'Yes, sir.' But DI Findlater looked doubtful. 'As sure as we can be, sir.'

'What's that mean?'

'Well, short of him climbing down a drainpipe at the back, yes, he was there all night.'

Fox was clearly unhappy about that. He was convinced that Norton was involved not only in smuggling drugs, but in the four murders as well. 'I suppose,' he said thoughtfully, 'that Jock Cameron didn't turn up at the flats during the course of that night, Henry?'

'I don't know, sir.'

'What d'you mean, you don't know?'

'I don't know what Cameron looked like, sir. Never saw him.'

'Dammit, neither did you.' Fox stood up and paced about his office.

'There were a few comings and goings, sir,' said Findlater. 'It's a big block of flats. There are twenty-four served by that one entrance. Norton arrived at about nine o'clock. There were quite a few people who came in after that . . . and about four who left.'

'Right then, Henry,' said Fox, making a decision. 'Get

116

down to Princes Risborough, or wherever their mortuary is, and have a look at Cameron. See if you recognise him. Then I think I shall suggest to the Thames Valley Police that executing a search warrant at Mrs Daphne Lovegrove's flat might be a useful exercise.'

'But won't that alert Norton, sir?'

'It might alert him to the fact that Thames Valley are thrashing about a bit, I suppose,' said Fox. 'But only if Daphne Lovegrove tells him. And I've got that feeling she won't. She won't make a connection between Norton and Cameron . . . not unless she's involved. We can always spin her some fanny about a suspect seen to enter. All that stuff. Keep the warrant up our sleeves, just in case. Let Norton think that blundering Old Bill, in his big boots, is bending and stretching. You see, Henry, it's just when they're laughing fit to bust and telling their mates in the pub how they outwitted the poor old fuzz that you catch the bastards with their trousers down.'

'Do I get the impression that you're going to take over the Cameron murder, sir?' asked Findlater. It was more than a casual inquiry. He knew that if Fox took on extra work, he tended to spread it about. Fox was very generous like that.

'If that's the impression you've got, Henry, it's totally erroneous.'

'That's what I thought, sir,' said Findlater. That confirmed it.

The two prison officers who had accompanied Edward Farmer from Brixton prison to Bow Street police station concluded that he would be safe enough there, and adjourned to the canteen.

The uniform branch inspector conducting the identification parade had eventually assembled the appropriate number of volunteers – not without some difficulty – and had offered Rodney Bingham the requisite facility of picking his own place.

117

When everything was arranged, Farmer was brought out and asked if he could pick out the man who had paid so generously for his ancient Datsun. Three times he walked up and down the line, finally shaking his head. 'He ain't there, guv,' he said to the inspector.

'A great help you are,' said Fox afterwards. He was convinced that Bingham was his man and that Farmer was deliberately not pointing him out.

Farmer sniffed. 'Makes a day out, don't it, Mr Fox,' he said.

'Make the most of it,' said Fox darkly. And turning to the two prison officers who had reappeared, duly refreshed, he said, 'You can have him back, gents. He's no bloody use to me.'

'What do we do now, sir?' asked Gilroy.

'Charge Bingham with the theft of the receipts from the garage in Wanstead and get him banged up.'

'The beak'll never stand that, guv'nor,' said Gilroy.

'No, he probably won't. In fact, with any luck he'll throw it out. No case to answer. But more to the point, Jack, it will have enabled us to get Bingham's fingerprints.'

'But if the case is chucked, guv'nor, we'll have to destroy the prints.'

A sinister smile crossed Fox's face. 'Speak slowly when you get to court, Jack,' he said, 'to give the fingerprint lads time to check them in the scenes-of-crime index. They know where to look, after all.'

Gilroy was amazed. It was quite out of character for Fox to let go that easily. 'But if Bingham's released, he'll be straight down to Cheltenham, telling Norton that we're on to him.'

Fox grinned. 'No he won't, Jack, because you're going to re-arrest him outside the court in connection with the murder of Leo Bridge. That'll do for a start. I know his sort, Jack. Full of piss and importance. He'll walk out of court thinking that he's had us over. And that's just when he'll come unstuck.'

*
118

Henry Findlater journeyed to Buckinghamshire and gazed upon the waxen features of Jock Cameron. Then he travelled all the way back again.

'Well?' said Fox.

'Never seen him before in my life, sir.'

'Damn!' said Fox.

Rodney Bingham's confidence had been restored by his solicitor's scathing criticism of the case against him as a rag-bag of hearsay unworthy of the court's time. As Fox had predicted, the magistrate had declared that there was no case to answer and had dismissed the charges. But the fine distinction between that and an acquittal eluded Bingham who did not immediately appreciate that the police could bring the same charges again . . . when they did have the requisite evidence. He decided to celebrate by lunching at Rules, a short stroll away in Maiden Lane.

'Rodney Bingham.'

Bingham looked scornfully at Gilroy. 'What d'you want now?' he asked.

'Rodney Bingham, I am arresting you in connection with the murder of one Leo Bridge at Wandsworth on the morning of—' But that was as far as Gilroy got. Bingham collapsed at his feet in a dead faint.

'Tommy.' With an absent gesture, Commander Alec Myers pushed his glasses back on to the bridge of his nose and stared down at the form on his desk.

'Yes, sir?'

'How in the name of God did Denzil Evans incur an incidental expense of two quid buying a toothbrush in Gloucestershire?'

'He's Welsh, sir,' said Fox.

Chapter Twelve

'You were right, sir,' said Evans.

'I usually am,' said Fox, 'but what in particular are you talking about now?'

'Bingham's prints were in the Montego, sir. Got a positive ID from Fingerprint Branch.'

'Well there you are, Denzil. Everything comes to those who wait. Incidentally, I think the Commander might want to examine your toothbrush.'

The morning following their alcoholic outing with *Delegado* Vicente Sanchez, Williams and Martino – both nursing hangovers – spent an anti-climactic few hours going through the Drug Enforcement Administration's Brazil files in the hope that they might contain some snippet of information that would help the British customs officer's inquiry, but to no avail.

Williams was despondent. 'You reckon this Sanchez as an informant, do you, Sam? I must say, he seemed a bit laid-back to me.'

Martino poured more coffee and sat down at his desk. Then he lit one of the foul-smelling Brazilian cheroots to which he had become addicted. 'If anyone's going to turn up some dirt on your guys, it's Sanchez, John,' he said. 'You gotta remember, these South Americans work a darn sight slower than you and me. It's the *mañana* principle. Don't do today what you can put off till tomorrow . . . or better still, next week. But if there's anything to find, Sanchez'll dig it up.' He shrugged.

'What the hell else is there? There's one hell of a lot of people making one hell of a lot of money out of drug trafficking. The penalties are high, but so are the profits. It makes 'em damned careful, I can tell you.'

'It's just that I hate kicking my heels waiting,' said Williams.

'That's what you came for, wasn't it? Just to turn around and go back on the London flight. If anything turns up while you're waiting, that's a bonus.' Martino stood up and slipped on a light linen jacket. Williams noticed that it barely covered the bulge of his .45. 'Let's go get a drink some place.'

The next three days were like that. Martino knew just about every bar in Brasilia, and by the time they had finished, Williams reckoned he knew them too.

But they heard nothing from Sanchez.

'Can't you give him a ring, Sam?' asked Williams.

'Nope. It don't work that way. If Vicente's got anything, he'll come across.'

And so on the Friday morning, still having heard not a word from the Brazilian *delegado*, a disappointed Williams packed his bags and took the internal flight from Brasilia to Rio de Janeiro.

Williams was not altogether surprised to be met by Sanchez at Rio, and the Brazilian policeman explained that he'd had a phone call from Martino giving him details of Williams's flight. At the departure desk, Sanchez used his not inconsiderable influence with an attractive check-in girl of his acquaintance to get Williams a seat with a good view of the galley. Then he shook hands and promised to keep in touch.

Williams boarded the aircraft and settled himself down for the long flight back to England.

Sherry Martin, along with the other stewardesses, went through the take-off drills with well-rehearsed but unconvincing vivacity and then got on with serving meals and looking glamorous.

Williams found it hard to keep awake throughout the

121

long night and even with the good vantage-point that Sanchez had secured for him, he was aware that he wouldn't necessarily see everything that happened in the galley. But he was more than ever convinced that an overnight flight, with dimmed cabin lights, provided ideal conditions for a stewardess intent on hiding something that had come on board at Rio de Janeiro International.

'I don't know anything about a murder.' A white-faced Bingham sat in the interview room.

'Don't pussy-foot about,' said Fox. 'The Montego car that you helped to ring was found outside Edward Farmer's house when we arrested him. And your fingerprints are on it, my son. Farmer has been particularly helpful to the police, and I now know you were involved, so you can start by accounting for your movements on the morning in question.' It was pure hypothesis, particularly as Farmer had declined to identify Bingham, but it had an electric effect on him and he slumped back in his chair, a cold sweat forming on his brow.

'Look here, I had absolutely nothing to do—'

'Oh, I nearly forgot,' said Fox. 'Anything you say will be recorded and may be given in evidence.'

When Williams's flight from Rio arrived at Heathrow, Ramsay's investigators were in place, together with a token presence of police. Reynolds, the suspect engineer, boarded the aircraft, but appeared only to assist in its servicing. No toolbags were thrown over fences, and the customs surveillance of Northern Perimeter Road failed to spot any suspect vehicles.

All in all, it seemed to Williams that his trip to Brazil had been a waste of time. And an expensive one. At least, that was the view taken by Duncan Mayfield, the Chief Investigating Officer, when he passed Williams's expenses . . . and wondered how he was going to justify them to the holders of the Customs and Excise purse strings.

'I think we should continue to keep observation on the Rio flights,' said Ramsay, 'and the next time a tool-bag goes over the fence, nick Reynolds, Sherry Martin . . . and whoever picks the bag up.'

'Well, that's the easy way out,' said Fox, 'but nothing happened after your man went off on his expensive wild-goose chase to Brazil.' He grinned. 'I know you customs chaps are keen to do something positive,' he continued, 'but that sounds like panic.'

'We might yet get something from Rio,' said Ramsay defensively. 'We had to give it a try.'

Fox smiled benevolently. 'Of course you did, dear boy,' he said, but he didn't look as though he meant it. 'The point is, though, that it won't get you any nearer arresting Norton even if you do thrash about nicking the foot-soldiers.'

'If Norton's got anything to do with it.'

'Must have,' said Fox, unwilling to believe that his prime suspect was innocent. 'He's got form for smuggling.'

Ramsay laughed. 'Yes, I know, but there's a hell of a difference between bringing in booze and porn and smuggling cocaine. If we worked on that basis, we'd have half the old-age pensioners in the country on CEDRIC.'

'On what?'

'CEDRIC,' said Ramsay. 'It's our computer. It lists suspected drug-traffickers.'

'Oh, really? You got Norton on it?'

'Yes,' said Ramsay.

'Well, there you are then,' said Fox.

'But only because you thought he was at it,' said Ramsay. 'We're thinking of taking him off again.'

For some time, Fox had been fretting over the fact that on the night that Jock Cameron had been murdered,

Charles Norton had been with Daphne Lovegrove in her flat at Stokenchurch. And Stokenchurch was about five miles from Princes Risborough where the body had been found.

Finally, Fox convinced himself that a talk with Daphne Lovegrove might be profitable. However, given that the murder of Jock Cameron was not his inquiry, it was necessary – as a matter of inter-force courtesy – to persuade Detective Chief Inspector Donaldson of the Thames Valley Police that it might be a good idea.

'Kevin, dear boy,' he began.

Donaldson may have construed this familiarity as a sign of Fox's rising confidence in him. If he did, it was a mistake . . . as Gilroy could have told him. 'Yes, sir?'

'This Daphne Lovegrove whom my officers have discovered is Charles Norton's sleeping partner . . .'

'Sorry, sir, not quite with you.'

'On the night that Cameron was killed, my officers followed Norton from his hotel to an address in Stokenchurch – Daphne Lovegrove's address – where, so they say, he spent the night with her.'

'Yes, sir?' Donaldson sounded doubtful. He could not see what Fox was driving at.

'Well, according to my map, Stokenchurch is but a short haul from Princes Risborough. And your pathologist says that Cameron was killed elsewhere and dumped on the golf-course. With me so far?'

'Yes, sir.'

'Good. Now the thing is—'

'But surely, sir, there's nothing to connect your man Norton with the death of Cameron, is there?'

'Oh dear.' Fox shook his head. Slowly. 'They were friends, dear boy. Friends. Or perhaps acquaintances would be a better term to use.'

'Yes, I know, but if your blokes were keeping obo on Norton all night . . .' Donaldson paused. 'That is what you said, sir, isn't it?'

'Ah!' said Fox, 'you do remember. Yes, that is so.'

'Well how could Norton possibly have murdered Cameron?' Donaldson seemed genuinely puzzled by Fox's theorising.

'Don't know,' said Fox nonchalantly. 'But he's a villain, this Norton.'

'Yes, I know that too,' said Donaldson, sitting down. The strain was beginning to tell. 'But what exactly are you suggesting, sir?'

'I am suggesting that it might be to our mutual benefit – yours and mine – to go and have a chat with Muzz Lovegrove. Might solve your problem . . . and it might well solve mine. Got the drift, Kev?'

'I'm not sure, sir,' said Donaldson, now totally bewildered by it all. 'It seems a bit obscure to me.'

'Never mind,' said Fox. 'I'll guide you through. All we need now is a warrant.'

'A warrant?'

'Of course. Can't search property without a warrant,' said Fox with a grin. 'Well not down here, anyway,' he added.

'Search it?' Donaldson stood up again. 'Bit heavy, isn't it, sir? I mean we've got no evidence to connect Daphne Lovegrove with Cameron's murder. How can we justify a search warrant?'

'Easy. Cameron knew Norton. Norton knows Lovegrove. And you won't find evidence by pussy-footing about, old son,' said Fox confidently. 'But I'll tell you what we'll do. You and I will go and see the lady. Let her think that we're thrashing about. Just ask a few questions. Spin her some fanny totally unconnected with the Cameron murder . . . or with Norton for that matter. You know the sort of thing. Only use the warrant if we have to. Better safe than sorry. OK?' And before Donaldson had time to reply, Fox added, 'Well, that's settled then.'

Fox knocked confidently on Daphne Lovegrove's door.

There was no answer. He rang the bell of the flat opposite.

'Yes?' The woman who answered the door was about sixty and grey-haired. She looked curiously at Fox and Donaldson, apparently unable to decide whether they were selling encyclopaedias or seeking converts to some exclusive religion.

'Good afternoon, madam,' said Fox. 'We're police officers.' The woman still looked doubtful and Fox wafted his warrant card in front of her face. Quickly, so that she wouldn't see his rank. Detective chief superintendents from Scotland Yard did a lot of things, but investigating domestic burglaries in another police area was not one of them. 'We are investigating a number of burglaries in the area,' he continued smoothly. 'I wondered if you might be able to help us.'

'But I haven't been burgled.'

'You're very fortunate, madam,' said Fox with a comforting smile. 'But have you seen anything suspicious? Sunday evening two weeks ago is the time we particularly have in mind.' He waved a hand to include Donaldson in his concern.

The woman looked doubtful. 'Well,' she began, 'there was something . . .'

Fox looked up and down the small hallway. 'D'you think it might be better if we came in?' he asked.

'Oh, yes, I suppose so.' The woman led them into a sitting-room that looked out on to the back of the building. 'It was down there,' she continued, pointing out of the window.

'What, in the car park?' Fox stared down on to the tarmacadam parking area at the rear of the flats.

'Yes. It must have been about midnight, I suppose. My husband had just turned off the television when we heard voices. A few moments later we heard a noise that sounded like a car boot being closed.' She paused for a moment. 'Well, we're not ones to pry, you know . . .'

126

'Of course not,' murmured Fox.

'But our curiosity got the better of us.' The woman smiled guiltily. 'And we looked out. Just in time to see a man getting into a car. Then he drove away.'

'You didn't happen to notice what sort of car it was, I suppose?' asked Fox. 'Or the number?' he added hopefully.

'No, I'm afraid not. It was very dark. We just assumed that it was a visitor going home. But it was unusual. It's always so quiet round here. Well, it's in the lease, you see.'

'What's in the lease?' Fox looked puzzled.

'That residents shouldn't make a noise. The staircase committee's very strict about that.'

'I suppose you didn't recognise the man you saw getting into the car.'

'No, I'm sorry. As I say, it was very dark.'

'Never mind,' said Fox. 'Thank you for your time.' At the front door he turned and paused. 'By the way, you don't happen to have seen Mrs Lovegrove today, do you? We particularly wanted to have a word with her.'

'Mrs Lovegrove?'

'Yes,' said Fox with a sigh. 'She lives opposite.' He indicated Daphne Lovegrove's front door with a wave of his hand.

'Oh, her. Not seen her for a week or so. I think she must have gone away. She's very punctual, you see. Goes out to work at half-past eight every morning and comes back again at half-past five every night. But not lately.'

'Do you know where she works?'

The woman pondered for a moment or two. 'Yes, of course,' she said, the recollection suddenly coming to her. 'She works at a building society.'

'In Stokenchurch?'

'I think so.'

127

It was hard work, but Fox was getting there. 'I don't suppose you happen to know which one.'

'No, I'm sorry, except . . .'

'Yes?'

'Well I think it's in Stokenchurch. She always walks to work.' The woman paused. 'Of course, she might catch a bus. But she does have a car, so I wouldn't have thought so.'

'Thank you, madam,' murmured Fox. 'You've been most helpful.' He waited until the door was closed before turning to Donaldson. 'I do love people who keep themselves to themselves,' he said. 'They seem to know everything, Kev.'

Suddenly Williams's trip to Brazil paid off. A coded signal from Martino in Brasilia to his opposite number at the United States Embassy in London was passed on to Williams immediately.

'Well?' said Ramsay when Williams strolled into his office clutching the message.

'Our friend Sanchez has come good after all, Peter.'

'Worth what it cost to send you out there?'

'I think so.' Williams sat down, still reading.

'Well, don't keep me in suspense. What does he say?'

A smile spread across Williams's face. 'Great stuff,' he said. 'Just listen to this. Sanchez – and God knows how he's managed to get informants like this – says that the cocaine is put into discreetly marked sugar bags at the in-flight catering depot and loaded on to the aircraft as part of their normal supplies. During the flight one of the stewardesses . . .' He looked up. 'He doesn't say which stewardess, but I reckon we can guess. One of the stewardesses transfers the marked packets to a tool-bag and leaves it in the galley. She just walks off the aircraft and one of the maintenance crew takes the bag out.' Williams threw the message on to Ramsay's desk. 'Couldn't be simpler,' he said.

'Well we'd guessed most of that,' said Ramsay, 'but

128

what it does do is to confirm that it's cocaine. Until now we'd been assuming that it was.' He stood up and thrust his hands into his pockets. 'It's not bloody fair, is it? We do all this training, learning how to find drugs in every conceivable type of hiding place, and this bloody lot just thumb their noses and do it the easy way. The bastards. Have they no pride?' He paused. 'This Sanchez . . . doesn't want a job over here, does he?'

'No,' said Williams, 'but he would like to know when we're going to pull this lot. According to that . . .' He pointed at the message. 'According to that, he intends to nick the little team at his end, but he doesn't want to bugger up our job. So he's prepared to wait until he gets word.'

After his unsuccessful attempt to interview Daphne Lovegrove, Fox had decided that he wasn't going to waste his valuable time traipsing the streets in search of her. That would be left to an officer of lesser rank.

He sent for Gilroy.

And Gilroy sent for Fletcher.

And Fletcher eventually reported back to Fox.

'Well, Perce? Found her?'

'No, sir,' said Fletcher.

'Oh, that's a pity.'

'Yes and no, sir. I found the building society she works at, but she's done a runner. Not been seen since the day Cameron's body was discovered. They haven't had any word from her, either. They rang her flat, thinking she might be sick, but got no answer.'

'And is that all they've done?'

Fletcher grinned. 'No, sir, they checked the books to make sure she hadn't seen them off for a few grand.'

'Good God!' said Fox. 'Gives a whole new meaning to staff welfare, doesn't it, Perce? Right then. Message to all forces and all ports. I want that woman found. I've got this gut feeling that she has something to tell us. Something quite important.'

Chapter Thirteen

When Fox heard the information that Williams had received from Brazil about the sugar-bag ruse, he rubbed his hands in glee. 'Got the bastards,' he said.

But they hadn't.

Blanket surveillance was mounted to cover the arrival of the next two Rio flights on which Sherry Martin was a member of the crew and when Reynolds was one of the engineers servicing the aircraft.

But nothing happened. And once again, no suspect vehicles were seen on Northern Perimeter Road.

'Well, that was a waste of bloody time,' said Ramsay. 'The bastards have changed the route,' he added despondently.

'That, if you'll forgive me for saying so,' said Fox, 'is a brilliant observation.'

'So what do we do now?'

'My suggestion,' said Fox, 'not that smuggling is my problem . . .' He smiled at the disconsolate Ramsay. 'My suggestion is that you get someone to have another chat with the bold Sanchez. See if he has any further and better particulars.'

'I think that might be easier said than done.'

'Not at all,' said Fox cheerfully. 'Have a word with the Drug Enforcement Administration's man at the embassy – the American Embassy – and ask him to bell this Martino chap in Brazil. Couldn't be simpler. In the meantime, maintain the observation.'

'Is there any point?'

'Only that we'd look right bloody fools if another load came in and there was no one watching.'

Ramsay looked doubtful. 'Got nothing to lose, I suppose,' he said gloomily. 'What are you going to do while we're waiting, Tommy?'

'I think it's time I put the frighteners on Charlie Norton.'

'Is that wise?'

'You got a better idea, Pete?'

It was probably as well that Fox was side-tracked from striking fear into Norton. Gilroy had thought it unwise – at this stage in the inquiry, anyway – and had said so. He knew Fox, and knew that there came a point in every investigation when Fox began to get impatient. When he was likely to do something rash. Fortunately, the diversion arrived at the crucial moment.

'It's Edward Farmer, sir,' said Gilroy.

'What is?'

'A message from the prison, sir. He wants to see you urgently.'

'Oh does he, the little toe-rag? Well I've got news for him. If he thinks he can bugger me about, he's got another think coming.'

'The prison officer stressed the importance, sir.'

'And what the hell does a bloody screw know about it, then?' Fox was clearly in an uncompromising mood this morning.

'I'm only repeating what I was told, guv,' said Gilroy apologetically. 'The prison officer said Farmer was very agitated.'

'Was he indeed? If he thinks Farmer's agitated now, tell him to stick around. Right, Jack. Ring the prison and tell them you've got a message for Farmer . . . from me. Firstly, what he wants to see me about had better be important. Secondly, I'm not having that bloody mouthpiece Isaacs poking his nose in.'

'The message said to tell you that Isaacs wouldn't be there, sir,' said Gilroy with a grin.

Fox glared at the opposite wall with a sour expression. 'Sod the little bastard,' he said.

'I've got several pieces of advice for you,' said Fox, as he strode into the interview room at Brixton prison. He swung a chair round and banged it down on the floor with such force that the escorting officer stuck his head round the door and inquired if everything was all right. 'And my advice,' continued Fox, waving an assuring hand at the prison officer, 'won't cost what your brief costs. Which, I would remind you, comes out of my bloody income tax.' He shook his head. 'To think that people like Mr Gilroy and I have to pay for people like you to come up with arguments to try and stop me from putting you where you belong. But it won't work.'

Farmer was visibly shaken by this heavy onslaught. 'Honest, it's important, Mr Fox,' he whined.

'What's important, Ted, is that you're going up the steps for the murder of Leo Bridge. So get that into your thick skull, and put all else into perspective therewith. Got it?'

'No, Mr Fox,' said Farmer who was having great difficulty in following the detective's irate outburst. 'That topping's definitely not down to me.'

'In that case, Ted, you'd better convince me otherwise. And I don't want any bloody fairy stories. No ifs, buts and maybes.'

'That job's down to Bingham, Mr Fox.'

'What?' Fox stared at Farmer, an expression of stark disbelief on his face. 'You mean to sit there and tell me, you little sod, that after all that bloody palaver at Bow Street, with you walking up and down that ID parade, you get me here just to spew out that load of crap? You've got more bloody front than Selfridges, you have.'

'Stand on me, Mr Fox. It's the God's honest truth.'

'Well you'd better come across with a bit more than

that, old son. Frankly, I don't believe it. If that's the case, why didn't you pick him out when I had him binned-up?'

''Cos he threatened me.'

Fox scoffed. 'He did what?'

'On the line-up. When I got close to him, he whispered out the corner of his mouth. He said if I fingered him, he'd make sure I got done. Here in the nick.' Farmer suddenly looked very concerned. 'I want protection, Mr Fox. This is a dangerous place, you know.'

'Yeah, I know, Ted. It's full of villains. Well, don't stop there.'

'But can I have protection?'

'All right. I'll fix it with the prison governor. If your little tale's worth it.'

'The night before that drum got done in Wandsworth, Bingham come down my place. Come in heavy, he did. Had a shooter. Said as how he was staying the night and we'd got a job to do the next morning. Well, he didn't need the shooter, I can tell you—'

'Why not?' Fox's eyes narrowed.

'Well, I was working for him already, wasn't I?'

'Doing what?'

'Jobs,' said Farmer miserably.

'All right, I'll come back to that. What happened?'

'Well, like I said, he wanted a hand out with this job. Well I never knew it was no topping. I wouldn't have had nothing to do with a topping . . . not if I'd known. Anyhow, next morning, we drove down Wandsworth and parked in this street. Next thing I know, he disappears round the back of this drum. Gone for about ten minutes, he was. Then he comes out again, hops in the motor and says to get me foot down.'

'And did he tell you what it was all about?'

'Not till I asked him.'

'What did he say?'

'He just laughed and said listen for the fire engines. I thought it was a joke, but then he said he'd torched

133

the place. That'll teach the bastard, is what he said. And I thought to meself, Jesus, I thought.'

Fox nodded. 'Yes, I imagine you did, Ted. Did he tell you what he was teaching this fellow?'

'Nah, he never said.'

'Did he have petrol with him?'

Farmer wrinkled his brow. 'That's what it must have been,' he said.

'What must have been what?'

'He got something out of the boot before he went round the back of the house.'

'Out of the boot of your car. That's what you're saying, isn't it, Ted?' Fox glared at Farmer suspiciously.

'He must have put it in there the night before, when he came down my place.'

Fox laughed. 'And no doubt, Ted, when we question him about all this, he'll put it firmly down to you.' But without waiting for what he knew would be a valueless answer, Fox continued. 'You said just now that you'd done other jobs with Bingham.'

'I did?'

'Don't bugger about, Ted.'

'Yeah, well, they was nothing jobs.'

'I'll be the judge of that. What were they?'

'Only pick ups, like.'

'Don't tell me,' said Fox. 'You drove a blue Montego out to Heathrow Airport and picked up a toolbag you just happened to find in the long grass.'

Farmer stared at Fox in astonishment. 'You must be physic, Mr Fox,' he said.

'The word is psychic, Ted. But tell me, as a matter of passing interest, why weren't your dabs on this Montego?'

Farmer looked as though Fox had impugned his professional expertise. 'Well, I wore gloves, didn't I. Stands to reason.'

'And you took this mysterious toolbag to a hotel in Gloucestershire, I suppose,' continued Fox.

Farmer looked puzzled. 'No,' he said. 'Not a hotel. We made a meet with some other geezer at Windsor and handed it over.'

'Very interesting,' said Fox. 'Tell me, what made you change your mind about fingering Bingham?'

'When I found out what was in the bag, Mr Fox.'

'And what was in the bag?'

Farmer hesitated. Being a member of the criminal fraternity, he was well aware of the weight of sentences attaching to the illegal drugs trade. 'It was cocaine.'

'And why should that have changed your mind?'

'Well that ain't on, is it? I mean a bit of honest thieving's all right. But drugs and topping people, well, that's a no-go area as far as I'm concerned.'

'Good God!' said Fox. 'A villain with a social conscience. And how did you find out what the bag contained?'

'I heard it in here, Mr Fox.'

'Really? And who told you, Ted?'

'Dunno his name. Anyhow, he got sent down for a stretch last week.'

'Terrific,' said Fox. 'And I don't suppose you know the name of this finger you handed the bag to in Windsor either.'

'No. He never said.' Farmer looked apologetic. 'But he was a bit of a toffee-nosed bastard.'

Fox paced up and down his office like a caged lion. 'It's got to be that prat Studd, Jeremy Studd,' he said.

'Could have been anyone, guv'nor,' said Gilroy.

'Farmer said he was toffee-nosed.'

'I should think just about everyone is from where Farmer's standing,' said Gilroy.

'He's the only one I know who's a mate of Norton and Bingham,' said Fox. 'And Cameron's dead.'

'He wasn't at the time, sir.' Gilroy looked pensive. 'But I can't see Studd getting into the heavy side of trafficking. A user maybe, but—'

'I don't care if he's a poofter, even,' said Fox. 'I reckon it's down to him.'

'Well he's not a poofter, guv,' said Gilroy. 'Ron Crozier reckons he's having it off with Letty Norton.'

'Seen him at it, has he?' asked Fox angrily. 'All Crozier saw was her going into Studd's room. Doesn't prove anything.'

Gilroy thought that this was not the moment to point out that if Fox was demanding proof, he hadn't got much to show that Studd was dealing in drugs either. 'Well, what's next, sir? Have another go at Bingham?'

'Maybe, Jack.' Fox looked thoughtful. 'All we've got so far is Farmer telling us a tale, probably with a view to getting out from under himself. But that's certainly enough to put Bingham on the sheet. In the meantime, I want you to trace every prisoner from the remand wing at Brixton who's gone down since Farmer was admitted. And I want every one of the bastards interviewed. I want to know who told Farmer that there was cocaine in those toolbags. And I want to know how he knew. Take Percy Fletcher, then it shouldn't take long. All right, Jack?'

It was far from all right in Gilroy's view, but he knew it had to be done. It was even less all right in Fletcher's view. He knew who would be doing most of the work.

The telephone rang at half-past one, just as Fox was trying to escape from the office for a pint and a pie.

'Fox.'

'It's Kevin Donaldson, sir, from the incident room at Princes Risborough. We've found the car.'

'What car?'

'Cameron's, sir.'

'Where?'

'In a public car park in Stokenchurch, sir.'

No less than one hundred and thirty-two prisoners had passed through the remand wing of Brixton prison between the time that Edward Farmer was sent there and when he identified Rodney Bingham as the man who had set fire to Leo Bridge's house. Of those prisoners, all but twenty had been either acquitted, transferred to other holding prisons, been later released on bail, or were still there. The twenty had been convicted. Two of them had been given heavy fines and were no longer in custody. That left eighteen. And they had been spread around prisons all over the place.

'Sod it,' said Gilroy when he heard where his man was.

Fox arrived in Stokenchurch in as short a time as could possibly be managed by the complaining Swann who had been obliged to leave behind the finest poker hand he'd had all week.

The road leading to the car park had been closed and canvas screens erected around Cameron's car while on-site scientific tests were carried out. Shortly, it would be removed to the nearest police laboratory where it would be subjected to an even more thorough examination.

'Anything, Kev?' asked Fox.

Donaldson was standing some distance from the car while the photographers, fingerprint men and scenes-of-crime officers finished their work. 'Quantity of blood in the boot, sir. And we've found what looks like the murder weapon. Also in the boot.' He led Fox towards a Range Rover which had been set aside to take the exhibits. 'Let Mr Fox have a look at that nasty-looking implement we found, Joe.'

A white-coated SOCO produced the weapon, now carefully wrapped to preserve any fingerprints, and laid it on the tail-board. 'There you are, sir.'

'Well now, isn't that interesting,' said Fox. 'Unless I'm very much mistaken, that's an Army bayonet.'

'Yes, it is, sir,' said Donaldson.

'As issued to corporals, among others,' said Fox.

*

137

'Mr Fox, it's Bill Jenkins of Press Bureau,' said the voice on the telephone.

'How nice,' said Fox. 'What can I do for you?'

'We've had several calls this morning, wanting to follow up this story in one of the tabloids.'

Fox frowned. 'What story?' he barked.

'The story about the missing building society clerk.' There was a pause and a rustle of paper. 'A Mrs Daphne Lovegrove of Stokenchurch.'

'How the bloody hell did they get hold of that? What does it say?'

'The headline says "Police probe for missing Daphne", and goes on to say that police in Thames Valley are seeking the whereabouts of missing divorcée, Mrs Daphne Lovegrove, last seen at her flat in Stokenchurch the night before the body of Jock Cameron was found in Princes Risborough.' Jenkins paused. 'Looks like someone at the building society has opened his mouth, Mr Fox.'

'It does, doesn't it?' Fox was wondering what had led the press to make the same connection as he had made between Daphne Lovegrove and the death, five miles away, of Jock Cameron.

'But do you have any comment, Mr Fox?'

'Yes,' said Fox. 'But not one they'd want to publish.'

'Well, we ought to say something.' Jenkins was aware as always of the delicate position in which he found himself, wanting to oblige the media, but conscious of the need to protect a police investigation. And it was the police he worked for.

'Tell them to speak to Thames Valley police. It's nothing to do with this force. But wait until I've had a word with the local DCI.'

'So the Met does have an interest, then?'

'Whatever gave you that idea?' said Fox and immediately rang DCI Donaldson at Princes Risborough. 'Kev, the press are on to Daphne Lovegrove. For some reason they thought I ought to know all about it.'

'Yes, I know, sir. I saw it. As a matter of fact, I've had a couple of inquiries already.'

'What did you tell them?'

'That it's a missing person inquiry and has got nothing to do with anything else.'

Chapter Fourteen

'There's a con man called Lane doing two years in Gartree prison for a neat little scam, sir.'

'Is that so, Jack? Well, I don't suppose that's a first.'

'No, sir,' said Gilroy. 'But he's been interviewed by the local CID and admits speaking to Farmer while on remand in Brixton.'

'Ah, that's better. And how did he know about the cocaine?'

'Didn't get that far, sir. I didn't think it wise to tell the local Old Bill the full story. Just told them that we were trying to verify information that Farmer had given us and to check whether Lane had a conversation with him about anything. Lane admits to having had quite long chats, sir.'

'Did he, indeed. Well, Mr Lane is about to have a long chat with me. Gartree, you say? Leicester, isn't it?'

'Yes, sir.'

'Bloody well would be, wouldn't it?'

Gilroy grinned. 'Could have been Aberdeen, sir.'

'I've had a look at the map, sir,' said Findlater, 'and the car park where Cameron's car was found is the same one where Norton left his car the night we housed him to Mrs Lovegrove's address.'

'Well, Henry,' said Fox, 'isn't that interesting? And you're absolutely certain that Norton didn't leave that flat all night?'

'Absolutely, sir.'

140

'Even in a car from the rear of the flats?'

Findlater looked dubious. 'I suppose it's possible, sir. It was very dark.'

'Yes . . .' said Fox slowly. 'I wonder if friend Norton knows anyone called Houdini.'

'Has he got form, this Houdini chap, sir?' asked Findlater with a rare flash of Scots humour.

'Get out,' said Fox darkly.

The moment that John Lane entered the interview room at Gartree Prison, Fox could see why the reception officer had referred to him as 'Mincing' Lane. His hair was wavy and dyed blond and he strolled in with an affectation that would have got him a place on any catwalk . . . if he had been a woman.

'Well, hallo,' he said. 'Company. How lovely.'

'You were in the remand wing at Brixton at the same time as Edward Farmer, I'm told.' Fox lit himself a cigarette.

'May I?' Lane leaned forward expectantly and pointed at Fox's cigarette case.

'Help yourself.'

'You're from London then? You can always tell, you know. So worldly. They're all terribly provincial up here.' Lane dropped his voice. 'Even the screws.'

'Farmer tells me that you and he had a discussion about drugs. What exactly was said?'

'Well, we had so many discussions, you know.' Lane leaned back in his chair, crossed his legs and flicked a loose lock of hair out of his eyes.

Fox crooked a finger at Lane and waited until the prisoner leaned forward again. 'I haven't come all the way up here to be treated to a performance of dramatic art by a raving iron,' he said. 'But I'm quite willing to hike you out of here and put you on the sheet for conspiracy to smuggle cocaine. And that's worth about eight . . . at least. And if you really upset me, I'll arrange for you to do it in Holloway.' He leaned back

141

again knowing that there was no truth in what he had just said, but knowing also that Lane wouldn't be prepared to gamble on it. 'There, sunshine, that worldly enough for you?'

Lane puffed nervously at his cigarette. 'I had nothing to do with any smuggling,' he said hurriedly, panicking because this butch policeman seemed to have got hold of the wrong end of the stick entirely. 'It was just idle chatter. The poor dear needed cheering up.'

'Tell me about it.'

'We were talking one day and I asked Eddie what he was in for. And he told me all about these little jobs he'd been doing with this young man—'

'What young man?'

'I don't know his name, but he and Eddie were picking things up out at Heathrow. Well, I didn't like the sound of that, and I said so.'

'How did you know that the bags contained cocaine?' Fox was beginning to get extremely irritable with Lane.

'Oh, I didn't. I just guessed.' Lane leaned forward and stubbed out his cigarette. 'Well, it stands to reason, doesn't it? Near the airport, and people throwing things over the fence to be picked up. Had to be drugs. Wouldn't be condoms, now would it?'

'But how did you know it was cocaine as opposed to any other drug?'

'I didn't. Like I said, I guessed. I was really only saying these things to make conversation. It was so nice to have someone to talk to, you see.' Lane examined his fingernails. 'Generally, people are very unfriendly to me in prison.'

'Well, you do surprise me,' said Fox.

'The DI from Basingstoke's just been on, guv'nor,' said Gilroy. 'Apparently his DCS told him to give us a ring.'

Fox groaned. 'Don't tell me he's got problems with the press as well.'

142

'No, sir. Not yet, anyway. But he's had a strange burglary. Actually sounds more like criminal damage.'

'Tell him to keep taking the tablets,' said Fox. 'I suppose he wants me to pop down and clear it up for him, does he? Sometimes, Jack, I get the impression that I'm the only detective in the country.'

'Know how you feel, guv,' said Gilroy, and got a hard stare from Fox, 'but I think you might just want to have a look at this one. The victim's our friend Stanley Reynolds.'

'Is it now?' Fox was suddenly interested. 'So what happened there then?'

'The story's a bit confused, sir, but apparently Sherry Martin got in from the airport. Been to Jakarta, or some such place, and found that the house had been done over.'

'Coincidence, is it?' Fox's eyes narrowed.

Gilroy shook his head. 'Doesn't look like it, guv. Nothing taken, but a lot of damage done.'

'And what did the bold Stanley have to say about it?'

'Nothing yet, sir.' Gilroy grinned. 'He's still at work apparently.'

'Or at his other abode in Harlington. The DI got any theories?'

'Not that he mentioned, guv, but I've asked him to keep me posted.'

'You can do better than that, Jack.'

'I can?'

'Yes. Pop down to Preston Candover and see what it's all about.'

'Got a call at about half eleven this morning,' said Detective Inspector Phil Kirby during the drive from Basingstoke police station to Preston Candover. 'From his missus.'

'Sherry Martin, was it?' asked Gilroy.

'Sherry Reynolds, according to the message,' said Kirby. 'Put up a nine double nine. She's an air hostess

143

apparently. Just finished some overseas flight, and when she got here she found that the place had been wrecked.'

'How did they get in?'

'The patio doors, round the back. Took the whole thing out of its frame. Very professional.'

'And nothing taken, you said on the phone.'

'Not as far as we know. His missus was in a rare old state – naturally – and we haven't been able to get any sense out of her. Not yet, anyway,' said Kirby. 'Of course, they may have been after something particular, but until this Reynolds bloke turns up, we shan't know for sure.'

'You've not tracked him down yet then?'

'No. His missus said he was at work, but she didn't know how to get hold of him.'

'She's not his missus,' said Gilroy.

Kirby shrugged. 'OK,' he said. 'So she's the bird he's living with. I know a few coppers doing it these days. Even get the allowances.' Kirby must have been nearly fifty years of age, and had joined the force when it was almost a disciplinary offence for a married officer to look at another woman. Gilroy got the impression that he was annoyed that he'd missed out.

'He's got a wife – a real one – living in London. Well, Harlington.'

'Cunning bastard,' said Kirby. 'That must cost him a bob or two. Still, judging by his pad, he's quite well-heeled.'

'He's a maintenance fitter at Heathrow Airport.'

Kirby shot a sideways glance at Gilroy. 'You're joking,' he said.

Gilroy lapsed into silence for a moment or two. 'I think I'd better tell you the story so far,' he said eventually, and told the Hampshire DI what the Flying Squad knew about Reynolds.

'Doesn't surprise me,' said Kirby. 'I had a word with the local PC, and he reckons that Reynolds hasn't got any visible means of support. In fact, it was because the

144

PC said that your guv'nor had an interest that I rang you. So, you got any ideas?'

'It's got to be connected with this drugs business,' said Gilroy.

Kirby laughed. 'That'll shake the Women's Institute,' he said, and laughed again. 'Stone me! Drug traffickers in Preston Candover. Whatever next?'

Sherry Martin had been taken to hospital suffering from shock, but the PC who had been left to guard Reynolds's house let them in. It was a wreck. Whoever was responsible for the attack had systematically damaged as much of the property as they could. The walls were sprayed with paint, tables had had their surfaces gouged, furniture and bedding had been ripped open, and almost everything breakable was broken. The television set had a large hole in the screen and the Bang & Olufsen would never play the violin again.

'You see,' said Kirby, sauntering round the house with his hands in his pockets. 'There's silver and stuff all left here, money in the bureau even.' He nodded towards a secretaire with its front stove in. 'And her ladyship's jewellery is all still upstairs in the bedroom. Looks like a vendetta, a warning, if you like. And you ought to see the Porsche in the garage. Gave that a right going over.'

'Any prints?'

'The fingerprint lads have been over it, but you can bet that the only dabs they'll find will be his and hers.' Kirby perched on the edge of the dining-table. 'Got any ideas, Jack?' he asked hopefully.

'Yeah, lots,' said Gilroy, 'but proving it'll be another matter altogether. What did the hospital say about Sherry?'

'Haven't heard anything yet.' He glanced at his watch. 'Six o'clock. I'll give them a ring. Should know something by now.'

'They didn't cut the phone then?'

'They pulled out the one in here and stamped on it,'

145

said Kirby pointing to the splintered remains of a telephone lying in the middle of the floor. 'And did the
same to the one in the bedroom. But they didn't cut the
wire, so we brought our own and plugged it in.' He
walked over to the phone on the floor and dialled a
number.

While Kirby was talking to the hospital, Gilroy
wandered about upstairs. The scene of destruction there
was much the same as on the ground floor, and two
pictures on the landing – which might or might not have
been valuable – had been ripped with a knife.

'Nothing wrong with her, which comes as no surprise,
but they're keeping her in overnight just in case,' said
Kirby when Gilroy returned. He gazed round the dining-
room with renewed interest. 'Well, if he's a drug smug-
gler, serve the bastard right. Unfortunately, he's entitled
to the full protection of the law, but if it happens to work
against him, that's bloody hard luck.' Kirby yawned and
stretched his arms above his head. 'Fancy a pint?'

'Well that's all very interesting, Jack. Have Hampshire
got hold of Reynolds yet?'

'No, sir. I suggested that they should wait until he
went down to Preston Candover. I thought it might upset
our job if Mrs Reynolds – the real Mrs Reynolds – got
to hear about the other bird he was shacked up with in
the country. DI Kirby wasn't too happy about it, but
he's agreed to hold off.'

'When is Reynolds next off duty?' asked Fox.

'According to the roster that Henry Findlater got hold
of, sir, it'll be another three days.'

Fox looked thoughtful. 'I'm beginning to wonder
whether they've changed the route, Jack. Perhaps the
whole thing's fallen apart.' He looked depressed at the
possibility. 'Maybe we're going to have to start all over
again.'

'I'm not so sure about that,' said Gilroy. 'There's been
an interesting development.'

146

'Oh?'

'Phil Kirby went to the hospital in Basingstoke last night to see if he could get some sort of a statement from Sherry Martin—'

'And?'

'She'd discharged herself and gone to work. Got to the airport in time to go out on the twenty-two fifty flight to Rio.'

'Ah!' Fox rubbed his hands together. 'Get on to the airport, Jack, and find out when that flight comes back in.'

'I did, sir. Just after half-past twelve tomorrow.'

'Well now,' said Fox, 'I do believe it's all coming together. If she was so anxious to go out on that flight, it's a racing certainty that a consignment's coming in on the return journey. And she had to be there to make sure that it got put in the bold Stanley's little toolbag.'

Chapter Fifteen

Fox had mustered a full team, and so had Peter Ramsay, the customs investigator. They would have preferred to wait, but that sixth sense that most investigators seem to possess had told them that this could be their last chance. If they didn't make a move now, they might have to go back to the beginning and start all over again.

The huge Boeing taxied to a standstill and the handful of passengers alighted, making their weary way down the finger into the arrivals lounge.

DI Kirby from Basingstoke had been invited to join the party, Fox being aware that the Hampshire officer had a case of criminal damage to clear up. That though was likely to take a back seat compared with what the Flying Squad and customs had in mind.

Ten minutes after the passengers had left the aircraft, the crew came down the finger, the gaggle of stewardesses – Sherry Martin among them – laughing and joking with each other.

Kirby stepped forward. 'Miss Martin?'

'Yes, that's me.' Sherry Martin switched on her be-nice-to-passengers smile.

'I'm Detective Inspector Kirby of the Hampshire Constabularly. I'd like a word with you.'

'Oh!' Sherry stopped. 'Catch you up, girls,' she said to her colleagues, and then turned to face Kirby. 'Is something wrong?'

'It's about the incident at your house at Preston Candover the day before yesterday.'

The girl shrugged. 'Oh, that,' she said. 'I told the policeman who came to the house all about it. What else can I say?' She sat down on one of the bench seats in the arrivals lounge. 'Have you caught anyone yet?'

'Not yet, Miss Martin, but we're working on it.'

'Can we make this quick then? I am rather tired. It's a long haul from Rio, you know.'

'They're off!' said Fox who was studying the inbound Rio flight through binoculars. Twenty pairs of eyes focused on the figure of Stanley Reynolds as he climbed the ladder set against one of the forward hatches of the Boeing. There was a hushed silence as they waited until he emerged with a tool bag. The routine was exactly the same as before. Reynolds dropped the bag on the tarmac and left it for a minute or two while he wandered around the aircraft, apparently intent on checking various parts of it. Then he picked up the bag again, got into a truck and drove off. Watchers in different parts of the airport waited expectantly as the fitter drove along the fence near Northern Perimeter Road and casually tossed the bag over into the long grass.

'Gotcha, you bastard,' said Fox under his breath.

'D'you want him nicked, guv?' DS Buckley's voice crackled through the personal radio.

'Not yet, Roy,' said Fox. 'We'll wait until after the pick up. We want to be sure that the right stuff's in the bag before we go mad.'

Denzil Evans and his team were secreted along Northern Perimeter Road and watched as a white Vauxhall Cavalier stopped long enough for a man to leap from the passenger seat and recover the tool bag. Evans grabbed for his personal radio. 'They've taken it, guv.'

'Right, go for it, Denzil.' Fox smiled and lit a cigarette. 'That's it, Pete,' he said to Ramsay. 'Make-or-break time.'

Out on Northern Perimeter Road, Evans switched channels on the main force radio and called up the marked police car that had been waiting in nearby Sipson Road. The white Vauxhall drove out on to the Bath Road and turned left, driving within the speed limit. Its driver was suddenly disconcerted to see flashing blue lights in his rear-view mirror and, hoping that it was nothing to do with him, followed the practice of all good road-users and pulled over to the nearside. That the police car stayed behind him and switched on its siren told him that he had hoped in vain.

As the suspect vehicle pulled into the kerb, three Flying Squad cars arrived. One pulled ahead and stopped, another drew alongside and the third mounted the pavement and stopped on the nearside. With the traffic car right behind it, the Vauxhall was effectively boxed in.

'Out! And keep your hands where I can see them.' Revolver in hand, DI Evans had approached the driver's door from the rear of the car, moving stealthily. Four people had died already in connection with this little enterprise and Evans was going to make damned sure that he didn't become a fifth.

'What's this all about?' The driver of the Vauxhall got awkwardly out of the car, his hands going quickly into the air as he did so.

DS Ron Crozier and DC Joe Bellenger hauled the Vauxhall's passenger unceremoniously out of his seat, and the two suspects found themselves facing each other across the roof of the car as the police quickly searched them. Then, just as quickly, they were handcuffed and put into separate Flying Squad cars.

The two traffic officers who had brought the Vauxhall to a standstill were now out in the road vigorously waving on traffic in an attempt to prevent open-mouthed sightseers from causing an accident. Meanwhile, Evans and his team conducted a cursory examination of the Vauxhall. On the floor behind the passenger seat they found the tool bag. Inside it were six one-kilogram bags of sugar. At least that's what it said on the labels.

150

Evans grinned at one of the prisoners. 'You got a sweet tooth or something?' he asked.

'I want to know what we've been nicked for. What's this, a bleeding police state, or something? If you nick us, you're supposed to tell us what we're nicked for. I saw that on telly.'

Evans poked his head into the car. 'You're nicked for the unlawful possession of six kilograms of sugar,' he said.

'What?' The prisoner scoffed. 'You must be bloody joking.'

'No, I'm not,' said Evans. 'We happen to know that those six bags of sugar were nicked off an aircraft that just arrived from Rio de Janeiro. Anyway,' he added, 'that'll do for starters.'

Hoping against hope that the substance would turn out to be cocaine – or at worst something that came within the ambit of the law – Fox had ordered the arrest of Stanley Reynolds. Not that Reynolds knew that he had been arrested. DS Buckley had been sent to the maintenance fitters' duty room to tell him that a policeman from Hampshire wanted to talk to him. 'Some problem about your house in Preston Candover, mate,' Buckley had said.

Sherry Martin was already talking to Phil Kirby and he was passed a discreet message asking him to make sure that she didn't go anywhere.

Reynolds had a certain air of confidence about him. He was thirty-five years old, slightly built and had he been dressed in a suit rather than overalls could have passed for an estate agent, accountant or bank clerk. Fox gazed at him pensively for some time. But he did not intend to take any part in the proceedings. Not yet anyway.

'We've had trouble getting in touch with you, Mr Reynolds,' Kirby began. 'Your wife . . . Sherry?' He raised an eyebrow and Reynolds nodded. 'Your wife called the police the day before yesterday.'

'What for?' Reynolds tensed slightly.

'Your house at Preston Candover has been broken into. She discovered it when she got in from work.'

'Christ!' said Reynolds. 'Was there much taken?'

'Nothing, as a matter of fact.'

'Oh, well that's all right then.' Reynolds relaxed again.

'But the place was wrecked,' said Kirby. 'From top to bottom. It seems to me,' he continued, 'that you've got some enemies, Mr Reynolds.'

'What d'you mean, wrecked? Was it squatters?'

'I wouldn't think so. The furniture was smashed, as well as crockery, glassware, the television. And your hi-fi's had it. The carpets were ruined and there's graffiti all over the walls. It was systematic destruction.'

'Bloody hell,' said Reynolds. 'Who would do a thing like that?'

'I was hoping you'd tell me,' said Kirby mildly.

'And this was the day before yesterday?'

Kirby nodded. 'Yes,' he said. 'We'd have contacted you earlier, but I gather that you were at your other house.'

'My other house?' Reynolds looked shiftily at the detective.

'Yes, the one in Harlington. We didn't want to call on you there in case it alarmed your other wife.' Kirby smiled and Fox nodded approvingly.

'Look,' said Reynolds, an element of hostility creeping into his voice, 'my private arrangements are my business.' He shot a quick glance at Fox. For some reason which he couldn't understand, Fox made him feel uneasy.

'Exactly,' said Kirby. 'As I say, that's why we didn't get in touch with you there.'

'It's a mystery to me and no mistake,' said Reynolds, shaking his head.

'You've no idea why anyone should want to do this to your house?'

'No, no idea at all.'

'Nobody made threats? You've not upset anyone recently? Nothing like that?'

Reynolds gave a good impression of a victim of crime who was completely baffled by the whole affair. 'What did Sherry say about it?'

'I haven't spoken to her yet,' said Kirby. 'She was taken to hospital suffering from shock.' He thought it unnecessary to tell Reynolds that he had been speaking to Sherry Martin only ten minutes previously and that she was now sitting in a detention room not ten yards from Reynolds.

'But she—'

'Don't worry, she was well enough to discharge herself in time for the Rio flight out that night.' Fox spoke for the first time in the interview and Reynolds shot a frightened glance in his direction. 'And to come back with it this morning.'

Reynolds leaned back in his chair. 'Oh, that's all right then,' he said, trying to look confidently unconcerned.

'Well, it isn't really,' continued Fox, standing up. 'A crime has been committed – a quite serious crime – and it would help this officer if you could give some thought to why it might have happened.' He glanced at Kirby. 'Must just make a call,' he said and left the room in search of a telephone.

Peter Ramsay was in the customs suite at Terminal Three where the six sugar packets had been taken for a field drug test.

'It's Tommy Fox, Pete. How's it going?'

'The substance has reacted positively to the cocaine test, Tommy,' said Ramsay, 'but we'll need a proper analysis before we can take it to court. I'm getting it up to the lab at Teddington now, if that's OK with you. Be quicker than Lambeth and if they pull out all the stops, we'll have a result before close of play today.'

153

'Does that mean we've got to wait until we hear from them?'

'Not a bit of it. The blokes here have seen so much cocaine, Tommy, that they'll put their pensions on it being the real stuff. And so will I.'

'Brave men,' said Fox. 'What's the grand total?'

'There's six kilos altogether. Street value about half a million quid, give or take.'

'Jesus Christ!' said Fox. 'They don't muck about.'

'How's the interview going?'

'I'm just about to find out,' said Fox. 'Come over and join the party, why don't you?'

Reynolds looked up apprehensively as Fox and Ramsay came into the room. 'Look, I've got to get back to work,' he said plaintively. 'I can't sit around here all day.'

'The toolbag you threw over the fence contained six kilograms of cocaine, Stanley dear boy,' said Fox, sitting down opposite Reynolds. 'Five hundred grand's worth. Now, what was your cut of that?'

'Eh?' Reynolds sat bolt upright. 'I don't know what you're talking about,' he said, but he was unable to disguise the anguish that Fox's bowel-twisting question had evinced.

'I'm talking about mysterious goings-on along the perimeter fence, Reynolds old sport.'

'I don't know anything about any toolbags.' Reynolds gave a nervous laugh.

Fox looked surprised. 'Oh dear, you're not going to be difficult about this, surely?'

'I tell you, I don't know what you're talking about.' But it was quite evident from Reynolds's demeanour that he knew precisely what Fox was talking about.

Fox shrugged. 'Have it your own way,' he said. 'In the meantime you'll be detained pending further inquiries.' And looking across at DS Buckley, added, 'Put him down, Roy.'

*

154

Fox had decided to leave the interview with Sherry Martin to WDC Rosie Webster. Rosie was six feet tall, well proportioned and beautifully dressed. She had been a member of the Flying Squad for some years now, and her size and poise had frightened the wits out of a fair few women prisoners. As for male criminals, they felt positively intimidated by her presence.

She settled herself at the table and lit a cigarette. Then she pushed the case towards Sherry Martin. 'Want one?'

The girl shook her head. 'I don't smoke, thank you.'

Rosie leaned across and switched on the tape-recorder. 'Anything you say will be recorded and may be put in evidence,' she said. 'Your friend Stanley Reynolds is in police custody,' she added mildly.

'Who?' Sherry Martin gave an affected toss of her head. It was obvious that the girl had been scared stiff by her detention, and thought that the safest course of action was to deny everything that was put to her.

'Now look . . .' Rosie leaned across the table. 'Let's not fool about, Miss Martin. We know that you live with Stanley Reynolds in a house at Preston Candover, a house which was wrecked the day before yesterday. We also know that you discharged yourself from Basingstoke Hospital the same day so that you could get the Rio flight that came back here today.'

'I don't like missing a day's work.'

'I see. Are your employers so hard-hearted that they'd sack you if you didn't turn up for work after an experience like that?'

'No, but—'

'So you had another reason for not wanting to miss that flight. What was it?'

'I'm not saying anything. I've done nothing wrong and you've got no right to keep me here.'

Rosie gazed at the girl opposite for some seconds before speaking again. 'D'you know,' she said eventually, 'I really think you don't know what's happening.

155

Police have just stopped two men in a car on Bath Road who had picked up a toolbag. Your friend Reynolds had just taken that bag from the aircraft you came in on and thrown it over the fence. We know that on several previous occasions you put certain marked sugar bags from the aircraft's catering stock into a toolbag and left it on the floor of the galley for Reynolds to collect.' Rosie didn't know that for certain, but she reckoned it was a damned good guess.

'But that was sugar. There was always some left over. It wasn't doing any harm.'

'Then why were the bags marked? Surely if you were stealing sugar, any six bags would have done?'

Sherry Martin let out a great sigh. 'All right,' she said, 'I may as well tell you. The bags contained watches and perfume, hidden in the sugar.' She spread her hands in a gesture of resignation. 'OK, so we were dodging the duty. That's no big deal.'

'That toolbag contained six kilograms of cocaine which has a street value of more than half a million pounds,' said Rosie. 'And you put the cocaine in the bag, Miss Martin.'

Sherry Martin's face blanched and her fingers, which were intertwined, gripped so hard that her fingernails showed white. 'I don't believe it,' she said in a whisper.

'Well you'd better believe it, Miss Martin. I am not threatening you, or intimidating you, but I want you to know that you are in serious trouble.' Rosie lit another cigarette. 'D'you suppose for one moment that the wrecking of the house you share with Reynolds was a coincidence? I'm afraid that you're in the middle of a rather nasty drug-smuggling ring . . .' She paused to give effect to her next statement. 'And four people have already been murdered.'

'Oh my God!' Sherry put her elbows on the table and rested her head on her hands. 'This is awful,' she said.

'I am authorised to say that if you assist the police,

156

some consideration will be given to recommending leniency when your case comes to court.'

'Court?' Sherry looked startled. 'You mean that I'll—'

Rosie nodded slowly. 'I'm afraid that people who smuggle drugs don't just walk away from it, even if they do assist the police. I can't make any promises – that's a matter for the court – but it might just make a difference.'

'Christ!' said Sherry. 'I could use a drink.'

'Well,' said Fox, looking round at the debriefing conference in his office at Scotland Yard, 'what d'you think of it so far?'

'I've got a statement from the Laboratory of the Government Chemist,' said Ramsay. 'It's cocaine all right. Forty per cent pure.'

'Is that good?'

Ramsay laughed. 'You won't do much better than that, Tommy. But I think that we've only got the tiddlers. Reynolds was obviously paid well for his part.' He turned to Kirby, the DI from Hampshire. 'What d'you reckon Reynolds's drum was worth, Phil . . . before they wrecked it, that is?'

Kirby shrugged. 'Close on three hundred K, I should think.'

'So,' continued Ramsay, 'they must have been at it for a while . . . if Reynolds made that much.'

Fox nodded. 'A big ring then.'

'Probably not, Tommy, but one which is bloody well organised.'

'But then the thieves fell out, I suspect. Hence the two bodies we found on the M4.'

Chapter Sixteen

The two men in the Vauxhall Carlton who had picked up the consignment of drugs from its temporary resting place alongside Northern Perimeter Road were small-time villains. Fox was convinced that they were front-line expendables and would have little to tell him, but he intended to go through the motions just the same.

'So you're Billy Dawkins.' Without even bothering to sit down, Fox riffled through the printouts of the prisoners' criminal records. 'And you're Wayne Gibbs,' he added, switching his gaze to Dawkins's partner. 'Congratulations, lads, you've finally broken into the big time.'

'I dunno what you mean.' Dawkins's mean little face stared up at Fox apprehensively.

'What I mean,' said Fox, tossing the papers on the table and putting his hands in his pockets, 'is that after a short lifetime of thieving you've at last gained the respect of the criminal community.'

'What you going on about?'

'The bag that you kindly picked up on Northern Perimeter Road contained six kilograms of cocaine which has a street value, as far as you're concerned, of about twelve years. That's what I mean.'

'You're joking.'

Fox shook his head gravely. 'I fear not, sunshine. Now where were you going to take it?'

'The police station,' said Gibbs. 'S'what you're supposed to do with anything you find, isn't it?'

158

Fox glanced at Gilroy. 'Oh dear, Jack,' he said, 'I fear we have a comedian among us.' He turned a beaming smile on Dawkins's companion. 'Well, old sport, if you want to take it on your own, that's your problem. Charge them both, Jack.'

'Right, guv,' said Gilroy.

'Here, hold up,' said Dawkins, sudden fear gripping him. 'We never knew what was in that bag.'

Fox smiled and shook his head. Slowly. 'So where were you going to take it?'

'Some hotel down Gloucestershire, near Cheltenham.'

'Well there's a surprise,' said Fox. 'And what was the name of the person you were supposed to hand it to once you arrived?'

'Dunno. We was told someone would contact us when we got there.'

'Oh dear!' said Fox. 'He must be getting very anxious by now. But tell me, who gave you these wondrous instructions?'

'Dunno that neither.' Dawkins lapsed into silence.

'Well don't keep me in suspense. How did this good fairy contact you? I say good fairy because presumably he came bearing riches.'

'A bloke come up to us in a boozer, down Dulwich, and asked if we wanted to earn a grand.'

'Oh dear,' said Fox, 'that's so hackneyed it's got to be true. Did he have a name, this charity worker?'

'Nah! Well, I mean he had a name, but he never told me what it was.'

'And you got the money up front, did you?'

Dawkins looked sorry for himself. 'Nah! He said as how we'd get the cash when we delivered the gear.'

Fox laughed. 'Oh, what a crying shame. You must almost have been tempted to make off with the goodies.'

'No chance of that,' said Dawkins miserably. 'He said there'd be someone watching all the time, so's if we'd got any ideas of welshing to forget it.'

159

'Very wise,' said Fox. 'Personally I'd trust you about as far as I could sling a Bosendorfer.'

'You wouldn't get me anywhere near one of them German dogs,' said Dawkins.

Rodney Bingham had been charged with the murder of Leo Bridge and remanded in custody. But Fox knew that to secure a conviction he needed more evidence than Edward Farmer's statement about their visit to Bridge's house in Wandsworth. The word of one alleged co-conspirator against another was just not good enough. In the meantime, Bingham was saying nothing. But now that the arrests of Reynolds and his girlfriend, Sherry Martin, had been effected, Fox decided that it was time to have another talk.

'We arrested Stanley Reynolds yesterday, Rodders old son,' said Fox, smiling benignly. 'And Sherry Martin too. She of the gorgeous body but little else.' Fox swung a chair round and sat down opposite Bingham. 'And she's been telling us all sorts of interesting things.'

'Is that supposed to mean something to me?' asked Bingham in a loftily disdainful voice.

Fox contrived to look surprised. 'You're not going to tell me that those names mean nothing to you, surely?'

'Well they don't.'

'Oh dear!' said Fox and turned to Gilroy. 'Have you got that statement there, Jack?' he said.

Gilroy made a big thing of ploughing through the sheaf of papers in his briefcase before extracting a wodge of about fifteen sheets. 'That the one, guv?'

'That's the one,' said Fox. 'Now, Rodders, let's just have a quick scan through this little lot. The young lady mentions you once or twice . . .' He glanced up. 'Not with any affection, though.'

'Really?' Bingham's attitude implied that he was intellectually superior to this ebullient policeman with the cockney accent and that nothing he said could possibly be of the slightest interest.

160

'Oh yes. Now then . . .' Fox turned over a few sheets. 'Yes, here we are. There was one occasion when you approached her, she says, and invited her out to dinner—'

'That's a bloody lie.' Bingham sat up sharply.

'Don't interrupt,' said Fox, 'it's very rude. She says that she accepted your kind invitation and—' Fox stopped and thumbed back a few pages. 'Ah, there it is. Yes, she says that you approached her at the airport and invited her out. That's it. She also says that you tried to get her into bed . . .' Fox looked up and grinned. 'I thought you'd like to know she mentioned that. It's not really relevant, but it does add flavour and credence, don't you think?'

'Look here—' Bingham began.

'But the crux of it all, the young lady seemed to think, was your abiding interest in when she was next flying in from Rio. In her innocence, Miss Martin presumed this to be born of a desire to take her out to dinner yet again. However, when we pointed out to her what your real interest was, she got quite upset.' Fox flung the statement down on the table. 'It's terribly insulting to a young lady to let her think that you want one thing, and then it turns out that you want something entirely different. Not at all public school . . . or is it?' Fox smiled at Bingham.

'I don't know what all this is leading up to—'

Fox held up a hand. 'Be patient, dear boy. We're getting there.' He opened his cigarette case and politely offered it to Bingham before lighting a cigarette for himself. 'So I started to puzzle over all this,' he continued, 'and I wondered whether it might just have anything to do with the fact that we relieved yesterday's merry little team of about half a million quid's worth of cocaine.' He surveyed Bingham through a haze of smoke and smiled blandly.

'I don't know what you expect me to say,' said

161

Bingham. 'You've charged me with murder, so what's in it for me?'

'But that was an accident, surely. That's what you said, wasn't it?'

Bingham was unable to hide his astonishment. 'You mean you're not really charging me with murder?'

'I didn't go that far,' said Fox, 'but a good brief will quite probably put forward the argument that you were convinced that poor old Leo Bridge's house was empty, and that the only evidence against you,' he added gravely, 'is the statement of a worthless villain.' He looked into the middle distance. 'I can see it now,' he continued. 'There was no intent, members of the jury, and my client was utterly distraught when he discovered that not only was Mr Bridge in the house at the time, but his common-law wife also.'

'What?' Bingham went pale. 'What common-law wife?'

'Oh, didn't I mention that?' said Fox. 'How remiss of me. No, as a matter of fact, Rodders, we were keeping it up our sleeve in case the charge *in re* Bridge, as the lawyers say, went moody on us. But we also found the body of one Mary Gibbons. She was a retired prostitute as it happens . . . not that that affects the possible charge. Very hot on the sanctity of human life, Her Majesty's judges.' Fox smiled at Bingham. 'After all,' he continued, 'we're all equal under the law, aren't we.' For a moment, he pondered that concept. 'Although some do seem to be more equal than others.'

'Look, are you trying to tell me that I could get off with this?'

Fox pursed his lips and tutted. 'Now I'm not in a position to make promises, as you well know, Rodders, but let's say that we might not push it too hard.'

'I hope all this is going down on tape,' said Bingham, glancing at the tape-recorder.

'No, it's not,' said Fox airily, 'because you're not

162

making a statement . . . yet. If you wish to do so how-ever, I'll happily turn the machine on.'

'But you're not allowed to question me now that I've been charged, except to resolve ambiguities.' Bingham sat back with a triumphant smirk on his face.

'Oh God,' said Fox in an aside to Gilroy. 'Another bloke with an A-level in law.' He turned back to Bingham. 'You haven't been charged—'

'But—'

'Not with conspiracy to smuggle cocaine, but that's only a matter of time . . . I should think. And the interesting thing about that is that you'll get a substan-tive sentence – about twelve years, I should think – not one of those airy-fairy life jobs so that the Home Sec-retary can spring you when he's feeling in a good mood. Which reminds me,' Fox continued relentlessly, 'I do believe that an officer from the Thames Valley Police wants to talk to you about another murder.'

'Another murder?' Bingham looked aghast. Fox's con-stant onslaught was beginning to wear him down.

'Yes. Jock Cameron by name. I think you knew him.'

Bingham's jaw dropped. 'I had nothing to with that.'

'They all say that,' said Fox.

'The problem,' said Fox, 'is where to go from here. We've got Reynolds and Martin in custody, along with two foot-soldiers, and we've got Bingham and Farmer banged up for Bridge's murder . . . not that I think we'll get far with that, given that they each accuse the other.'

'Pay Charlie Norton a visit?' asked Peter Ramsay.

Fox shook his head. 'Not unless we want to make fools of ourselves,' he said. 'What have we got? The only hard information is that the first time we did a following job, the two villains turned up at his hotel, and the two we nicked the other day said that's where they were going. All right, so we front Charlie Norton with that. What's he going to say?'

'Search me, guv,' said DI Evans.

163

'Exactly, Denzil, and when we do, what are we going to find? I'll tell you. Sod all with a leavening of righteous indignation. No, my friends, we've got to have more than that before we go pounding down to Cheltenham.'

'What about Bingham?' asked Ramsay.

'He's stewing nicely,' said Fox. 'We had a little chat and I left him to consider his position. It's just possible he might decide to co-operate.'

But before that happened, *Delegado* Vicente Sanchez of Brazil had a word with Sam Martino of the DEA.

'You wanted to see me?' Fox looked down at the miserable figure of Billy Dawkins.

'Yeah, well, it's all getting a bit heavy, guv.'

'Yes,' said Fox, 'that seems a reasonable assessment of the situation.'

'Well, I thought as how it might help if I give you the complete SP—'

'Help who?'

'Me?' The expression on Dawkins's face was not as confident as he would have liked it to be.

'If you've got something to say, Billy, you'd better get on with it.'

'Yeah, well . . .' Dawkins paused to wipe his nose on a filthy handkerchief. 'I done one of them runs before, see.'

'One of what runs?'

'Like the one I got picked up for this time.'

'Did you now?' Fox did not believe in giving too much encouragement to the criminal fraternity.

Dawkins struggled on. 'Yeah, me and a bloke called Leo.'

'Leo Bridge, would that be?'

'Yeah, that's the geezer.'

'Shame about him,' said Fox.

'What happened to him then?' Dawkins looked nervous.

'Got topped,' said Fox in matter-of-fact tones. 'His

164

house caught fire. Well . . .' He paused. 'More a case of someone setting fire to it while poor old Leo was in bed.'

'Gawd strewth!' said Dawkins.

'This run you did. Where did you take the stuff?'

'Down Cheltenham way. Some flash hotel it was. The geezer what set it up—'

'Name?' demanded Fox.

'Dunno,' said Dawkins. 'He wouldn't tell us. He said as how no one knowing no names was safer.'

'Your English grammar is awful,' said Fox mildly. 'And what did you do with the gear when you arrived there?'

'Nothing.'

'What d'you mean, nothing?'

'Well this geezer said we was to book into the hotel for the night and leave the bag in the room when we left like . . . in the wardrobe.'

'And what did you get paid for that little jaunt, may I ask?'

'Two grand . . . each.'

'And did you know what the bag contained?'

'No, guv. Didn't want to neither. There's such a thing as knowing too much in this game.'

'Yes,' said Fox. 'Not that you're ever likely to fall into that category. Is that it then?'

'No,' said Dawkins. He spoke slowly as though having doubts about the wisdom of deciding to come clean. 'We done a job down Hampshire.'

'We? Who's "we"?'

'Me and another bloke. I'd never seen him before. Funny geezer, he was. Never said a word.'

'Do leave off,' said Fox. 'What was his name?'

Dawkins underwent a bronchial spasm and stubbed out his cigarette. 'Wayne Gibbs. The bloke I got nicked with.'

'Oh yes, Billy,' said Fox, 'I do know who you mean. And what was this job?'

'We had to go down this drum and wreck it.'

'Was this at Preston Candover?'

'Yeah, that's right. How d'you know that, guv?'

'Because I'm very, very clever,' said Fox. 'And where did you meet this bloke? The one who gave you this exciting job.'

'The Bush.'

'Would that be the Bull and Bush . . . or Shepherds Bush?'

'Shepherds Bush,' said Dawkins, a look of puzzlement on his face. He was not on Fox's wavelength when it came to humour. 'Bleeding shame though.'

'What was?'

'Wrecking that drum. Smashing place it was.' Dawkins looked up hopefully. 'D'you reckon that'll help me, telling you all that?' he asked.

'Doubt it,' said Fox. 'The owner of that drum's locked up in the next cell. You'd better just pray you don't both finish up doing your porridge in the same nick.'

'Got another cable from Sam Martino in Brazil, Peter,' said Williams.

'Really?' Ramsay sounded less than enthusiastic.

'The route's changed.'

'What route?' Ramsay had at least twelve different investigations under his control at any one time, and was mildly irritated when his subordinates assumed that his only interest was in the job they were doing.

'The cocaine run. You know, the one that Reynolds, Sherry Martin and company were nicked for at Heathrow.'

'Oh, that one. Well, what does he have to say?'

Williams sat down and spread his papers on his knees. 'According to Vicente Sanchez, well-known Brazilian policeman, they've given up on the air route. Sanchez said that something's happened to alarm them.'

Ramsay laughed. 'No prizes for guessing what that was,' he said. 'So what's this Sanchez got to say?'

'According to his informants—'

'Yeah, yeah. Cut the crap, John.'

'It seems that the consignments are still coming across, but now they're going overland . . . he thinks.'

'How does one get overland from South America to the UK, as a matter of interest?' Ramsay asked sarcastically.

'By sea, I suppose,' said Williams unabashed. 'Sanchez's informant reckons that long-distance freight lorries are involved . . .' He looked up. 'Not that that's our problem, but the crunch is that eventually the gear is put on a yacht somewhere and sails into the UK with all the appearance of some rich punter on holiday.'

'Where in the UK?'

'He doesn't say, but I'd guess at the south coast. The traffickers seem to think that our people don't visit yachts unless the skipper practically begs them to come aboard.'

'Do they now,' said Ramsay. 'Well that's their first mistake . . . but it won't be their last.'

'Oh, that's bloody terrific,' said Fox when he heard Sanchez's information. 'And what are you doing about it, Pete?'

Ramsay looked serious. 'I've alerted all our south coast officers to the possibility of coopering.'

'What in hell's name is coopering?' Fox looked suspiciously at the customs man.

'It's when a vessel drops anchor at dead of night and the contraband is rowed ashore, usually in a dinghy. And there's often someone along the coast waiting to collect it.' Ramsay gazed at the detective without a trace of humour.

'Really,' said Fox. 'How fascinating. And one of your mounted officers rides along the beach and captures them, I suppose. Have you told the local police?'

'Thought I'd leave that to you, Tommy.'

'That's what I like about you revenue men,' said Fox,

'always so bloody generous.' For a moment he stared at the ceiling. 'Bloody hell,' he said. 'That means we'll have to inform Chelmsford, Maidstone, Lewes, Winchester, Dorchester and Exeter.'

'But the action's on the coast,' said Ramsay.

'You stick to your coopering,' said Fox, 'and I'll deal with the police work.'

Chapter Seventeen

'Is this going to help me?' Bingham was slouched in the chair, deflated. He had obviously done a great deal of thinking since Fox had seen him last and it looked as though he might now be prepared to talk about his part in the affair.

But Fox never gave the impression that he was indebted to anyone, least of all criminals. 'That rather depends,' he said.

'On what?'

'On what you have to tell us. On what the Director of Public Prosecutions thinks about it. But above all, what the judge at your trial thinks about it. You see, Rodders, old sport, it's a bit of a gamble, but considering what you've been up to recently, I should think that twist-and-bust is a reasonable chance to take. Never know, you might come up with a five-card trick.'

'You mean that you're not going to offer me anything?'

'It would be worthless, dear boy. Out of my hands entirely. I might just as well try selling you Nelson's Column. I don't have the authority you see, so it wouldn't mean anything. Follow my drift, do you?'

Bingham shrugged. 'Oh well,' he said. 'In for a penny, in for a pound.'

'That's it,' said Fox. 'Put a brave front on it. Have a cigarette,' he added and pushed his case across the table.

Bingham lit the cigarette and blew smoke into the air. 'OK,' he said, 'let's go.'

Fox nodded to Gilroy who turned on the tape recorder. 'Rodney Bingham, I must caution you that anything you say will be recorded and may be put in evidence.'

'I only want to talk about Jock Cameron,' said Bingham.

'So talk.'

'I first met Jock in South Africa, about five years ago. I'd been working out there selling expensive cars, but there was a lot of talk about sanctions and suddenly the bottom fell out of the market.'

'Was he living there?'

'I don't think so. He was there on some business trip. I think that's what he said. Anyway, he gave me his address in England and said that if I was ever there to look him up.'

'And you did, presumably.'

'No. He found me, some years later. I was on my beam-ends when I got back here, but I managed to find a job. Well a succession of jobs actually—'

'Selling cars?'

'Not all the time. I was even a male stripper once.'

'Jesus, how awful,' murmured Fox, whose sympathy immediately went out to the women who had been obliged to witness Bingham's foray into show business.

'Anyway, I got that job at the car dealers in Wanstead. I'd been there for about three weeks, I suppose, when Jock turned up. God knows how he tracked me down, but he did. And he suggested that I went into business with him. Said I was just the sort of chap he was looking for.'

'What was this business?'

'Import and export.'

Fox grinned. 'Thought so,' he said. 'What did it involve . . . for you?'

'Well, nothing at first. He paid me a retainer to carry on working at the car showrooms.'

'So it was obviously bent from the start,' said Fox.

170

Bingham looked as though he might challenge that assumption but then changed his mind. 'Yeah, I suppose so.' He shrugged. 'So what? I was desperate for money.'

'Did you know it concerned drug smuggling?'

'Not at first.'

'But you found out later, I presume?'

'Yeah, sure.'

'But you didn't mind that?'

'Frankly, I didn't give a damn where the money came from so long as it kept coming. These junkies are going to get the stuff from somewhere whatever happens,' Bingham added with a sneer, 'so I thought I might as well have some of the action.'

'So when did you get involved . . . with drugs?'

'After I got the sack from the garage. It was over that business of the duff receipts. There was absolutely no proof that it was me, but that bloody MD thought he'd get shot of me anyway. He was bogus and he knew I knew it. Beer-gut, moustache, going bald and always talking about his golf handicap.'

'Who else was in this little ring?'

'I said I'd only talk about Cameron.'

'Who were they?' Fox leaned forward slightly. 'Was Charlie Norton one of them?'

'I'm not prepared to name names.'

'Why not? Are they still at it?'

Bingham shrugged. 'I'm just not, that's all.'

'Afraid you might get blown away like Leach and Collins?'

Bingham stared down at the tabletop for some moments as though seeking an answer in its scored wooden surface. Then he looked up. 'That was Jock,' he said.

'Are you saying,' began Fox, wishing to have this vital piece of information crystal-clear, 'that Cameron was responsible for the murders of Leach and Collins?'

'Yes, that's exactly what I'm saying.'

171

'How d'you know that?' Fox fixed Bingham with a gimlet-like stare.

'Because I was there.'

'I must remind you that you have already been cautioned that anything you say—'

'Yeah, sure, I know,' said Bingham. 'But I didn't have anything to do with it. Jock and I were going out to the airport in his car. He said we were going to pick up some gear. A bag that had been slung over the fence, as a matter of fact. Anyway, we arrived and waited for a few minutes, but then this other car stopped and picked up the bag. At first, I thought that they'd beaten Jock to it. It was only later I found out that Jock was intending to take it off them, not pick it up. I think he was trying to make a point.'

'He did that all right,' said Fox drily.

'Anyway,' continued Bingham, 'he chased the other car down the M4 and ran it off the road. Far enough so there'd be no witnesses. Then he leaped out and grabbed a shotgun from the boot. I'd no idea he'd got it, but then, as I said, it was his car. And he just blasted those two chaps, straight through the windscreen. I was absolutely bloody stunned, I can tell you.'

'Yes, I can imagine,' said Fox mildly. 'Enough to unnerve a lad of your sheltered background, I should think. Then what happened?'

'Jock opened up the tail-gate of the other car – it was an estate – and grabbed the toolbag. But the damned thing wasn't done up properly and one of the bags fell out and split. Jock went bloody potty, swearing and trying to scoop it all back into the bag. Then he jumped into our car and we took off.'

'Where did you go?'

'To Windsor. Jock had a pad there.'

'What happened to the cocaine after that?'

Bingham shrugged. 'No idea,' he said. 'Jock told me to push off and said he'd see me later . . . at the hotel.

172

Charlie Norton's place just outside Cheltenham. That was our usual meeting place.'

'What happened after that?'

'Well, I hadn't bargained for murder, and I told Jock I wanted out, but that was when he started to put the frighteners on. He said that I'd been involved with those two murders and that I'd better co-operate.'

'What did he mean by that?'

'Seems he was a bit pissed off with the cut he was getting and had decided to take over the operation. Needless to say, the others weren't too happy about the idea.'

'And you're still not going to say who those others are?'

'Not likely. They'd kill me. It's not an amateur dramatic society, you know.'

'Are they the ones who killed Cameron?'

Bingham looked at Fox with a despairing look on his face. 'What do you think?'

'Right, Reynolds,' said Fox, 'I'm not going to bugger about. I have here a full statement from Sherry Martin which I now serve on you.' He dropped a sheaf of paper on the table. 'Read it.'

'But I—'

'Read it,' said Fox sternly.

Reynolds picked up the statement and started to go through it, the expression on his face telling Fox that Sherry Martin hadn't lied. When he had finished, Reynolds dropped the statement on the table and looked at Fox. 'That's a load of cobblers,' he said.

'I could tell it rang true,' said Fox. 'Now then, I'll tell you something else. Rodney Bingham, who with Edward Farmer has been charged with the murder of Leo Bridge, volunteered the information that Jock Cameron murdered Leach and Collins, the two unfortunates who were carrying one of your previous consignments. Then, lo and behold, Mr Cameron gets his come-uppance.

173

Dreadful, isn't it? But the fact that your gaff at Preston Candover got done over a couple of days ago tells me that you suddenly found yourself on the wrong side of the fence. Want to tell me about it? Or do I just let you go and wait for them to top you too.' Fox had no intention of releasing Reynolds, but Reynolds didn't know that.

'Bloody Cameron cocked it all up. Greedy bastard.'

Fox nodded sympathetically. 'Hard world, isn't it?' he said. 'But do go on. You've whetted my appetite now.'

'Everything was all right until he muscled in. He wanted more, you see.'

'Would you care to expand on these rantings of yours, Stanley, dear boy?'

Reynolds glared malevolently at Fox. 'If you're so bloody clever, I'd've thought you'd have known all this.'

'Never very good at jigsaw puzzles, so you'll have to explain it all very simply,' said Fox.

'We'd got this system going nicely. Like she said, Sherry'd pick out the marked bags when they came on at Rio and put them in the toolbag. Then I'd have them away at Heathrow and chuck 'em over the fence. Easy.'

'Yes, very commendable.'

'But like I said, Cameron wasn't satisfied with his share and started cutting up rough. I'm not surprised that it was him who rubbed out the two on the M4, and that's what started it all going wrong. That bastard Bingham tried to find out from Sherry when the next load was coming in — he was obviously working for Cameron by then — but she wasn't having any—'

'So she said,' murmured Fox.

'Then that bloke got burned down at Wandsworth. I reckon that was Cameron too.'

'What makes you think that?'

Reynolds shrugged. 'Got to be, hasn't it?'

'Who's running the ring?' asked Fox. 'Is it Norton?'

'I'm saying nothing,' said Reynolds.

'Why's that?'

'Because I'd rather stay alive, thank you very much.'

'But you'll be quite safe in here,' said Fox, 'and on my reckoning you'll be here for anything between eight and twelve years.'

'You must be joking,' said Reynolds. 'You never heard of anyone being croaked in the nick?'

'I've solved the murder of Jock Cameron for you,' said Fox cheerfully. He wedged the telephone receiver between his collar-bone and chin and lit a cigarette.

'Really, sir?' said Donaldson.

'There's only one drawback,' continued Fox. 'I don't know his name.'

'Oh!' There was a pause, and then, 'We've received an anonymous letter, suggesting that we make inquiries about a certain individual who's recently lost an army bayonet.'

'Well, well,' said Fox, 'and does it suggest who this bayonet-loser might be?'

'Yes, sir.' Donaldson chuckled. 'A certain Mr Charles Norton who apparently keeps a hotel somewhere near Cheltenham.'

There were eight officers altogether. Fox had five detectives with him, and DCI Donaldson was accompanied by a detective sergeant. It was, after all, Donaldson's inquiry. But Fox had come mob-handed in case there was some need to tear up floorboards, pull down ceilings, inspect chimneys and generally poke about in the sort of recesses that might reveal something of evidential value.

Fox was reluctant about the whole business. He had not wanted to confront Norton at this stage of the investigation, but the anonymous letter to the Thames Valley Police could not be ignored.

But even setting that aside, it was too much of a coincidence in Fox's book that Cameron, an acquaintance of Norton, should have been murdered when

175

Norton was in Stokenchurch. In fact, it was almost too good to be true. And the irritating thing about it was that Detective Inspector Henry Findlater was the one who could testify to Norton being there, a fact that at once provided Norton with an alibi. The sort of alibi that is a gift to defence counsel and would probably convince a jury. But it did not convince Fox. He knew all about alibis and to him Norton's apparent tryst with Daphne Lovegrove had all the hallmarks of an elaborate plan.

And then there was Bingham. Unfortunately, Edward Farmer's statement implicating Bingham was most unlikely to hold up in court. Not without corroboration. But some of that corroboration might turn up this morning too.

Donaldson and his sergeant had been shown into Norton's office while Fox gave his team a last-minute briefing. He was letting the Thames Valley officer beat on the ground, secure in the knowledge that if anything came up that was of interest to the London officers they would be on hand to seize it. But he couldn't resist the temptation to interfere.

'Mr Norton, I am Detective Chief Inspector Donaldson of the Thames Valley Police and this is Detective Sergeant Douglas—' At which point the door opened and Fox walked in. 'And this is Detective Chief Superintendent Fox of Scotland Yard,' added Donaldson.

Norton's mouth opened in astonishment. 'But I thought you were a professional rat-catcher,' he said.

'I am,' said Fox. 'Very professional. In fact, I think I might be catching a few this morning.'

Norton was obviously thrown by the whole business. 'What the hell's this all about?' he asked.

'I am here in connection with the death of John Cameron, known as Jock.'

'He used to drink here, quite regularly, but apart from that I don't see how I can help you,' said Norton.

176

'I am told that you possess an army bayonet, Mr Norton,' said Donaldson.

Norton looked suspiciously from Donaldson to Fox. 'Just what's this about, old boy?' he asked.

'I should answer the question if I were you . . . old boy,' said Fox.

'Well, yes, I do have a bayonet somewhere. It was a souvenir from my early days in the army—'

'I suppose you used it mainly for opening the general's packing-cases when they got back here,' said Fox. He was beginning to enjoy himself, and hoped that Donaldson's straight-laced county attitude was not going to interfere with his fun too much.

'General's packing-cases? What are you talking about now?'

'I'm talking about when you got nicked for using the general's kit to smuggle in your porn . . . Corporal Norton.' Fox held up a hand as Norton was about to speak. 'Don't bother to say anything . . . old boy. I had a long chat with Colonel Lloyd of the Royal Military Police. Remembers you with some affection it seems. So don't come the old ex-officer, ex-public-school bit. The only thing public about Elgin Road Comprehensive was the fact that the public were admitted.' Fox grinned insolently. 'Usually on their way to some corrective establishment, I should imagine.'

Norton laughed. 'That's business, old boy. After all, the punters would much prefer to think that mine host was a public school ex-officer than a bloody corporal, what?'

'Where were you the night that Cameron was killed?' asked Donaldson.

Norton hesitated. 'I take it that this is between ourselves,' he said eventually.

'At the moment,' said the Thames Valley DCI stiffly, 'but I can't make any promises that it will remain so.'

There was another pause before Norton answered. 'I was with a woman,' he said with some reluctance.

177

'Who was she?'

'I'm not prepared to say.'

Donaldson shrugged. 'Up to you,' he said. 'But where was it?'

'I'm not telling you that either.'

'Very well,' said Donaldson. 'In that case, perhaps you'd produce this army bayonet.'

'No problem,' said Norton, opening a drawer. 'I keep it in the desk here. Used to use it as a letter-opener, but it's a bit too big.' He started to search the drawer, moving things about. Then he started on the other drawers, but eventually looked up, his original expression of confidence waning. 'I can't find it,' he said.

'That's probably because we found it, Mr Norton,' said Donaldson and held his hand out in DS Douglas's direction.

Douglas opened his briefcase and produced the murder weapon, still shrouded in its protective plastic sheathing. He laid it on the edge of the desk and glanced up at Norton. 'That the one?' he asked.

Norton leaned forward and stared at the bayonet. 'Yes,' he said softly. 'I recognise the scratch on the handle. Where did you find it?'

'In the boot of Cameron's car, Mr Norton,' said Donaldson. 'The car itself was found in a car park in Stokenchurch and the blood on the bayonet matches that of Cameron.'

Norton's shoulders drooped and he laid his hands flat on the desk. 'Anyone could have taken that bayonet from this office,' he said.

'And how many people knew it was there?'

Norton shrugged. 'I don't know,' he said. 'It was no secret that I had it.'

'Where is your wife?' asked Fox suddenly.

Norton turned blank eyes on Fox. 'My wife?'

'Yes. Where is she?'

'Oh, she's gone off on some show-jumping thing.

Somewhere near Tewkesbury, I think.' Norton sounded as though he didn't care.

Donaldson stood up. 'Charles Norton, I am arresting you for the murder of John Cameron. Anything you say will be given in evidence.'

Norton stood up too. 'This is ridiculous,' he said.

DS Douglas studiously wrote down those few words in his pocket-book and glanced at his DCI. 'Search, sir?'

'Yes,' said Donaldson. 'We propose to search these premises, Norton,' he said.

'Have you got a search warrant?'

Donaldson smiled. 'In the circumstances, we don't need one,' he said, 'but as it happens we've got one.'

It was a pointless task. Even with the assistance of Fox's five detectives it took two hours, and then it was only a cursory search. Fox knew instinctively that there would be nothing there to interest him, and he was not yet ready to talk to Norton about drug trafficking. Not until he had some positive evidence. Neither was there anything to help him with the case of murder against Bingham.

And Donaldson had got as much as he was going to get. He'd got Cameron's body, the murder weapon and a prisoner. But he knew that he was nowhere near going to court. Knew it because Fox's DI, Findlater, would be able to put Norton in a flat with Daphne Lovegrove. But he had no alternative but to make the arrest. He just hoped that Norton could be persuaded to say something in his defence. The Thames Valley officer was convinced that Norton knew more about the affair than he had said.

And, as Fox frequently said, when the chips were down, suspects did tend to start thrashing about a bit.

Chapter Eighteen

It was too much to hope that the arrest of Charles Norton would pass unnoticed by the press, particularly when it had occurred in so public a place as a hotel, and by the time Donaldson and his prisoner arrived at High Wycombe the police station was besieged by reporters.

Once Norton was safely locked up, Donaldson made a brief appearance and trotted out the time-honoured phrase that a man was assisting police with their inquiries into the death of Jock Cameron.

But he didn't assist them much.

He stuck to his story that he had spent that night with a woman, refused to elaborate, and demanded the presence of his solicitor. But Donaldson shared with Fox the nagging doubt that, surveillance or not, it was possible that Norton had left the flat in Stokenchurch, committed the murder, and returned just as covertly. And the evidence of the woman in the flats who had seen a man leaving the rear car park at about midnight tended to support that proposition. An incident which neither Findlater nor his officers had witnessed.

But it so happened that the presence of the press turned out to be useful. To Norton anyway.

At eight o'clock that same evening a woman in her early thirties walked into the police station and told the officer on duty that she was Mrs Daphne Lovegrove and that she wished to see someone in connection with the arrest of Charles Norton which she had read about in the evening paper.

'Did he tell you that he'd spent that night with me?' Daphne Lovegrove was a very self-assured woman and gazed at Donaldson with large brown eyes.

'Not exactly. But he did say that he was with a woman.'

'Well it was me. He arrived at about eight o'clock on Sunday evening and left at about eleven the following morning.'

Which was exactly what DI Henry Findlater had reported.

'And did you or he go out at all during that period?'

'No.' Daphne Lovegrove smiled without a trace of embarrassment. 'We were in bed practically the whole time,' she said.

'And would you be prepared to go into court and swear to that?' asked Donaldson.

'I hope that won't be necessary, but if it is then yes, I would.'

'You sound hesitant.'

'Well of course I am. Charles is a married man.'

'Does he intend to divorce his wife and marry you?'

Daphne Lovegrove looked surprised and gave the question some thought. 'I'd like to think so,' she said, 'although I don't see what that's got to do with you. But to be honest it's unlikely.'

'Why?'

'I think he likes things the way they are.'

'And that doesn't worry you?'

'I can't really argue, can I? The other woman is always there on sufferance.'

'Tell me, Mrs Lovegrove, why did you disappear straight after the murder of Jock Cameron?' Donaldson leaned back in his chair and gently tapped the edge of the table with a pencil.

'It was Charles's idea. He rang me and said that he

thought someone was trying to get him, and that they might just try to do it through me.'

'What did he mean by that?'

'I've no idea, but he sounded very serious on the phone, very concerned. It rather frightened me.'

Donaldson leaned forward and rested his folded arms on the table. 'When did he ring you?'

'It was the Monday afternoon, just after lunch as a matter of fact.'

'And what exactly did he say? Can you recall?'

After some consideration, Mrs Lovegrove said, 'Yes, he told me that a friend of his had been murdered and he thought that someone might try to frame him for it. Then he said it would be a good idea if I went away for a few weeks until it was all sorted out.'

'What did you say to that?'

'I made all sorts of excuses, mainly about my job, but he said I wasn't to worry. He said that I could always get another job, that he'd see to it, and that I was to find a quiet hotel and ring him to let him know where I was.'

'Let me get this straight, Mrs Lovegrove. Norton, a hitherto normal, rational individual, rings you up with some bizarre story about being in danger and asks you to abandon your job and move out of your home on an open-ended arrangement. And you just go?'

'Yes. I'd never heard him so concerned before.'

'And that was all it took?'

Daphne Lovegrove twisted an eternity ring which she wore on the third finger of her left hand. 'He's always been sincere and I believed him,' she said.

'Had he ever given you any hint previously that he might be in some sort of trouble?'

'Never.'

'And did he mention the name of this friend of his? Did he say it was Cameron?'

'No. In fact I didn't know until I saw it in the paper this evening.'

'And does that name mean anything to you?'

'No, not a thing.'

'So where did you go?'

'A hotel in Somerset. Charles said he would pay for it, but that I was to keep out of the way until the fuss had died down.'

'Did he get in touch with you at all, while you were there?'

'He rang me once or twice.'

'What did he say?'

'Nothing in particular. Just wanted to know if I was all right, and whether anyone had tried to contact me.'

'And had they?'

'No.'

'Why did you come back then?' Donaldson glanced across at Douglas to satisfy himself that the sergeant was keeping up with his note-taking.

'I told you. I read about Charles's arrest in the evening paper. I knew that he couldn't possibly have killed Cameron, so I came straight back here to tell you where he had been that night.'

'Mrs Lovegrove called here to see me,' said Donaldson. 'She made a statement saying that you spent the whole of that Sunday night with her.'

'I told you I'd spent the night with a woman,' said Norton. 'Where is she? Is she here now?'

'No, she's gone back to Stokenchurch.'

'Is she all right?'

'She appears to be. But she said that you were concerned that someone was trying to frame you and that they might try to put the murder of Cameron down to you. What did she mean by that?'

'I haven't the faintest idea,' said Norton.

'Did you say that to her on the phone?'

'No.'

'Then why did she suddenly leave her job, go down to Somerset, and put up in a hotel? She said that you

183

suggested it. In fact, she said she only did it because you were concerned about her safety.'

Norton laughed. 'Sounds like a bit of romancing to me,' he said. 'I suggested that she took a holiday. As a matter of fact I said that I would join her down there if I could, but I wasn't able to get away.'

'And you paid the bill, I understand.'

'Yes. Why not? You'll have gathered that Daphne and I are having an affair. Well, old boy, little pleasures like that have to be paid for.' It was obvious that Norton now believed himself to be in the clear, and his confidence was rapidly returning.

'When did you last see the bayonet that you say was in the drawer of your desk?' asked Donaldson.

'At a guess,' said Norton with a frown, 'about six months ago.'

'And have you any idea who might have taken it?'

Norton laughed. 'Over that period of time, any one of a few hundred guests, to say nothing of the staff.'

'And you still maintain that Mrs Lovegrove was talking nonsense when she claimed that you thought you were going to be framed for Cameron's murder.'

Norton laughed. 'You know what women are,' he said. 'Always imagining things.'

'What are you going to do with him, Kev?' asked Fox.

'Kick him out, sir,' said Donaldson. 'That anonymous letter was obviously intended to stir things up for him and from what you've been saying it's got to be connected with the drug smuggling.'

'Well the only person that I can think of who might have sent it is that prat Studd. I think he needs a talking to.'

'What are you going to do, pull him in?'

'No.' Fox laughed. 'There's no evidence. Not for my job. But if you want to have him off, that's your business. I think I'd've been inclined to have another go at Norton though. He knows more than he's telling, and

184

he knows who's gunning for him. Wouldn't surprise me if he did a bit of personal sorting out once you bail him.'

Donaldson looked apprehensive. 'I've got nothing to hold Norton on, sir. The only evidence against him was the bayonet. If he had been guilty, he would have denied ever seeing it before, but he admitted that it was his. That seems pretty genuine. Added to which there are two people who can vouch for his whereabouts on the night in question. And one of them's a police officer.'

'Yes, I know,' said Fox. 'Bloody shame, isn't it?' He stood up and stared out of the window. 'If you're going to pull Studd,' he said, 'I suggest you do it before you release Norton. Stop the buggers comparing notes.'

There was no doubt that Detective Chief Inspector Donaldson was out of his depth. The intricacies of the case which Fox was investigating were beyond anything that the Thames Valley officer had experienced and he wished, not for the first time, that Cameron had been murdered in the Metropolitan Police District. Nevertheless, he decided that he would question Studd about the Cameron killing. But he asked Fox if he wanted to sit in on the interview.

'Wouldn't miss it for anything,' said Fox. 'But I probably won't say much.'

Donaldson and DS Douglas took Studd to Cheltenham police station and then Donaldson telephoned High Wycombe to order the release of Norton. Fox sauntered into the room and had to go through the business of explaining that he was, in fact, a police officer and not a rat-catcher, before Donaldson settled down to some questioning.

Beneath his foppish manner, Jeremy Studd was completely composed. He relaxed, as far as was possible on the hard wooden chair in the interview room, and surveyed the detectives with a supercilious smile. 'I shall give you the benefit of assuming this to be some heavy-handed joke,' he said in a sneering tone. 'But I'm not

185

sure that my solicitor will take the same view when we come to consider the question of wrongful arrest.'

'You haven't been arrested,' said Donaldson. 'You've come here quite voluntarily to assist the police in their inquiries . . . as any conscientious citizen would do.'

Fox, sitting quietly in the corner, gave Donaldson a few points for that bit of quick thinking.

'In that case, I take it I am free to leave whenever I wish to do so.'

'Of course,' said Donaldson, 'despite the construction we may put on your apparent unwillingness to assist us. You will appreciate, of course, that I am investigating a serious crime – a case of murder – and that certain questions remain unresolved.'

'Such as?' Studd crossed his legs and assumed a bored expression.

'Such as the bayonet with which Cameron was killed.'

'What can that possibly have to do with me?'

'It was Charles Norton's.'

'Then perhaps you ought to talk to him about it.'

'We have,' said Donaldson.

'Oh!' That seemed to surprise Studd. 'Well what d'you want from me then?'

'Did you know where it was kept?'

'I didn't even know of its existence.'

'Norton said that it was kept in the drawer of his desk . . . in his office. Did you ever see it there?'

'Really? Well, I've never been in his office. The bar is as far as I ever get.' Studd brushed absently at a speck of fluff on his knee.

'Where did Charles Norton go that night?' Donaldson asked.

Studd seemed slightly disconcerted that the police thought he should know. 'I've no idea,' he said. 'Mrs Norton said that he'd gone away on business, but why don't you ask him?'

'And for that matter, where were you?' Donaldson knew the answer to that question. Or thought that he

186

did. The fact that DS Crozier had seen Letitia Norton entering Studd's room just after midnight did not necessarily mean that she had spent the night with him, or that Studd had been there at all.

'I stayed that night at the hotel,' said Studd, a little too quickly.

'Alone?'

Studd lifted his head slightly and looked down his nose at the detective. It accentuated his sneer. 'Of course,' he said. 'Who else would I spend it with?'

The questioning went on for some time, Donaldson asking about Studd's acquaintanceship with Norton, how well he knew him, how long he had known him, and what sort of relationship had existed between Norton and Cameron. It was all rather innocuous and left Studd thinking that he had been too hasty in jumping to the conclusion that he was the suspect rather than Norton.

Donaldson glanced at Fox who shook his head. Then he turned back to Studd. 'Well, I don't think that I have any further questions for you, Mr Studd. Thank you for your assistance.' He stood up. 'I'll get someone to drive you back to the hotel . . . unless there's anywhere else you'd rather be dropped.'

Studd rose to his feet, a little unsure what the interview had been about, but silently regretting his outburst about wrongful arrest. Although not very bright, even he had the wit to realise that if the police had any suspicions about him, his behaviour had merely served to harden those suspicions.

'Oh, Mr Studd,' said Fox as Studd reached the door. 'Where in Windsor did Mr Cameron live?'

Studd turned slowly and stared at Fox. Eventually he said, 'I'm sorry, I didn't even know that he lived there.'

'I can tell you where Cameron lived,' said Donaldson when Studd had departed. 'We searched the place.'

'I know,' said Fox, 'but I was curious to see whether Studd knew. Or more to the point, whether he was prepared to admit knowing. Incidentally, did you find anything interesting in Cameron's drum?'

'There were no traces of drugs anywhere. In fact nothing of interest at all, but we went through his papers. It seems that he spent quite some time in Hong Kong. I've asked the Hong Kong police if they've got anything on him.'

Fox shrugged. 'Never know your luck,' he said, 'and every little helps.'

'What now then, sir?' asked Donaldson.

'Our interview with Studd will have put the frighteners on . . . I hope. Jeremy Studd will leg it back to the hotel and tell them the strange story of the rat-catcher who turned out to be Old Bill. He and Norton will compare notes and they'll start wondering what I was doing there. Then they'll start wondering if Evans and Crozier were coppers as well.' Fox laughed. 'Wouldn't mind being a fly on the wall,' he said. 'Right now I reckon there's a bit of panic down at Charlie Norton's hotel.'

'Ron,' said Fox, 'that night you saw Letitia Norton going into Studd's room . . .'

'Yes, sir,' said Crozier.

'You don't know if he was actually there, do you?'

'No, I don't, guv.'

'When did you last see him that night?'

Crozier thought for a moment or two. 'It must have been about eleven thirty, I suppose. That's when I left the bar to go for a walk round the grounds.'

Letitia Norton had one tomato juice, gave Studd a lingering glance and went off to play with her horses. Now that Cameron was dead and Bingham was in custody, the usual coterie of regulars had been somewhat depleted.

'I want to talk to you . . . in the office,' said Norton.

'Can't we talk here?' Studd languished against the bar.

188

'No. In the office.' Norton turned on his heel and walked away.

Reluctantly, Studd followed and watched apprehensively as Norton slammed the door and locked it. 'Now, mister.' Norton swung round to face Studd. 'I spent a few uncomfortable hours in a bloody police station yesterday. For no reason at all.' All traces of his pseudo-captaincy had disappeared and he was suddenly very much the ex-corporal. 'Someone's trying to stitch me up, and my money's on you.'

Studd held up his hands. 'Look, Charlie—'

'And I know you've been screwing my missus.'

'So what? You've been giving that woman in Stokenchurch a seeing-to.'

'How did you know about that?' Norton's eyes narrowed and he took a pace closer.

'Well I—'

But that was as far as Studd got. Norton delivered a crippling blow to his solar plexus and followed it with a forearm smash that dropped Studd to the floor. Whatever else he had forgotten of his army training, he could still look after himself. 'If I ever see you anywhere near my wife again, I'll bloody well kill you, Studd,' he said. 'In fact, I'll kill you if I ever spot you within miles of this place. Now get out.'

Chapter Nineteen

Vicente Sanchez helped himself to another glass of wine and looked across the table at Sam Martino. 'I have got more information for you,' he said. 'Good information.'

'I suppose you want paying for it as well,' said Martino with a grin.

Sanchez shrugged. 'It did not cost me anything. This man – this informant – he owed me a favour. He thought it might be a good time to settle the bill, eh.'

Martino did not inquire what sort of debt Sanchez had called in to get the particular information he was about to offer. Knowing Sanchez as he did, he thought it better not to inquire too deeply. But there was little doubt in his mind that somewhere along the line someone had got hurt. Or was going to get hurt. 'What's it about, Vicente?'

'About the cocaine that's going to England.'

Martino laughed. 'Great,' he said. 'Here's Uncle Sam paying for information from a Brazilian snitch that's only any good to the limeys.'

Sanchez looked slightly puzzled. 'I suppose that means something when translated,' he said, and drained his wine glass.

'Well, what have you got?'

Sanchez looked disappointed. 'Aren't we going to eat?'

'OK!' Martino beckoned a waiter. 'I should have known better than to get anything out of you on an empty stomach.'

Sanchez worked his way through several courses before leaning back with a satisfied expression on his face. 'OK, Sam,' he said, 'now we talk. You remember I told you that the stuff is going overland from now on. Well, the next consignment is going to be put on a plane at Rio . . . but not the usual plane—'

'Where does it come from?'

Sanchez spread his hands. 'That much I don't know,' he said. 'Does it matter?'

'I suppose not. At least not for the moment. And then?'

'This flight goes to Madrid, and from there by truck up through France to a French port.'

'Christ!' said Martino. 'That's a bloody long haul. Are you sure?'

Sanchez just nodded. 'I am sure.' He laughed, a deep rumbling laugh. 'If it's wrong, I kill my informant.'

Martino thought he probably would. 'Yeah, go on.'

'At the French port,' continued Sanchez, 'the drugs are put on to a yacht owned by a . . .' He paused, searching for a word. 'Playboy?'

Martino nodded. 'Some playboy,' he said.

'And is taken across to . . . ah!' Sanchez banged his forehead. 'Wait.' He pulled a slip of paper from his inside pocket. 'Is taken to some silly islands. That means something to you?' He looked up with a puzzled expression on his face.

'That's a damned cockamamie description, Vicente. I reckon your snitch is screwing you.'

'Never!' Sanchez spoke with such vehemence that Martino almost felt sorry for the anonymous informant.

'OK.' Martino shrugged. 'Maybe it'll mean something to the Brits,' he said. 'How much candy is there in this consignment?'

'Is eight or ten keys,' said Sanchez.

'Not bad.' Martino nodded approvingly. It was the respect of a Federal agent for his professional enemy. 'There's only one thing you haven't told me. The name

191

of the goddam yacht . . . and when it gets there.' He grinned at the Brazilian policeman, not expecting a reply. Which was just as well.

'What you want for your money, a bonanza?' asked Sanchez.

'I suppose it could mean the Scilly Isles?' said Fox when he read the signal that had come from Martino via the US Embassy in London.

Ramsay stirred his coffee. 'Your guess is as good as mine,' he said. 'But it wouldn't be a bad place for a drop. We've only got the one officer there, and on top of everything else, he's the immigration officer, the Receiver of Wreck and God knows what else.'

'And how do they get it from there to here?'

'Three main routes. Helicopter or boat to Penzance. Or there's a flight from St Mary's to Plymouth for most of the summer. All scheduled services, but internal of course. There's no routine customs examination when they arrive on the mainland. Most people make the mistake of thinking that once they're in, that's it. But customs can give them a pull any time they feel like it. And if we feel like boarding her, we will . . . even if she's tied up at Teddington Lock.'

'Splendid,' said Fox enthusiastically. 'So what d'you reckon?'

'I've alerted the *douane* and the Police de l'Air et des Frontières, but it's a long shot when you think how many yacht basins there are over there. Or over here, for that matter.'

'What about Madrid?'

'Thought I'd leave that. If the *guardia civil* start poking about at Madrid Airport, it could ruin everything. I'd rather wait and capture them here.'

'But where is here? We're just guessing at the Scilly Isles.'

'That's the problem,' said Ramsay. 'It could be anywhere on the south coast that has facilities for yachts. And there are plenty of them.'

'The answer,' said Fox, 'is to put surveillance on both Studd and Norton. They're going to be involved somewhere along the line.' He grinned hopefully. 'Might even go and collect it themselves, now that we've locked up those foot-soldiers who haven't been topped.'

'I suppose that's all we can do. In the meantime, I'll play a hunch and put some of my chaps down at St Mary's in the Scilly Isles, and persuade the powers that be to move one of our cutters down there.'

'Just our luck for the bloody thing to sink in some freak storm or get run down by a tanker,' said Fox gloomily.

'You're a miserable sod at times, Tommy,' said Ramsay. 'But what about your murders? Think you'll clear them up at the same time?'

'Maybe,' said Fox. 'I don't think there's any doubt that Leach and Collins were down to Cameron, or that Bingham was responsible for toasting friend Bridge. The only tricky one – which thank God's not mine – is Cameron himself. That alibi of Norton's is too bloody good to be true.'

'But your man reckoned he didn't move all night.'

'Yes,' said Fox darkly, 'but I have known policemen make mistakes.'

'So have I, Tommy,' said Ramsay. 'So have I.'

As the sole customs officer in the Isles of Scilly, Geoff Fielder was usually left to get on with his job without interference. Mainly because very little happened in St Mary's. Very little of interest to Her Majesty's Customs, that is.

But suddenly he was invaded. A small team of officers from the Investigation Division arrived and having been smartly snubbed by Mrs Fielder when they suggested that they put up in the large Custom House, went in search of accommodation in the hotels and boarding houses of St Mary's.

The local populace was aware that something was going on, but then Scillonians are historically sensitive to anything involving the customs. It tends to run in their blood. None of this mattered, however, because it was not for a moment suspected that anyone living in St Mary's was implicated. Ramsay and Fox were convinced that the cocaine would finish up at Charles Norton's hotel in Cheltenham. But what really interested them was where it went from there. It was apparent that a lot of people were making a lot of money. And the combined resources of police and customs were determined that not only would they put a stop to it, but that several of the leading players would go to prison. For a long time.

'But how long will this go on for, sir?' asked Findlater plaintively.

'No idea, Henry,' said Fox. 'Till they come home to roost, I suppose.'

Findlater looked unhappy. 'Norton and Studd,' he said, just to confirm the instructions that Fox had given him for mounting surveillance on the two principal suspects.

'That's it. You look as though it's a problem.'

'It needs to be very discreet, sir.'

'Absolutely, Henry. That's why I picked you. You're not telling me that you're not up to it, surely?'

'It's the manpower, sir. If I'm to keep this going, possibly for weeks, it'll take a lot of men.'

'And women!' Fox grinned.

'Yes, sir. And women.'

'In that case, Henry, I'll talk to Commander McGregor of SO 11 and see if we can borrow some of your old mates.'

Findlater brightened at the mention of Criminal Intelligence Branch's surveillance team. 'That would certainly help, sir. Help a lot.'

'There you are then, Henry,' said Fox. 'There's a way out of everything. Of course, if Mr McGregor's chaps happen to be committed already . . .'

It was a difficult and tiring operation, but Findlater got little sympathy from Fox.

'Well, Henry, and how's your little holiday in the country going?'

'We've been running it for three days now, sir. And for the whole of that time, Norton's remained at his hotel. I've booked a DC and a WDC into the hotel and told them to pretend that they're on honeymoon or something.'

'You've done what?' Fox sounded horrified. 'And you a strict Calvinist.' It was not the moral issue that bothered him, but he knew what fun defence counsel would have with the impropriety of two single police officers sleeping together while engaged in a surveillance operation.

'They're married to each other, sir.' Findlater smiled. He felt that the balance was slightly redressed.

'Oh, good. What's Norton doing? Hanging round the bar as usual, I suppose?'

'Mostly, sir, yes.'

'With Studd and the lovely Letitia?'

'Neither of them are there, sir. Mrs Norton went off this morning to some three-day horse event in Wiltshire. And Studd's hardly moved. As you know, he's got a flat just outside Gloucester. On the Cheltenham side.'

'I wonder why he's not at Charlie Norton's place,' said Fox, knowing nothing of the threat that Norton had made to kill Studd if he ever saw him again.

'He certainly doesn't seem to have a job,' said Findlater. 'Which confirms Percy Fletcher's information.' Fox nodded. 'He goes out each morning for a newspaper. Then he goes out to lunch, always close by, but a different restaurant each day, and he goes out to dinner in the evening.'

Fox was not disappointed at this pattern of behaviour. 'I think he's waiting for something to happen, Henry. Like a telephone call to tell him that a certain consignment is due to arrive somewhere . . . by sea. Carry on the good work.' He paused, thinking. 'Should have put a tap on his phone really. Still, it's too late now.'

'Yes, sir.' Findlater turned to go.

'And Henry . . .'

'Yes, sir?'

'Don't lose them when it all starts happening.'

It happened the very next morning. Or at least it started to.

'Just got a call from the lads on the phone taps, guv'nor,' said Gilroy as he entered Fox's office.

'How nice,' said Fox.

'Letitia Norton's been abducted.'

'Now that's what I call interesting,' said Fox. 'And from where has she been abducted?'

'From some bloody horse show in Wiltshire I should think.'

'Thank God for that,' said Fox. 'For one awful moment I thought you were going to tell me it had happened in the Metropolitan Police District.' He paused. 'What d'you mean, you think it was in Wiltshire?'

'That bit's guesswork, sir. But Henry Findlater reported that she'd gone off to some three-day event early yesterday, so I presume she got kidnapped from there.'

'So he did. What do we know so far?'

'About eight o'clock this morning, the intercept picked up a call to Charlie Norton. Male voice from a public call-box—'

'Where?'

'Where what, sir?' Gilroy looked briefly puzzled.

196

'Where was the call-box?'

Gilroy glanced down at the sheet of paper in his hand. 'Croydon, sir.'

'How original,' murmured Fox. 'And it was obviously someone who knew Norton's private number. That's the only one we've got an intercept on, isn't it, Jack?'

'Yes, sir. Anyway the caller told Norton that his wife had been kidnapped and that they wanted half a million quid for her safe return.'

'Bit expensive,' said Fox, 'even for her. Any instructions about payment?'

Gilroy shook his head. 'No rendezvous was mentioned, sir. Just told Norton to get the money – in used tenners – and he'd get further instructions.'

'Used tenners! They must be joking.' Fox did a few calculations on his blotter. 'That'd fill a suitcase.'

'I understand that Norton said much the same sort of thing, guv,' said Gilroy drily.

'Has Norton reported this to the police?'

'I don't know, sir. Thought I'd let you know first before we start thrashing about.'

'We do not thrash about, Jack,' said Fox severely. 'We make intelligent inquiries.'

Gilroy thought that this was not the time to suggest that he did not always get that impression. 'I'll give the Gloucestershire police a ring then, sir, shall I?'

'No, Jack. I will. In the meantime, you have a word with Wiltshire. See if they've had any report that Letitia Norton's missing.'

Fox checked with the intercept team to make sure that Norton had not informed the police from his private line at the hotel, and then rang the detective chief superintendent at Gloucestershire police headquarters.

'Nobody's heard a word,' said Fox when Gilroy returned. 'You got anything?'

'Yes, sir. Apparently the local police in Wiltshire got a call from the show organisers about an hour ago saying that Mrs Norton hadn't turned up for today's events.

197

They were really inquiring whether police had any reports of an accident.'

'Anything else?'

'She took part in yesterday's dressage events. Did quite well apparently, sir.'

'Oh, splendid,' said Fox with heavy sarcasm.

'But she didn't show up this morning.'

'Where was she staying?'

'Local livery stables. It's quite a regular thing. Sort of bed and breakfast for horses and humans.'

'Wonderful,' said Fox.

'The police made inquiries there, but she's not been seen this morning.'

'Bed been slept in?'

'No, sir. Either that or she made it herself.'

'What's the story then?' asked Fox.

'She'd booked herself and her horse into these livery stables and was staying at the house. It's a farm as well. She told people there that she was having a meal out, but wouldn't be late. Anyway, by the time the folk there turned in – at about half-past ten – she still hadn't got back. When they went to call her this morning she wasn't there.'

'Did they notify the police?' asked Fox.

'No, sir. Her Range Rover was gone and they assumed that she'd left early. It wasn't until the show organisers rang that the people at the stables looked around. That's when they found that the horse and trailer were still at the stables. But there was no Mrs Norton.'

Fox looked thoughtful for a moment. 'I suppose there's no chance that the voice on the phone belonged to our friend Studd,' he said eventually. 'The ransom demand call, I mean.'

A brief smile flitted across Gilroy's face. 'No, sir. At the time the call was made, Studd was in his flat, and the call was made from Croydon . . . sir.' He stopped in the doorway. 'By the way, sir, Henry Findlater's just rung to say that Studd's on the move.'

Chapter Twenty

Fox's priority was the sudden movement of Jeremy Studd. Letitia Norton's kidnapping had occurred in Wiltshire and the ransom demand had been made to Norton's hotel in Gloucestershire.

And that meant that it was none of Fox's damned business. Perhaps.

But because he was convinced that it was in some way connected with his own investigation, he asked to be kept informed of any developments.

Unfortunately, the chief constables of those two forces quickly learned of his interest and asked the Commissioner of the Metropolitan Police for assistance in the hope that they might offload something which could go disastrously wrong. Which was a somewhat underhand ploy, given that both forces possessed highly qualified detectives of their own.

'Bloody hell, guv'nor,' said Fox. 'There are times when I think I'm running this police force all on my own.'

'I thought that's the way you liked it, Tommy,' said Commander Alec Myers. 'However, I have told the Commissioner that you're heavily engaged with this drug thing . . .' Fox sniffed. 'But that you will give such advice and assistance as is possible. So they've all come to an agreement. Wiltshire will investigate it, and you'll pass on anything about your job that might be relevant. D'you think there's a connection?'

Fox shrugged. 'I wouldn't mind betting on Studd being

behind all this, guv,' he said. 'What a lovely scam. Kidnap Letitia Norton away from the consignment that's due in, and distract police at the same time.'

'Even so, Tommy, we do have to consider the possibility that it's a coincidence.'

Fox scoffed. 'Not a bloody chance,' he said. 'I definitely smell villainy in all this.'

Myers peered over his glasses at Fox. 'I don't think there's much doubt of that, Tommy,' he said.

It was at about eight-thirty that Findlater and his team had seen Studd emerge from his flat and walk round to the garages. Minutes later, he had driven out in a grey Rover Sterling and made for the M5 motorway.

Police Constable James Braid pushed open the door of the pay-booth at Hyde Park underground car park.

The attendant, who was reading a copy of the *Sun*, glanced up. 'Morning.'

'Morning,' said Braid. 'Got any Range Rovers in here this morning?'

The attendant shrugged. 'Probably,' he said. 'Why?'

'We're looking for one.' Braid pulled his notebook wallet out of his back pocket and quoted a registration number.

The attendant shrugged again. 'Your guess is as good as mine, squire. Have a look round if you like. What is it? Nicked?'

'Yeah,' said Braid, not wishing to reveal details of a kidnapping that, so far, the press had agreed to withhold from publication.

A detective constable from the Flying Squad office knocked on Fox's door. 'Message from Hyde Park nick, sir. Letitia Norton's Range Rover has been found. Abandoned in the underground car park there.'

'Locked or unlocked?'

'Er, not sure, sir.'

'Keys in the ignition?'

'I don't know, sir.'

'Wiltshire police been told?'

'I'm sorry, sir, I—'

'Well, bloody well find out,' said Fox, 'instead of coming in here with half a story.'

'Yes, sir.' The DC went. Rapidly.

Fox swung round to Gilroy. 'You do it, Jack. Speak to the DCS in Wiltshire at wherever he's set up shop and make sure he's heard.'

'Yes, sir.'

'And find out what the latest is when you speak to him,' he added as Gilroy reached the door.

It took about fifteen minutes, during which time Fox fretted and drummed his fingers on his blotter. 'Well?' he said when Gilroy reappeared.

'There's been another call to Norton, sir. The lads on taps passed it straight to Wiltshire in accordance with your instructions.'

'Same caller?'

'Sounded the same, so they said. Wants Norton to go to a point on Banstead Downs, close to the Brighton Road, at ten o'clock this evening and leave the ransom under a bench. He gave precise directions.'

'Stupid sod,' said Fox. 'Some bastard'll nick it if he leaves it there for long. How long will it take Norton to get there from his hotel?'

Gilroy shrugged. 'Three hours to be on the safe side, I suppose. It depends on the traffic . . . and whether Norton knows where this place is.'

'And I suppose Wiltshire want us to cover it for them.'

Gilroy nodded. 'Yes, sir. Their Assistant Chief Constable's just spoken to the commander.'

'Bloody terrific,' said Fox. 'I'd better go and see him. See what he's got in mind.'

Commander Myers looked up as Fox entered his office. 'I thought it'd be you, Tommy,' he said. 'I've already spoken to Commander Campbell. The Anti-

Terrorist Branch are always telling me that they deal with kidnappings, so they can deal with this one. How's your job going?'

'Sort of pending at the moment, sir. Studd is on the move and once we get some idea of where he's going I shall descend on him. From a great height.' Fox grinned maliciously.

Gilroy was waiting in Fox's office. 'Studd's just skirted Exeter and switched to the A30, sir,' he said.

'That's it then,' said Fox. 'The bastard's making for Penzance . . . and the Scillies.' He walked across to his desk and seized the phone. 'Pete,' he said, when he got through to Ramsay. 'It's on. If you want to be in at the kill, meet me at Battersea Heliport about ten minutes from now.' He slammed down the phone and grinned at Gilroy. 'Right, Jack,' he said. 'Get on the trumpet and arrange for a helicopter to be at Battersea . . . like yesterday.'

'A helicopter, sir?' Despite the years he had worked with Fox, Gilroy was still occasionally stunned by his chief's swift decisions.

'Yes, Jack. One of those metal things with a fan on top. And get Swann to get the car up.'

When Jeremy Studd reached Penzance, he parked his car and sauntered across to the Queen's Hotel where he had a leisurely lunch. Then he drove to the heliport and caught a helicopter to St Mary's, unaware that Fox was there already. Waiting for him.

Detective Superintendent Marsden of the Anti-Terrorist Branch walked round the Range Rover which now stood in the yard at Hyde Park police station. 'Well?' he said to the scenes-of-crime officer. 'What can you tell me?'

The SOCO shrugged. 'Not a lot really. Almost certainly it was driven to the car park by someone who had the keys. There's no evidence that the ignition's been bridged.'

202

Marsden shrugged. 'So what? The bloke who took the girl took the keys as well. What about fingerprints?'

'Got a couple of sets,' said the SOCO, 'and I got Fingerprint Branch to do a priority search.'

'And?'

'And nothing. Not on record.'

'Bloody marvellous,' said Marsden.

Detective Chief Superintendent Carmody of the Wiltshire Constabulary sat down in the chair opposite Norton. 'Why didn't you tell the police that your wife had been kidnapped, sir?' he asked.

Norton, firmly believing that the police had called to discuss something else, sat up sharply. 'How the hell did you know about that?' he asked.

'She was reported missing by the organisers of this three-day event she's attending. She's not been seen since last night apparently.'

'But that doesn't necessarily—'

'Your wife is a horse-lover, Mr Norton, isn't she?' Norton nodded. 'Not the sort of person just to go off and leave her horse . . . at least, not without getting someone to look after it.'

'Well no, of course not, but that still doesn't—'

'Mr Norton,' said Carmody patiently, 'why didn't you inform the police that you'd received a ransom demand?'

'How did you know that?'

'I just assumed that you would have received one,' said Carmody, not wishing to tell Norton that the police suspected him of drug smuggling and that they had been monitoring his telephone calls under a warrant granted by the Home Secretary.

Norton slumped down in his chair. 'Yeah, I got two calls. One told me that she'd been kidnapped, the other told me to take five hundred thousand pounds and leave it under a bench at—'

'You won't, of course,' said Carmody.

'But what will happen if I—?'

203

'Oh, you'll go, Mr Norton . . . if you're agreeable to co-operating with the police that is. But your suitcase will be filled with newspaper.'

'Just as well,' said Norton. 'There's no way I can lay my hands on five hundred grand. Then what?'

'We will follow you, at a discreet distance . . .' Carmody looked sternly at the hotelier. 'Don't be tempted to try and lose us, Mr Norton,' he said, 'because the Metropolitan Police will be keeping the location under observation.'

'How do they know where to go?' asked Norton suspiciously.

Carmody smiled. 'Because you're about to tell me, Mr Norton.'

In the Isles of Scilly, Studd booked into a hotel. Then he walked around the small town of St Mary's, returned for dinner, and spent an hour in the corner of the bar with a pint and a newspaper. Then he went to bed.

It was a warm night but it had started to drizzle. Which was exactly what Detective Superintendent Marsden had predicted that it would do. Not that Marsden was a weather expert. But he had been a policeman long enough to know that it invariably rained on occasions of this nature.

Twenty detectives, some with night-glasses, had watched as Charles Norton pulled up at the roadside and walked across to the spot where the kidnapper – or his accomplice – had ordered him to leave the money. Norton had placed the suitcase under the bench seat that he had been told would be there, looked round self-consciously, and returned to his car. Then he had driven off to meet the police at Walton on Thames police station which was considered far enough away for the kidnappers to have given up if they had decided to follow him for a while.

At half-past nine the next morning, by which time th

204

watching detectives had run out of oaths, a tramp shuffled up to the bench and pulled out the suitcase. He examined its contents of newspapers with the cursory thoroughness possessed of all tramps and angrily kicked it back under the seat. At which point, to his astonishment, he was arrested.

Fox looked round the tiny back room of the stone cottage that was the police station in St Mary's. Evans, Gilroy, Crozier and Fletcher were there together with Ramsay and Fielder, the uniformed customs man, and Sergeant Doubleday of the Devon and Cornwall Constabulary who was known to the locals as the Chief Constable of the Isles of Scilly.

'As you know,' said Fox, 'Studd arrived here yesterday. So far he's done nothing. Earlier this morning he walked across to—' He broke off and glanced at Doubleday. 'What's that beach called?'

'Hugh Town, sir.'

'Right. He walked across to Hugh Town and had a swim. At this moment he's lounging on the beach, sunning himself and eyeing up the talent. So far, he appears to have spoken to no one who might have any connection with what we think he's here for. So we just sit and wait.'

'Any news on the Norton kidnapping, sir?' asked Evans.

'Yeah, of a sort, Denzil,' said Fox. 'A merry team of officers sat on the suitcase all night . . . and nothing happened.' He flicked his fingers. 'I tell a lie,' he said and grinned. 'They arrested a tramp. He was taken to the local nick, lightly grilled for about an hour and thrown out. Then Norton got another phone call, advising him that it was very silly of him to leave a suitcase full of newspaper on Banstead Downs, and that if he wanted his wife back, he'd do as he was told next time.'

'So who was the tramp, guv?' asked Evans.

Fox shrugged. 'Your guess is as good as mine, Denzil,

205

but the kidnapper obviously waited until this knight of the road had been kicked out, got his report on the contents and then gave Norton a bell. Either that or he kept observation on the thing as well. But there again, perhaps we're giving him credit for too much intelligence.' He sighed. 'However, to more important matters.' He glanced at Fielder. 'You've got a yacht scheduled to come in at fourteen hundred hours, haven't you?'

'Aye, we have that. Course it might not be the one you're waiting for. It's not like aeroplanes. They don't have to tell anyone they're coming.' Fielder's strong accent indicated that he had succeeded in getting the home posting that he had been seeking for years.

'I presume that it will hoist a yellow flag, indicating that customs are required on board?'

'Near enough. The yellow flag indicates that they've arrived in UK waters, that's all.'

'Then what?'

'I go out in the launch and board her. I'm also the immigration officer, so I do the necessary if they're foreigners. If they're British, I just have a quick look at their passports. Then it's like anywhere else. Remind them what they're entitled to, collect any duty or whatever, and Bob's your uncle.'

'D'you normally search?'

'Depends,' said Fielder. 'If they look a bit dodgy, then I might turn them over, but generally these folk have got so much money that they don't bother to avoid duty. Too much hassle, if you take my meaning.'

'Good,' said Fox. 'Well, if I may suggest . . .' He paused and glanced at Ramsay. 'If Mr Ramsay approves, that is, might I suggest that you don't look too hard. Of course we'd like to hear about anything out of the ordinary.'

Fielder nodded. 'No problem,' he said. 'Then I'll come off as normal and leave it to you, eh?'

'That's it,' said Fox. 'Sound all right to you, Pete?'

'Yes,' said Ramsay. 'Once Geoff's finished, we'll si

206

tight and see what happens. And let's hope the bastards don't get away from us this time.'

'I don't think there's much hope of that,' said Fox. 'We've got dozens of blokes – yours and mine – all over the place. There's only one thing that worries me though . . .'

'What?'

'Supposing they sus us out and put to sea again. What sort of power have these things got? I'm not talking about sail, but most of them have an auxiliary engine, haven't they?'

'Aye, they have that,' said Fielder, 'but it still takes them a while to get under way.'

'It's no problem anyway,' said Ramsay. 'I've arranged for one of our cutters to be standing out to sea. Just off Old Town. One word from us and that thing'll be down on them before you can say "Anything to declare?" '

'You seem to have thought of everything,' said Fox.

'We try to,' said Ramsay. 'Customs and Excise are like that.'

Chapter Twenty-One

Studd had remained on the beach at Hugh Town, eating
sandwiches from a packed lunch provided by his hotel,
and reading a book. But at half-past one, he had taken
a pair of binoculars from his sports bag and trained them
on a sleek white forty-foot yacht as it rounded Old
Town.

This sudden interest, witnessed by the surveillance
team secreted on the rocks above him, was reported to
the St Mary's Custom House by radio. Studd continued
to watch as the yacht dropped anchor and raised a yellow
flag almost before its auxiliaries had been switched off.
He had glanced at his wrist-watch as Fielder boarded
her and checked the time again when the customs officer
went ashore. Half an hour later, he dressed and
wandered back to his hotel, still unaware that his every
move was being closely observed.

Geoff Fielder had spent twenty minutes on board before
coming ashore to report to Custom House.

'Anything interesting?' asked Fox.

Fielder shook his head. 'Nothing out of the ordinary
for that class of vessel. Or for that sort of owner.'

'Meaning?'

'He's not short of a bob or two, I can tell you that.
Name of Ferguson – Jamie Ferguson – and that's his
date of birth.' Fielder laid his clipboard on the table,
turned it and pointed at an entry. 'Spends most of his

time in St Malo. That's where he's come from now, so he said.'

'What's he do for a living?'

'Bit vague about that,' said Fielder. 'Mentioned in passing that he was in television.' He shrugged. 'That covers a multitude of sins,' he added.

'But nothing that would make you think that he was up to no good?'

Fielder laughed. 'I'm a nasty, suspicious customs officer,' he said. 'As far as I'm concerned everyone's up to no good until I satisfy myself to the contrary.'

'I can see you're a man after my own heart,' said Fox warmly. He turned to Gilroy and handed him the clipboard with Ferguson's date of birth on it. 'Give that a run, Jack. See if he's got any form . . . but I'll put money on him being clean.' He glanced at Ramsay. 'Then you can let Pete give him to Cecil.'

'Who's Cecil?' Gilroy looked puzzled.

'It's our drugs computer,' said Ramsay, 'and it's called CEDRIC.'

But there was no record of Ferguson on either the Police National Computer or on CEDRIC. Which came as no surprise to the police or to Her Majesty's Customs and Excise.

'Now what do we do?' Ramsay, Fox and the others were seated at Geoff Fielder's kitchen table in Custom House drinking tea. 'All that's happened so far is that Studd's gone back to the hotel where presumably he's wallowing in a hot bath.'

'Patience, Pete,' said Fox. 'We've just got to wait and see.'

'Yeah, fine,' said Ramsay testily. 'But supposing nothing happens?'

'Look,' said Fox. 'Studd hangs about on the beach all morning. He swims, he watches the pretty girls and he reads a book. He has lunch. But he doesn't move an inch. Then he sees the yacht. There have been dozens of craft in his line of sight all morning, but suddenly out come the binoculars and he takes a passionate interest.' Fox stirred his tea. 'Got to be the one, Pete.'

One of Ramsay's investigators poked his head round the kitchen door. 'He's on the move, guv.'

'Who's on the move?' asked Ramsay. 'Studd?'

'No.` Ferguson. He's just left the yacht in an inflatable.'

'Aha!' said Ramsay. 'The game's afoot.'

'You've been reading detective novels again,' said Fox.

Jamie Ferguson beached his inflatable and walked towards the quayside. He was wearing a shirt and trousers, but was not carrying anything. Which was something of a disappointment to the watching police and customs.

'What's he up to now?' asked Ramsay of no one in particular. 'There's no way he's got eight kilos of cocaine secreted about his person.'

'Come ashore for dinner probably,' said Fox. 'Poor sod's got to eat.'

Ramsay looked gloomily at Ferguson's retreating figure. 'I'm beginning to think this is a blow-out,' he said.

But it wasn't. The surveillance team followed Ferguson as he wandered into the main street and into the foyer of Studd's hotel. Then he went into the bar. There were three members of the customs Investigation Division there already – two men and a girl – all attired in holiday clothes and apparently enjoying themselves immensely.

Studd was sitting at a table in the corner and stood up as Ferguson entered. He shook hands with the yachtsman, ordered some drinks, and then the two of them sat down. It was obvious that they weren't strangers to each other. Half an hour later, they went in for dinner.

It was eight o'clock. Which was the time when Norton got the next set of instructions about paying the ransom.

Charles Norton had agreed to the police monitoring his telephone, a comical piece of fiction which was necessary to protect the covert intercept that was still being maintained by Fox's men.

The voice, described by the police technician as having an 'unremarkable London accent', ordered Norton to obtain a bearer bond for half a million pounds and leave it, at eight o'clock the following evening, in the first emergency telephone box past Junction 15 on the M4 into London. The caller then added that if Norton involved the police on this occasion, his wife would be killed.

The call lasted long enough for the police to trace it to a telephone box in Purley, but by the time the local area car arrived the caller had gone.

Norton shook his head. 'What's he going to do with that, for God's sake?' he asked. 'Calmly walk into a bank and cash it?'

'He won't get the chance,' said Detective Chief Superintendent Carmody, 'because all you'll leave there is an envelope with a five-pound note in it.'

'But you heard what he said.' Norton sounded panicky. 'He'll kill Letty if I don't pay.'

'I think that's most unlikely,' said Carmody, 'because he'll be in custody.' And hoped that he was right . . . and that Norton believed him.

At ten o'clock Studd went to bed and Ferguson made his way, a little unsteadily, back to his inflatable and returned to his yacht.

'Now I'm sure it's a blow-out,' said Ramsay.

Fox shook his head. 'He's a villain,' he said. 'He'll come.'

But in fact he went. The following morning, Studd, carrying his grip, left the hotel and walked down to the

211

quayside where he hired a boatman who ferried him out to Ferguson's yacht. Twenty minutes later, Ferguson weighed anchor and the yacht, under power, moved slowly away from its moorings.

'Well I'm damned,' said Ramsay.

'He's a cunning bastard, that one,' said Fox.

It was late afternoon – evening really – before Ferguson's yacht sailed into Penzance Harbour, by which time Fox, Ramsay and the other members of their combined team were already there.

'It's just as I thought,' said Ramsay.

'What?' asked Fox.

'Ferguson thinks that because he cleared customs in the Scillies, he's fireproof and we won't touch him.'

'Does he really?' said Fox. 'What a silly fellow.'

Just before eight o'clock, Ferguson and Studd came ashore. Studd was carrying his grip, and this time Ferguson had one as well.

'That grip looks quite heavy,' said Ramsay.

'Yeah, about eight kilos heavy, I shouldn't wonder,' said Fox.

With the aid of powerful binoculars, the policemen positioned on the bridge – where the A345 crosses the M4 – had a clear view of the emergency telephone that Norton's caller had specified. At a minute to eight, Norton pulled on to the hard shoulder and quickly pushed the envelope into the small box containing the telephone. Then he drove on.

Minutes later, a Volkswagen stopped and a man got out. He walked across to the phone box, withdrew the envelope and got back into his car. Clearly anxious to get away, the needle of his speedometer was touching ninety when the man first saw the blue light of the patrol car which had come down on to the motorway from the bridge where the watchers had observed everything.

The driver of the police car strolled casually up to the

Volkswagen as its driver wound down the window. 'I made it ninety-three, sir,' he said.

The driver of the Volkswagen stared at the policeman. 'Surely not, Officer,' he said.

'Mind stepping out of the car, sir,' said the PC.

The man got out and slammed the door of his car, but before he had time to say another word, he was handcuffed. 'Christ!' he said. 'What the hell's this all about?'

'Don't know really,' said the PC cheerfully. 'You'll have to talk to my guv'nor.'

Studd and Ferguson got a taxi to the heliport in Penzance, collected Studd's car and drove to a nearby hotel. As they walked into the foyer Fox sent DS Buckley and WDC Webster ahead to keep an eye on them. He anticipated that Studd and Ferguson would have dinner and that Studd would then make his way back to his flat outside Gloucester with the eight kilos of cocaine that Fox hoped was in the bag that Ferguson had been carrying.

But then a woman walked into the hotel. 'Well I'm buggered,' said Fox. 'It's Letitia Norton.'

'So I found an envelope with a five-pound note in it. You seriously going to do me for that?'

'It's called stealing by finding,' said Carmody.

'I was going to hand it in.'

'Were you really? But you didn't tell the officer about it?' Carmody was an unimaginative officer who tended to be obsessed with the more trivial aspects of the law.

'I'd been nicked, hadn't I? Didn't have to say anything. Or have they changed that?'

'Why did you stop at that emergency phone?' asked Carmody.

There was a brief pause before the man said, 'I'd seen a woman in a car on the hard shoulder a way back. I

213

thought I'd better tell the police. You never know these days. There's all sorts of odd people about.'

'The control room hasn't received a call on that phone since eleven-thirty this morning,' said Carmody.

'Probably because it was out of order.'

'It was working perfectly. We tested it before you stopped . . . and afterwards.'

'Well it wasn't working when I tried it.'

'Where is Letitia Norton?'

'Who?'

Carmody sighed. 'Shall we stop messing about?' he said. 'Three days ago, Mrs Norton was kidnapped. Last night her husband, Mr Norton, received a telephone call telling him to leave a bearer bond at the emergency phone where you stopped. He was told to leave it there at eight o'clock. A short while later, you stopped at the same phone. You didn't make a call, nor did you attempt to—'

'I'm telling you—'

'Because the police were watching you the whole time. You just got out of your car, took the envelope, and then drove off again. Now then, kidnapping is a serious offence and carries a heavy penalty. And if anything has happened to Mrs Norton, you could well be facing a charge of murder.'

'Now hold on.' Sweat started to show on the man's forehead. 'I don't know anything about a kidnapping. It was all a scam.'

'Oh, was it indeed?' Carmody leaned back in his chair and smiled. 'Well perhaps you'd better tell me about it. And you can start by telling me your name and date of birth.'

Letitia Norton had not been in the hotel for more than ten minutes when Buckley came out. 'There's all hell let loose in there, sir,' he said to Fox. 'In a very restrained way.'

'What's that supposed to mean, Roy?'

214

'There's a hell of an argument going on about something, sir. The woman is having a right go at Studd.'

'What about?'

'Don't know, sir. I can't hear.'

'Terrific,' said Fox. 'Well, get back in there and see if your hearing's improved.'

The three suspects came out of the hotel at about a quarter to ten. Studd put both grips into the boot of his car and waited while Letitia embraced Ferguson and gave him a peck on the cheek. Then Studd and Letitia got into the car and Ferguson turned as if to walk away.

It was then that the police and customs closed in.

Buckley and Webster waited until Ferguson was some way away from Studd's car and quietly detained him, but it was Fox who approached Studd. He bent down and peered into the window. 'Well, well, Mr Studd, fancy seeing you here in darkest Cornwall,' he said.

Letitia Norton glanced across, a look of puzzlement on her face. Then she recognised him. 'Oh, God,' she said, 'it's the rat-catcher.'

'Yes, indeed,' said Fox, 'and working flat out.'

Studd fumbled with the keys and attempted to start the engine. But nothing happened. 'Sod it!' he said.

Fox grinned and opened the door. 'One of the fundamentals of motoring, Jeremy old sport, is that you have to have the sparking-plug leads connected before the thing will go.'

They found eight kilograms of white powder in a grip in the boot of the car. Everyone present – and that included Studd, if he was honest – was in little doubt that it was cocaine.

'I don't know where that came from,' said Studd.

'Nor do I,' said Fox, 'but the plain fact of the matter is that you have it in your possession. And for that, my son, you're nicked.' He glanced across at Ramsay. 'Won't Cecil be pleased about that,' he said.

For the first time in about a week, Ramsay grinned.

*

The man arrested by Wiltshire detectives on the M4 motorway for stealing a five-pound note in an envelope was called Burns, Michael Burns, and he was now a very worried man. The Police National Computer had told the Wiltshire detectives that Burns had several previous convictions, the most serious of which had earned him seven years for his part in a robbery.

'I have just received information that Mrs Norton has been arrested in Cornwall,' said Carmody, 'together with a man called Jeremy Studd. First reports,' he continued pompously, 'indicate that they were both intending to go abroad permanently. But unfortunately for them they were stopped by the police.'

'I don't believe it.'

'Studd had air tickets in his possession for the next flight from Heathrow to Miami,' continued Carmody. 'Which seems to indicate that you were unlikely to see him again.'

'The double-dealing bastard.'

'I take it you wish to make a statement, Mr Burns,' said Carmody drily.

Chapter Twenty-Two

Fox had announced to the assembled law enforcement officers that he didn't give a damn what the rule book said, he was taking his prisoners back to London.

'*Our* prisoners,' emphasised Ramsay half-jokingly. He could see the sense of what Fox said, but was unhappy about the legal aspects. 'And what about Ferguson's yacht?' he asked.

'Search it.' Fox waved a dismissive hand. 'And then give it to Geoff Fielder,' he said. 'He's the Receiver of Wreck . . . so you tell me.'

'Ah, but only for the Isles of Scilly . . .' Ramsay stopped when he saw that Fox was grinning at him.

'Jack,' said Fox, 'get a message to Special Branch at Heathrow. The two air tickets for Miami we found in Studd's belongings are for the flight that leaves at thirteen hundred hours today.'

'Right, sir.' Gilroy scribbled a few notes in his pocket book and looked up.

'According to the said tickets our Mr Studd was intending to fly to Miami along with a Miss Gillian Inwood. My betting is that Miss Inwood will be expecting to meet Studd at the airport. I want her nicked. On second thoughts,' Fox continued, 'be better if you went and did it yourself, just to make sure that it doesn't get cocked up.'

*

Donaldson had telephoned Fox first thing the following morning. 'I've got some interesting information, sir.'

'You'd better come up, Kev. Things are starting to develop quite nicely.'

And two hours later, Donaldson was there. In Fox's office.

'Well, Kev, and do you bring heartening news from the sticks?'

Donaldson grinned. 'I don't think it's much good to me, sir, but I think it might be useful to you.'

'Let's have it then.' Fox indicated an armchair and sat down opposite the Thames Valley DCI.

'As you know, we searched Cameron's flat in Windsor.'

'Naturally,' murmured Fox.

'And as I said before, there was nothing there to connect him with drug smuggling, much less the job you're involved with.'

'Too cunning by half, that bastard, I should think,' said Fox irritably.

'And you remember that we went through all his papers and there was a hint that he'd spent some time in Hong Kong. Well apparently, he came back about five years ago. In a hurry.'

'Oh?' Fox raised an eyebrow. 'What was that all about then?'

'I got in touch with the Hong Kong police and they have quite a file on our Mr Cameron. Kicked him out eventually.'

'Did they now? Why?'

'Reading between the lines, he'd got a bit too greedy.

'Too greedy for Hong Kong? Blimey!'

'It was more a case of not paying the right people Seems they don't much mind what you get up to so long as you share it. But if you try to keep it all to yourself Well . . .' Donaldson spread his hands expressively.

'OK,' said Fox, 'so he was bent. But what was he up to?'

218

'Drugs.' Donaldson looked pleased with himself. 'Cameron was running an import and export agency. On the surface it was quite legitimate, but he was using it as a cover for a quite sophisticated drug-smuggling operation. It was all right while he was greasing the right palms, but when he decided he was big enough to dispense with the help he'd been getting, they started to get a bit shirty. And they were too big for him to fight. They'd got all the power, it seems. All the way up.' Donaldson interrupted himself briefly. 'When I was at the Police College, I had several long chats with an RHKP officer who was on my syndicate. I tell you, sir, the things he told me would make your hair stand on end.'

'I doubt it,' said Fox drily. 'So what happened to Cameron?'

'He got a visit.' Donaldson grinned. 'I think you can work out what sort of visit.' Fox nodded. 'And it was made very plain to him that if he valued his liberty, he would pay a substantial fine – unofficial, of course – and leave the colony.'

'Or?'

'Or he'd get topped, I imagine.'

'So he left, I presume.'

'Like a rocket, sir.'

'Yeah, well, that's all very interesting, but does it get you any nearer solving your murder. I mean, what are you suggesting here? Triads, or some damned thing?'

Donaldson looked slightly perturbed at that. 'Christ, I hope not,' he said. 'But there was one other piece of information that might interest you, sir . . .'

'Yes?'

'The Hong Kong police tell me that while he was out here, he was very friendly with a European girl. So friendly in fact that they were living together. And she got chased out at the same time . . . and for the same reason.'

'Anyone we know?'

'Name of Pearson, sir. Letitia Pearson. Now Mrs Norton, of course.'

'What an astounding coincidence,' said Fox. 'We nicked her last night . . . along with the aptly named Studd. Perhaps you'd better sit in on the interview.'

'Perce,' said Fox as DS Fletcher came through the door, 'I want a full run-down on Letitia Norton. I want to know everything there is to know about the woman.'

'Right, sir,' said Fletcher. 'When by?'

'Yesterday,' said Fox.

Gilroy approached the girl at the British Airways desk and produced his warrant card. 'Has a Miss Gillian Inwood booked in for the flight to Miami?' he asked.

The girl didn't even bother to consult the list in front of her. 'She tried to,' she said, 'about five minutes ago. But she hadn't got a ticket. Said she was waiting for a man friend.'

'D'you know where she went?'

'Yes, she's over there.' The girl pointed. 'The tall woman with striking auburn hair . . . and an emerald-green dress.' She wrinkled her nose. 'And black shoes. Quite the wrong thing, if you ask me.'

Gilroy laughed. 'Thanks,' he said and turned to go.

'Will she be travelling?' asked the check-in girl.

Gilroy laughed again. 'Yes,' he said, 'but not to Miami . . . and not by British Airways.'

Detective Sergeant Percy Fletcher started pounding the pavements of Chelsea in pursuit of information about Letitia Norton. But it wasn't easy. Fletcher could find no one who seemed to know her, let alone tell him anything about her. He rang Fox and told him.

'Never mind, Perce,' Fox said. 'Beat on the ground long enough and something's bound to come up.'

Then Percy Fletcher remembered his favourite informant.

*

'The night that Cameron was murdered, Jeremy Studd claims to have spent the night with you.' Fox put his cigarettes and lighter on the table and sat down. He hadn't interviewed Studd yet, but thought that he would make use of the fact that DS Crozier had seen Letitia entering Studd's room that night.

Letitia Norton looked suitably shocked. 'Oh, did he? Well, he—'

Fox held up a hand. 'Before you say anything,' he said, 'I must tell you that this officer' – he indicated DCI Donaldson with a sweep of his hand – 'is thinking of charging Studd with Cameron's murder.'

Fox's glib lie took Donaldson completely by surprise. Right now, there was nothing further from his mind.

'Oh!' Letitia faltered. 'I didn't realise that it was that serious,' she said. 'Yes, I did spend the night with him.'

'Between what times?'

'From about midnight to about eight the next morning, I suppose.'

'I see.' The answer came out too quickly for Fox's liking. 'You're certain about that?'

'Of course.' Letitia spoke haughtily as though, having admitted to adultery, she was angry at being disbelieved.

'But you don't deny that you conspired together to stage your own kidnapping.'

'What are you talking about?' Letitia Norton seemed genuinely surprised.

'What I am talking about,' said Fox patiently, 'is your disappearance – after day one – from the three-day event in which you were competing, and the subsequent telephone calls to your husband demanding a substantial amount of money in ransom.'

'That's absolute nonsense.'

'Then perhaps you'd care to explain how your Range Rover came to be found parked in Hyde Park underground garage.'

'I parked it there.'

'Why?'

'I had an appointment, but that's my business.'

'You're not being very helpful, Mrs Norton.' Fox paused. 'It may interest you to know that the Wiltshire police have arrested a man called Michael Burns. Mr Burns, very wisely I may say, has made a statement in which he said that he was paid a sum of money by Studd to make a number of phone calls to your husband explaining that you had been kidnapped and that Mr Norton should pay half a million pounds to get you back. Mr Burns, it seems, was promised a quite substantial share of this half million.'

'Half a million!' The amount obviously stunned Letitia Norton. 'You must be joking.'

'I thought it rather excessive myself,' said Fox mildly. 'Even for you.'

'But I knew nothing about this.'

'Right then,' said Fox. 'Just so that I've got this right, you say that the night Cameron was murdered Studd slept with you . . . and you know nothing about this so-called kidnapping. Is that the up and down of it?'

'Yes, it certainly is.'

'It might interest you to know, Mrs Norton,' Fox continued, 'that when we arrested Studd last evening, we found two air tickets for Miami among his possessions.'

'Really?' Letitia Norton contrived a look of disdain.

'One for him . . . and one for a Miss Gillian Inwood.'

Letitia tensed slightly. 'Who?'

'Gillian Inwood.' Fox inclined his head. 'The name doesn't mean anything to you?'

'No.'

'We arrested Miss Inwood at lunch-time today on suspicion of being involved with the illegal importation of drugs. She was at Heathrow waiting for Mr Studd . . .' Fox paused and turned to Gilroy. 'What did she say Jack?'

Gilroy thumbed open his pocket book. 'She said that she and Studd were going to Miami for a holiday.' He

222

glanced at Letitia. 'She also claimed that they were going to be married and possibly settle in the States.'

Letitia Norton could do nothing to disguise the expression of anger on her face. 'The bastard,' she said.

'Would you now care to revise your previous statements, Mrs Norton?' Fox lit a cigarette and waited.

There was an aura of hopelessness about Letitia Norton as she looked up into Fox's face. 'Jeremy didn't spend the night with me,' she said. 'He killed Cameron that night. He took Charles's bayonet from the drawer in his desk – for self-protection, he said – and arranged to meet him in Stokenchurch. When he got back he told me that there'd been an accident and that Cameron was dead.'

'Interesting,' said Fox. 'And what was he meeting Cameron for?'

'To collect some drugs, apparently. Jeremy was heavily involved in cocaine.'

'Yes,' said Fox, brushing at his sleeve. 'I'd rather gathered that from the little haul we took off him in Penzance last night. But tell me, why Stokenchurch?'

Letitia Norton faltered. 'I – er – I don't know,' she said.

Jeremy Studd's public school reserve had started to ebb, but he still managed to regard Fox with a malevolent sneer.

Fox however, was immune to such attitudes and gazed at Studd as though he were some sort of interesting specimen of humanity. Which indeed he was, as far as Fox was concerned. 'Where were you on the night Cameron was killed?'

For a moment Studd looked as though he wasn't going to answer. That the question was so farcical that it was beneath serious consideration. Then he shrugged. 'I was in bed with Letitia Norton,' he said.

'I have interviewed Mrs Norton,' said Fox, 'and she denies that she slept with you that night. Furthermore,

223

she denies any involvement in drug smuggling, her own kidnapping, or in the murder of Cameron. As a matter of fact, she blames you for all of it. Reckons that you killed Cameron.' Fox grinned insolently. 'As for Mr Michael Burns, the loathsome individual arrested by the Wiltshire police, well, he's leaping about like a soul demented. Reckons he's been had over, old son.'

'It was all her idea.' Studd blurted out the accusation and lit a cigarette. Fox noticed that his hand was shaking.

'I think you've got that wrong, sport. You're not seriously suggesting that a refined lady like Mrs Norton, whose only interest seems to be horses, could have been involved with the sort of chicanery that's going to earn you a fair old dollop of porridge, surely?'

Studd laughed, a jeering sort of laugh. 'Well you'd better believe it,' he said.

'Well you'd better tell me about it,' said Fox and ostentatiously switched on the tape recorder.

'She knew that Charles was having an affair with Daphne Lovegrove and that rankled. You see she'd financed him . . . all the way along. Bought the bloody hotel and everything. To use as a base.'

'Where did she get the money for that?'

Studd laughed. 'From cocaine, for Christ's sake. Where d'you think?'

'Really?' Fox sounded unconvinced.

'She and Cameron had been at it in Hong Kong. Then the pair of them got chased out and so they set up over here. I got dragged in and so did Rodney Bingham.'

Fox scoffed. 'You sound like unwilling accomplices.'

Studd ignored that. 'But then Cameron tried to take over. He started by hi-jacking a consignment near the airport—'

'When Leach and Collins got blown away?'

'Yeah.' Studd just nodded. He seemed unconcerned at the demise of the two messengers. 'Then it started to get a bit nasty. I think Bingham was with him when that happened. Anyway, Cameron had got some sort of hold over him. Then Bridge got killed. He was another messenger . . .'

'By whom?'

Studd shrugged. 'Your guess is as good as mine. Cameron, I suppose . . . or Bingham. Then Reynolds's place at Preston Candover got the treatment. That was a couple of Cameron's hoods that he sent there to put the frighteners on.'

'Yeah, I know. It was Dawkins and Gibbs . . . who also worked for you.'

'Christ, the bastards—'

'Why did you go to Stokenchurch to meet Cameron?'

Studd looked up sharply. 'I was supposed to—'

'You were seen, you know,' lied Fox. 'I have a witness.' Secretly, he knew that the woman who lived in Daphne Lovegrove's block of flats and who claimed to have seen a man getting into a car would be destroyed the moment she stepped into the witness box.

For some moments Studd stared unseeing at the table. Then he looked up. 'It was Letty's idea,' he said. 'She wanted Cameron out of the way. Because he was trying to take over. She got me to make an appointment to meet Cameron at the back of the flats. The idea was that I should kill him, but that Charles would get the blame. She knew he was going to see Daphne and she was sick of his philandering.'

'What a lovely old-fashioned word,' said Fox. 'But it was all right for you to have it off with the lovely Letty. And you were, weren't you?'

Studd shrugged. 'Why look a gift horse in the mouth?' he said with unconscious humour.

'And Cameron suspected nothing?'

'Why should he?'

'Bit of a strange place for a meet . . . the back of someone else's block of flats.'

Studd shrugged. 'In this game, nothing's a surprise. A drug runner'll meet you anywhere.'

225

Fox thought that was probably true. 'And the kidnapping?' he asked. 'What was all that in aid of?'

'To take the heat off. Once you'd arrested me – the first time – we knew you'd been taking an interest in our activities. We needed that one last consignment and then we were going. We thought that to stage a kidnapping might take the spotlight off what we were doing . . . and see Norton off for a few quid at the same time.'

'Where were you going? Once you'd laid your hands on the last consignment.'

'Abroad. South of France perhaps. I don't know. We hadn't decided for sure.'

'What about the air tickets you've got for Miami?'

Studd had obviously forgotten the tickets. 'What about them?'

'D'you deny that you and Miss Inwood were going to Miami to get married?'

'I certainly do deny it.'

'Oh dear.' Fox chuckled to himself. 'Well, when Detective Inspector Gilroy arrested her at Heathrow Airport earlier today, she seemed firmly under the impression that nuptials were very much in the offing.'

'What did you arrest her for?' That piece of news clearly upset Studd.

'Suspicion of drug smuggling,' said Fox.

'But she had nothing to do with the—' Studd stopped suddenly realising that he was about to talk himself into further trouble.

'No, we know. She was just taken in by you. But where did Charles Norton feature in all this?'

'Nowhere. He's completely bogus. All this crap about having been an army officer and having gone to public school. It's all rubbish. Once he found out it was drugs and not booze, he didn't want to know. He said that if Letty didn't stop, he'd tell the police. But he was quite happy to take the money. He's just a parasite, really. Hanging round the bar all day, getting in the bloody way.'

226

'Why did you send an anonymous letter, suggesting that the police speak to Norton about his missing bayonet?'

'Because we knew that he wouldn't have an alibi for that night. Not unless he wanted to involve Daphne Lovegrove, which he wouldn't.'

Fox laughed. 'You were right about that. But Daphne Lovegrove decided to do something about it herself and came to see the police. All you succeeded in doing was to draw attention to yourselves. We had Norton under observation all that night, so we knew that he hadn't killed Cameron.' Fox stood up. 'All in all, old son, you haven't been terribly bright about all this, have you?'

Chapter Twenty-Three

'Well, Percy, my dear, we don't often see you in this part of the world. Chelsea's not exactly your scene, is it?' Claire Seeley took a sip of champagne and smoothed her dress with the other hand.

'Needs must where the devil drives,' said Fletcher with feeling.

'How long is it now?'

Fletcher looked thoughtful. 'About ten years, I suppose.'

The girl nodded. 'Yes, I suppose it must be. And I'm still grateful.'

Fletcher shrugged. 'I hope you've stayed clean.' Ten years previously, he had been involved in a drugs raid on a West End club. Claire Seeley, then a seventeen-year-old hostess, had been rescued by Fletcher and restored to her parents. Since then she hadn't ever smoked, let alone taken drugs, but her present job as the manageress of a rather up-market club made her useful to Fletcher . . . on occasions. 'What d'you know about Letitia Norton?' he asked.

Claire laughed. 'Oh, Lady Godiva.'

Fletcher took a mouthful of Scotch. 'Why d'you call her that?' he asked.

'It's near enough,' said Claire. 'Her two great activities in life involve her being either naked or on a horse. What d'you want to know about her?'

'Is she a supplier?'

'So it's said. She's got an awful lot of friends

Chelsea . . . and a lot on the eventing circuit. That's where she supplies cocaine.'

'But surely, they don't—'

'Oh, not the riders. But next time you go to a three-day event, have a look round . . . at the Chelsea set, with glazed expressions and no interest in the horses. It became well known. If you wanted a fix without having to resort to some grubby supplier who might blackmail you, Letty Norton was the one to see. So you just popped along to some horsy event. Or better still, you invited her to dinner. And she had a very wide circle of friends. It couldn't have been easier.'

'How long have you known about this?' asked Fletcher.

'I don't know about it, Percy, darling,' said Claire. She smiled and took another sip of champagne. 'It's just a wicked rumour.'

'How long were you and Cameron in the drug business before he decided that he wanted more than he was getting?'

Letitia Norton laughed outright. 'What an extraordinary thing to say,' she said in her affected drawl. 'He was a friend of my husband. I had nothing to do with him, and I'd no idea what he was involved in.'

'Apart from when you were living with him in Hong Kong, of course. Before the pair of you got chased out for failing to share your drug-smuggling profits with certain persons there who had helped you in the past.'

'Oh God!' Letitia Norton pushed her hands up through her hair and for some moments said nothing further. 'That had nothing to do with it,' she continued. 'That's all in the past. It's pure coincidence that he turned up again.'

'Good try,' said Fox, 'but not good enough. Jeremy Studd has been charged with Cameron's murder, and he has made a statement.' He dropped a sheaf of papers on to the table. 'I suggest you study that carefully,' he said.

Letitia spent some time reading through Studd's statement. Then she set it to one side, slowly, and gazed at Fox with a cool expression. 'That's all nonsense.'

'He's made a second statement in which he tells us everything about your drug-smuggling activities.' Fox dropped more sheets of paper on the table. 'And we know from recent inquiries that you have been supplying cocaine to a great number of people in the Chelsea area . . . and to your horsy friends.'

Letitia Norton let out a great sigh and ran her hands through her hair once more. 'I should have known that pansy would let me down in the end,' she said.

'You were seen going into his room at the hotel the night Cameron was killed, but he wasn't there.'

'No.'

'So what were you doing?'

'Waiting for him to come back . . . and I was prepared to say that he'd been with me all night.'

'But you now withdraw that statement?'

'Yes.'

'Why did you go to London, the day you left your Range Rover at Hyde Park, Mrs Norton?'

'Jeremy had told me that he was collecting the next load of drugs and I was to meet him in London. It was going to be the last consignment, then we were going to France together to live. Jeremy came up with this idea of pretending that I'd been kidnapped . . . to try and get money out of Charles. My money really. And to put you off the scent. But the bloody fool overdid it by asking for too much. And involving this man Burns. Anyhow, by then I was beginning to get suspicious that Jeremy was trying to take over where Cameron had left off. So I checked to see where the stuff was actually coming in—'

'How?'

'There's someone I ring in Madrid.'

'Name?' demanded Fox.

'Lopez,' said Letitia. 'At least, that's what I know him by. I don't think it's his real name. I can give you his phone number if you like.'

'Thanks a lot,' said Fox sarcastically.

'Anyway, Lopez told me the consignment was arriving in the Isles of Scilly on a yacht.'

'Did he say it was Ferguson's yacht?'

'Yes, I think so.'

'And did you know Ferguson?'

'No, I'd never met him before. Hadn't heard of him either. We'd never done a run that way before, you see. So I went there.'

'You were in St Mary's?' Now it was Fox's turn to sound surprised.

Letitia nodded. 'Yes. I left the Range Rover at Hyde Park and caught the train to Penzance. I went over on the chopper the day that Ferguson came in and watched what happened. Then I knew Jeremy was welshing on me. I realised that they were making for the mainland, so I went back to Penzance and confronted Jeremy in the hotel.'

'What did he say?'

'He said it was all a mistake and that at the last minute they'd had to use a different route. Well, I knew that was rubbish.'

'What has made you change your mind and implicate him then?'

Letitia Norton smiled. 'A woman called Gillian Linwood,' she said.

'How did it go, Tommy?' Commander Myers dropped his pen on the desk.

'So so, guv'nor,' said Fox. 'Studd got life, but Bingham's brief talked the jury into believing that he honestly thought that Bridge's house was empty when he set fire to it.'

'So what did he get?' asked Myers.

'Ten for bloody manslaughter, would you believe. But at least he got twelve for his part in drug smuggling. Marvellous, isn't it, guv? You get more for drugs offences now than you do for a topping.'

'Concurrent?'

'Of course,' said Fox. 'I thought he was a bit unfortunate not to get a pound out of the poor box as well.'

Myers shook his head and smiled. 'And the others, Tommy?'

'Farmer, Jamie Ferguson and Reynolds all got twelve apiece, and Michael Burns got seven. So did Dawkins and Gibbs, the pair that Denzil Evans nicked picking up parcels on the Bath Road. They'd coughed to the criminal damage at Stanley Reynolds's house at Preston Candover as well. Sherry Martin got three with eighteen months suspended. Silly cow didn't know what it was all about.'

Myers nodded. 'What about Letitia Norton?'

'Oh, she got eighteen years,' said Fox. 'Conspiracy to murder and smuggling cocaine.'

'That'll put a stop to her equestrian activities,' said Myers with a smile.

'I doubt it,' said Fox. 'She'll soon be mounted again . . . once the dykes of Holloway get hold of her.'

Myers wrinkled his nose at Fox's coarseness. 'And what did Charles Norton get?'

Fox laughed. 'Oh, he got the hotel. But only until Her Majesty's Customs and Excise sort out his drinks bill.'

'His drinks bill?'

'Yeah. Studd told me that he's got some racket smuggling booze over from the continent in container lorries and using it behind the bar of the hotel. Quite made Pete Ramsay's day, that did.' Fox paused. 'I must say he got his hands on a very decent Courvoisier, though.'

Fox waited as the tall, silver-haired figure of Peter Frobisher, the Assistant Commissioner Specialist

Operations, got out of his car and made for the entrance to New Scotland Yard.

'Morning, Mr Fox.'

'Morning, sir.'

'I hear you're running an expensive dental hygiene programme in the Flying Squad,' said Frobisher. There was just the trace of a smile as he pushed his way slowly through the revolving doors 'Encouraging all your chaps to buy toothbrushes, I hear.'

Fox clenched his fists. 'You wait till I get my hands on bloody Denzil Evans,' he said to the uniformed PC guarding the entrance.

The PC saluted impassively. 'Yes, sir,' he said, convinced that all members of the CID were either bent or mad.